"No," Jordan said, the sound startling in the quiet, and she reached up to grab his hair in her fists. Ruthlessly, she pulled Paul's face over hers.

Only then did she comprehend that he was lying on the bed with her, his head and shoulders hovering over her, but he was carefully holding his body away from her. And she understood why. Paul wanted her to come to him. That was why his kiss had been incomplete. He wanted her to acknowledge her need for him.

Vaguely, Jordan was aware that the rest of her body had been awakened and was being drawn to the man like a moth to light. But she would deal with that after she had his kiss.

Her lips implored. Her tongue pleaded. A groan erupted from deep within him.

She had won.

Cherokee Summer

ANNE HENRY

A Love Affair from

HARLEQUIN

London · Toronto · New York · Sydney

First published in Great Britain in 1985 by Harlequin, 15–16 Brook's Mews, London W1A 1DR

© Anne Henry 1984

ISBN 0 373 16076 3

18-0685

Printed and bound in Great Britain by Richard Clay (The Chaucer Press) Ltd, Bungay, Suffolk

Chapter One

"Sure you wouldn't like to go someplace a little more private?" Jeff asked as he turned into the driveway and turned off the ignition.

Jordan did not bother to answer. She had already answered the same question in its many forms all evening long. She was ready to end her date with this amorous young man whose every word seemed laden with sexual innuendo. She eyed the front door longingly. A circle of yellow light pooled itself invitingly around the old-fashioned entrance with its sparkling clean leaded-glass panes.

Jordan inched across the car seat and reached for the door handle as she said, "It's been a lovely evening. I really enjoyed the dinner and the movie."

Before she accomplished her maneuver, however, and managed to extract herself from the front seat of Jeff's luxurious sedan, he had his arms about her and was pulling her toward him.

Jordan stiffened as he buried his face against her neck and whispered, "I've been wanting to get my hands on you all evening."

"I have an early class, Jeff," Jordan said firmly, trying to ignore the kisses which were dotting her neck. "I really need to go in now."

Ignoring her words, Jeff began to fondle her breasts

"Anyone ever tell you that you've got great breasts?" he asked in a voice growing husky with desire.

With a sigh, Jordan took his intruding hand in both of her own and said, "I don't want you to do that. And I really do have to go in now."

She placed his hand on the seat between them and once again reached for the door handle. But he pulled her back and began to push her skirt up over her thighs.

"Come on," he pleaded. "I spent $50 taking you out tonight. You owe me more than a polite thank you After all, it's not like you've never done it before."

Jordan jerked away, pulling down her skirt. She grabbed her purse and hastily fished out her billfold. She removed two bills and handed them to him.

"I owe you nothing," she said. "I'm sorry if you thought you were buying sexual favors in return for a meal and a movie. Here's my share of the evening's entertainment. This should make us even."

When he made no move to take the money, she tossed it in his lap and quickly pushed the door open and escaped from the confines of the vehicle. She ran lightly up the steps to the broad front porch. As she fitted her key in the lock, she heard the squeal of tires as Jeff made an angry exit from the drive and raced away. The roar of his motor interrupted the nighttime quiet of the sedate, tree-lined street.

Jordan closed the door and locked it, then turned off the porch light and leaned against the door for a minute, staring into the darkness. Another disastrous date, she thought. It seemed that every man who took her out assumed she would be an easy mark. After all, they apparently reasoned, she was a divorcee. And many men liked to think that divorced women were willing to have sex with any man who took them out.

Jordan was tired of it.

And Jeff had seemed so nice, exhibiting an almost

boyish charm the times they had gone for coffee together between classes. He was a graduate assistant in her anthropology class and had seemed genuinely interested in her progress in the class.

You'd think I'd be used to it by now, she told herself as she made her way down the dark hallway. But she felt disappointed. She had allowed herself to think that Jeff would be different.

She realized she was in for a bad time almost from the very minute he picked her up at the dress shop where she worked afternoons and evenings. He seemed to think that she was supposed to be grateful to him for taking her out. And he kept bringing up her divorced state, implying that it must be difficult for her to get along without a man after being accustomed to having one around all the time.

Of course, he was partly correct, Jordan admitted to herself as she pushed open the kitchen door. She did get lonely for male companionship, but she was certainly not going to get involved with every man who came along and wanted to go to bed with her. And there had been several of those in the two years since her divorce. But Jordan was lonely for someone who would be her friend as well as her lover, someone who would respect as well as desire her. Jeff obviously was willing to bypass friendship and head right for bed.

The clock in the hallway struck one o'clock. She really should go over her notes before going to bed. She was scheduled to give a report in her graduate seminar on the history of Franco-American relations.

But she would have a cup of tea first. It was hard to go from a date with Jeff to the escapades of Napoleon.

As usual, Aunt Sarah's kitchen was spotlessly clean due in great part to the scrubbing Jordan had given it last Sunday. Her aunt had very high standards, but sometimes Jordan thought she carried her cleanliness routine to ridiculous lengths. Jordan was grateful, however, for the many years she had been able to make her home with Aunt Sarah and Uncle Joe, so she usually tried to keep up with her aunt's endless list of chores as best she could.

The only thing out of place in the large, old-fashioned kitchen was a tray with two slices of apple pie on Aunt Sarah's blue Wedgwood china. Jordan smiled wryly at the sight. How pleasant it would have been to end her date by inviting the young man in for a piece of her aunt's truly fine apple pie. Too bad it had not turned out that way.

She appreciated her aunt's gesture nonetheless, especially since Jordan realized that Sarah had disapproved of her divorce. Jordan had left her husband, and women of her aunt's generation had difficulty accepting a woman's right to do that. Even though Sarah acknowledged Jordan's former husband's shortcomings—his womanizing, his drifting from job to job, his seeming inability to assume responsibility—she maintained it was a woman's duty to accept her lot.

"Your mother always has," Sarah would tell Jordan. "That father of yours never could stay in a job for very long, but Grace has stuck with him all these years. Of course, I'll admit your father's never seemed to keep a woman on the side like Clayton does, but maybe the boy's just sowing his wild oats. Some men just have to do that, you know. And you two got married so young, maybe he hasn't had a chance to get it all out of his system yet. At least Clayton isn't mean. You could do worse, Jordan. He'll probably settle down when the children start to come."

Perhaps her aunt was right, but Jordan did not want children born into an unstable marriage. And she knew that even if Clayton changed, they could never have the sort of love for which Jordan yearned. This she could never explain to Sarah. Her aunt would think her a romantic fool—which perhaps she was. But right or wrong, the desire to be Clayton's wife was no longer a part of her. That time had passed in her life. She hoped that someday she would find a man she loved enough to marry, but if she did not, she would remain single. She would rather go through life alone than married to a man she did not love.

Jordan started to heat some water for tea but changed her mind in favor of a glass of milk to accompany one of those pieces of pie. Jeff will never know what he missed, she thought after the first delicious bite. Well, it serves him right.

Her spirits improving, she reached for her mail, which her aunt had left propped up between the salt-and-pepper shakers where Jordan would be sure to see it. Jordan sorted through the envelopes as she savored her pie and milk.

One was a letter from the university library. That would be for the overdue book residing on her desk upstairs.

The second envelope bore the logo of a national oil company. It would contain a bill for gasoline that she would be hard pressed to pay, especially after the unplanned expenditure of $25 this evening and an unbudgeted trip to the dentist last week. She wished she could afford to buy a car that was more economical to operate than the elderly sedan she had bought following her divorce and on which she was still making payments.

But Jordan knew that a new car would have to wait until she graduated and got a job that paid better than the salesclerk wages she earned for working in one of Lincoln's better dress shops. The salary she earned for selling clothes to well-to-do coeds and stylish young matrons was in no way indicative of the garments' expensive price tags. But her salary, small as it was, covered her tuition, books, and other college expenses.

She would not have been able to afford graduate school at all if it were not for her aunt and uncle's kindness. They had insisted that she return to live in their big house on Maple Street following her divorce and once again make her home in the house where her mother and aunt had been raised and where Jordan and her mother had come to live off and on over the years when Tom Marshall was away working in an oilfield in Iran or on a ship in the Pacific or perhaps mining coal along the Amazon. It was only in the years since Jordan had reached adulthood that Grace Marshall had finally given in to her husband's urgings and joined him for some of his travels. She now lived with her husband aboard an excursion craft he captained in the warm waters of French Polynesia.

But while Jordan was growing up, Grace had refused to follow her husband on his foreign travels, insisting their daughter should be raised in a God-fearing American home. Jordan had often longed to at least visit her father in all those distant places from which his many post cards and letters had arrived. But only when he worked in this country, and once for a few months in Canada, had Grace budged from the town of her birth.

Jordan had accepted her aunt and uncle's invitation to share their home once again. She was grateful for the chance to pursue a graduate degree in American history and enhance her chances of securing a desirable teaching position at the high school or college level when she finished. She had fallen into the pattern of doing most of the heavy housework and yardwork for aging relatives, which, combined with her job and her studies, left her little time for much else.

The third letter was from Clayton's mother. Jordan placed it unopened with the two other envelopes. It could wait until tomorrow. Like Aunt Sarah, Clayton's mother did not approve of Jordan divorcing her son and had been trying for the past two years to manipulate a reconciliation. Jordan was simply not in the mood to read about how well her former husband was doing in his new job—whatever it currently happened to be.

The fourth and last envelope bore a return address from the department of anthropology and archaeology at the University of Oklahoma. That would be a letter informing her that she had not been awarded a summer fellowship. Well, they certainly had taken their time to let her know, not that she had really expected anything to come of her application.

She put it with the other unopened envelopes and took the last bite of pie. As she sipped her milk, she stared at that last letter. It had felt like more than one page. It only took one page to turn someone down.

But Jordan knew it had to be a refusal. They had probably been besieged with applicants. After all, the fellowship was for ten hours of graduate credit for a summer's work as well as the opportunity to participate in an archaeological excavation with all expenses paid, including transportation to and from the eastern Oklahoma site. Something like that did not come along every day. The fellowship even included a $100-a-month stipend to cover incidental expenses.

She picked up the envelope once again and felt it. There definitely was more than one sheet of paper inside.

You don't suppose...

Jordan ripped it open and rapidly scanned the two-page letter.

Then she reread it to make sure.

"Well, I'll be," she said aloud to her aunt's very clean kitchen. "I'm going on a dig."

The magazine lay unread on Jordan's lap as she watched the changing countryside from the window of the bus. She ignored the admiring glances of the man sitting next to her as she leaned forward, trying not to miss anything while the bus meandered its way along the winding, two-lane highway.

She pushed a curtain of silvery blond hair away from her face and absently unbuttoned the jacket of her navy linen suit—an outfit she had been able to purchase with her store discount at the end of last season for less than cost. She had felt quite smartly attired when she boarded the plane in Omaha and hoped that for once she would not be mistaken for a teenager. Jordan knew she looked much younger than her twenty-six years, and not at all like a woman who had spent three years trying to make a marriage work and two more as a divorced woman on her own in the world.

But right now, she admitted, she did feel more like a teenager for this was the first time in her life that she had ever gone on a trip by herself. It was the first time she had ever done anything quite so daring. It felt good.

With a small sigh of contentment, Jordan leaned back in her seat and began to absently turn the pages of the fashion magazine she had purchased at the Tulsa airport, but her vivid turquoise-blue eyes kept straying back to the window.

The landscape was wooded and lushly green, not yet scorched by the relentless summer sun that was inevitable in this part of the country. Jordan watched the miles of tree-covered hillsides punctuated by an occasional small farm roll past her window. How different it all was from eastern Nebraska, whose orderly, flat countryside and squared-off fields of corn and wheat marched row after endless row across the prairie.

And the towns. As the bus wound its way southward from Tulsa through the hills of eastern Oklahoma, it stopped at each small community along the way. Such sleepy little towns they were, some with aging court-houses in a central square and memorials to war dead providing roosts for dozing pigeons.

Many of the towns looked as though progress and prosperity had long since moved away, along with many of their residents. Boarded-up store fronts and run-down buildings were not unusual and contrasted sharply with the bustling prosperity Jordan had observed around the city of Tulsa where more oil wells than trees pushed their way skyward, and modern glass-and-steel buildings had the look of new money and a bright future.

But the further the bus took her into Oklahoma's hill country, the smaller and more worn out the towns became. Many of them bore Indian names—Coweta, Broken Arrow, Tullahasee, Oketah, Checotah. Jordan peered out of her window during each brief stop, half-expecting to see blanketed squaws and painted braves, although she realized today's Indians probably differed greatly from the image Hollywood movies had long ago placed in her head.

She smiled to herself as she watched two frolicking colts race each other across a rolling meadow while their elders grazed in the shade of a cottonwood grove. It was grand to be going someplace again, really grand, Jordan mused as she ignored the open magazine in her lap.

Such a rut her life had fallen into—attending college, working in the dress shop, and helping with the yard and housework. Of course, there was an occasional date, but more often than not, they ended up like the one with Jeff.

She pushed a strand of pale hair back from her fore-head and mentally chastised herself. Here she was feeling sorry for herself when she was embarking on an adventure!

Not only was she going to earn ten hours of college credit this summer, putting her goal of a graduate degree in her chosen field that much closer—and at no cost to her—but she was also getting a chance to do something she had always wanted to do. It was a dream come true.

Jordan gave up on her magazine and put it in her satchel, exchanging it for a map of Oklahoma, which she used to follow the bus's progress through the next few towns.

The bus crossed a narrow bridge over the Fourche Maline River, and Jordan's eyes scanned its banks. Somewhere along the banks of that river was the place where she would spend her summer excavating the remains of a long-dead civilization, learning about people who lived in this land thousands of years before there were roads and bridges and towns.

It wouldn't be long now. Seneca was the next stop. Jordan put the map back in her satchel and consulted her compact mirror. Quickly she brushed her hair and applied a pink gloss to her lips. She smoothed her skirt over slim hips and was ready to get off the bus long before it rolled into the quiet town of Seneca, county seat of Cheyenne County and the end of her ride.

Seneca was much like the other county seats she had seen during her bus ride. Its courthouse stood in the town square, which was rimmed by most of the town's business district. Several elderly men sat on park benches, enjoying the shade of the square's spreading elms as they whittled away their afternoon making sticks smaller with their penknives.

Two blocks past the courthouse the bus pulled into a service station, which apparently doubled as a bus station. Jordan gathered up her purse and satchel, then said good-bye to her seatmate.

She stepped down from the bus into the warm Okla-

homa sun and waited for the driver to retrieve her suitcases and bedroll from the luggage bin.

"Expecting someone, miss?" the driver asked as he
set out her two cases. "You did mean to get off in Seneca?" he asked as he took in her smart suit and high-
heeled sandals, which were apparently not the usual attire for passengers who got off in this town.

"Yes," Jordan answered. "Someone is supposed to
meet me."

But as she looked up and down the broad street, all
she could see was a red hound strolling down its
middle.

"Someone will meet me," Jordan repeated. "They're
probably just late. I'll call a cab if they don't come."

At this, the driver laughed. "Not in this town, you
won't. Well, if there's been a mixup, there's a small
motel 'bout two blocks on down the street, and there'll
be a northbound bus 'bout ten in the morning."

Jordan thanked him and watched as the bus motored
down the wide, empty street, sending the hound scurrying and leaving a billowing trail of dust in its wake.
She shouldered her purse and satchel, tucked her bulky
bedroll under her arm, and picked up her two suitcases
before carefully crossing the gravel driveway of the service station, her high-heeled sandals making footing
difficult on the loose gravel.

A stout, gray-haired woman was watching through
the station's front window. Jordan put her luggage on a
bench by the door under a faded metal sign that announced Coca-Cola was sold within.

The inside of the station was not air-conditioned, but
just being out of the sun made Jordan feel cooler. She
bought a Coke and asked the woman if she could please
wait inside for her ride.

The woman nodded pleasantly and eased herself
into a wicker rocking chair. "Who you waiting for,

honey?" she asked as she fanned with a folded newspaper.

"Someone from the excavation site is supposed to
pick me up. I'm here to join an archaeological project
that's located a few miles from here."

The woman nodded. "Four miles south of town on
Chester Wilson's place. Folks from the university are
running it."

"That's right," Jordan agreed. "I understand it's
been under way for a couple of weeks now."

Jordan walked over to the window and looked out.
"I wonder if they've forgotten I was coming."

"Oh, I expect Cookie'll be along shortly. He's my
cousin, and I've never known him to be on time in
sixty-seven years. He works out there for the university
folks." With that, she unfolded her newspaper and began to read, her curiosity about Jordan apparently satis-
fied.

Jordan leaned against a glass case that held a display
of dusty fishing lures. What if no one comes, she
wondered. She supposed she could hire someone to
drive her out to "Chester Wilson's place." She hated
to use what little money she had brought with her for
that. She was counting on the fellowship stipend to
cover all incidental expenses, but she was not sure
when she was to receive the first installment.

Her worry ended, however, when a white van bearing a University of Oklahoma logo pulled into the
driveway, and an elderly man in overalls emerged from
the driver's side of the vehicle.

He strolled through the open door of the station,
glanced at Jordan, then greeted his cousin and asked if
a young fellow had gotten off the bus.

"No one got off but the young lady here," the
woman told him, "but she's the one you're after."

And to Jordan, she said, "Honey, this here's Cookie. He'll take you where you're supposed to go."

Cookie shook his head as he peered at Jordan over the rim of his glasses. He pulled a piece of paper from his pocket and consulted it. "I'm supposed to pick up Jordan E. Marshall from Lincoln, Nebraska," he announced.

Jordan smiled and said, "That's me."

The man looked down at her, his weathered face creasing in an answering smile. "Well, how about that! Professor Nicolle is sure going to be surprised. He thinks he's getting another fellow to work out there."

As Cookie loaded her suitcases and bedroll into the van, he explained his name was really Fred, but that everyone called him Cookie since his days in the Navy when he cooked on a destroyer.

"And I had a café for twenty-five years down on courthouse square 'til I retired. Been bored to death ever since. I was glad for the chance to sign on as the professor's cook, handyman, and errand runner. Worked for him summer before last when he had a dig over in Pushmataha County."

Jordan had a difficult time negotiating the high step into the van because of her pencil-slim skirt. Cookie gave her a hand, saying, "You're a little bit of a thing, aren't you? And pretty as a picture. Yep, the professor's going to have a real surprise when he sees you. You sure don't look like anyone I've ever seen at a dig. Hope you brought some other kinds of clothes," he said with a chuckle, "and those shoes'll never do."

Jordan stared down at her sandals with their narrow straps revealing pink-painted toenails. She supposed she did seem overdressed for the last leg of her journey, but she had wanted to look nice for her plane ride, although she had soon realized how unnecessary

that was when she saw her casually dressed fellow passengers. Her only other experience with air travel had
been years before, and people had dressed up more
then. Perhaps she would have a chance to change
clothes before she met Professor Nicolle and the
others.

Professor Paul Nicolle. Jordan remembered how she
had admired the man's name when the letter had arrived from him congratulating her on being selected for
the summer fellowship. And she recalled how intimidated she had felt by the academic degrees and titles
that followed his signature. His letter had explained
that the fellowship would provide ten weeks of on-site
experience at a small archaeological excavation located
on the Fourche Maline River in southeastern Oklahoma's Cheyenne County.

Professor Nicolle's letter went on to explain that he
expected the site to be a pre-Caddoan one, having been
occupied by predecessors of the Plains Indians who later lived in the region. He was hopeful that the site
would date back at least 5,000 years and told her to be
prepared for a summer of hot, dirty, yet rewarding
work combined with an intensive study of the culture
they would be unearthing and of archaeological methods. He had included a list of the clothing, bedding,
and supplies she would need, and explained that living
conditions at the site would be "primitive."

Jordan had been both surprised and delighted when
she read the letter. She never dreamed she would have
a chance at being selected when she entered her research paper and filled out the application at her anthropology professor's urging. And nothing Aunt Sarah
said about rattlesnakes or tornadoes or sunstroke could
dampen her enthusiasm.

Only now, as the van turned off the paved highway
and bounced its way along a rutted dirt road taking her

farther and farther from any vestiges of civilization, did Jordan begin to have a tiny doubt. Her aunt had said it was harebrained to give up the comforts of home and a good job to spend the summer in the wilderness digging up the bones of people who had been dead for thousands of years.

"It's the sort of thing your father would do," Aunt Sarah admonished when Jordan told her of the fellowship. "So impractical. The things my sister has had to put up with," she said with a shake of her head, the tone of her voice revealing her disapproval of Jordan's father.

And indeed, it had been her father that Jordan immediately thought of when her professor showed her the announcement of the summer fellowship. It was just the sort of thing her father would encourage her to do.

Her interest in archaeology had begun as a child. Her father was an amateur archaeologist of sorts, along with being an amateur musician, botanist, boat builder, ham radio operator, photographer, bird watcher, and historian. Her aunt was fond of saying that Jordan's father knew a little bit about lots of things and not much about anything. And perhaps there was some truth in her words. He had never stayed with anything for very long.

But as a small girl, Jordan thought her father knew just about everything. And archaeology held a particular fascination for him. He was always writing to Jordan about the various archaeological sites he had visited around the world. He even selected her name, Tom was fond of telling his daughter, after he visited the sites of some of the ancient civilizations that once had flourished along the famous River Jordan which flowed from the Sea of Galilee to the Dead Sea in the Holy Land. During his visits home Tom and his daughter had read many books together about prehistoric man and long-dead civilizations. Some of those books still resided on Jordan's bookshelf back in Lincoln.

And there had been that wonderful trip to Spiro, Oklahoma, when Jordan was ten. The present journey to Oklahoma was not her first visit to the Sooner state.

Jordan and her parents had been living in Decatur, Arkansas, where her father worked on a weekly newspaper. But Tom had not gotten along well with the editor, and he accepted a job teaching in a rural school in Missouri. On their way to the new job, however, the family had taken a side trip over the Oklahoma line to visit the famous Spiro Mounds. They checked into a small tourist court in the town of Spiro and spent the next four days inspecting the mounds—one of which was being worked by an archaeological crew from the University of Oklahoma—and visiting the area museums that displayed the artifacts unearthed at the site.

Jordan had been completely entranced with the romance and mystery of Spiro. Imagine, a civilization that had prospered long before Columbus discovered America, only to disappear, its remains hidden for centuries until curious archaeologists evacuated the strange earthen mounds, uncovering the vast collection of Spiro treasures.

Jordan had marveled at the intricacies of the artifacts and spent hours viewing bone carvings, elegant pottery, magnificent silver and shell jewelry, and skillfully made tools and weapons—all of which demonstrated that the Spiro people were far more advanced than the Plains Indian culture that later thrived in the area.

She never got over her fascination with prehistory and was always drawn to articles on archaeology in magazines and to archaeological exhibits in museums. During her undergraduate years, she had taken courses in archaeology and anthropology of the Americas to complement her major in American history, wanting to master the prehistory of America as well as that which had been recorded. And she had taken a course in Cultural Centers of Ancient America as part of her graduate program. Prehistory continued to be an area of constant fascination for her, and she would have liked to pursue a degree in archaeology if she could have justified it. But she was well aware that even a master's degree in a highly academic field like archaeology was not enough to secure employment in the field. And a Ph.D. would mean several years more of study and poverty. She was twenty-six years old. It was time for her to establish a residence of her own and start living like an independent, grown-up woman. She would complete her master's in American history and get a teaching job. And the sooner the better.

Jordan had worked hard on her research paper in Professor Miller's class. She chose the Spiro Mounds as her topic and wove her own reminiscences about the site into what she hoped was a knowledgeable and carefully researched paper.

Professor Miller had been impressed. He called her into his office, suggested that she submit the paper for consideration by a fellowship committee at the University of Oklahoma, and showed her the announcement for the competition in an archaeology journal. It was open to graduate students majoring in anthropology, archaeology, or American history. Applicants were to submit "an original paper which should effectively demonstrate a substantial knowledge of American prehistory and an affinity for the study of archaeology."

Jordan was flattered by Professor Miller's encouragement, even though she was certain her paper would not be scholarly enough to win.

But much to her surprise it had.

Professor Miller had been pleased. But her job at the

dress shop would not be waiting for her when she returned next fall, the store manager curtly informed her. Her arthritic uncle complained that he would not be able to tend his garden without her help. And Aunt Sarah had been counting on her to paint the front room and make new curtains for the kitchen. What about waxing the floors? And the windows?

"I swear, child," Aunt Sarah admonished, "you've got too much of your father in you for your own good. Such irresponsibility. Leaving good jobs for bad. Traipsing off after dreams."

Only her father approved. His letter came the day before she left Lincoln. "Reach out to life," he wrote, "because it usually doesn't come looking for you There's plenty of time to settle down when you're old."

Even her mother, in a brief postscript, had admitted that "life can sometimes be enhanced by a little travel."

Jordan realized her own life had become all too much like her aunt and uncle's. There were no surprises. Her days had a sameness about them. There were no breaks in her routine other than an occasional date or a Sunday afternoon fishing trip—always at the same marina with a stop at the same café on the way home. Her aunt would order fried chicken, and her uncle fried steak. And Jordan usually found herself nibbling at a mediocre fish platter.

It was time for a change, Jordan had decided. Over her aunt's dour warnings, Jordan had written to Professor Paul Nicolle, assistant chairman of the department of anthropology and archaeology at the University of Oklahoma, accepting the fellowship and stating the date of her arrival in Seneca. She carefully signed her name Jordan E. Marshall and mailed it.

It was done. She was committed. Maybe it wasn't the

right thing to do, but it was certainly exciting. It was going to be refreshing to climb out of her rut for at least one summer.

Her aunt and uncle had given her begrudging farewells wrought with warnings about plane crashes and natural disasters.

And now, here she was, tired and apprehensive and rapidly being covered with a layer of fine red dust as she bounced along a rutted country road sitting next to a man called Cookie on her way to a new experience.

The wind from the open window whipped her hair around her face unmercifully, but rolling up the window was out of the question in this heat.

"Is it much further?" she asked as she battled her hair.

"Right over the hill," Cookie answered. He looked over at her and grinned. "Better start getting prettied up."

Jordan tried. She tissued the dust from her fair skin and applied a touch of powder to her shiny nose. And she tried in vain to gain control of her blowing hair.

The van turned into the drive of a small, drab farmhouse with chickens pecking about the yard. This must be Chester Wilson's place, she told herself.

The chickens scattered with loud squawks as Cookie drove past a leaning barn and stopped to open a gate. The jostling Jordan had received before was nothing compared to the ride which followed, as Cookie took the van across a sloping, hillside pasture. Several dozen red and white cows, many with white-faced calves at their side, paused from their grazing long enough to watch the van go bouncing by.

Then through another gate and the river came into view. The Fourche Maline. Evil Fork. Jordan wondered at the Frenchman who had named the river. What had prompted such a forboding name?

Cookie explained that the river was the eastern fork of the Poteau River and was normally a sleepy little stream until a hard rain came and caused it to overrun its narrow banks with a vengeance. At times like that, he told her, the Fourche Maline deserved its name.

They followed the river for a time, leaving the fences and cattle behind them. The area on this side of the river appeared to be untouched wilderness, but across the river, Jordan could see an unfinished highway angling itself toward the opposite bank. Heavy road-building equipment stood idly by the roadbed. No workmen were in sight.

The highway ended abruptly just short of the towering bluff, looking as though it were ready to thrust itself across the beautiful, free-running river and continue its journey on the other side.

Directly across the river from the unfinished highway was what Jordan realized with a start must be the archaeological encampment. It was composed of three larger tents and several clusters of smaller tents, plus an assortment of parked vehicles.

That was all.

It was indeed primitive and, at this moment, deserted.

Cookie parked the van beside one of the larger tents and honked the horn.

"Well, here we are, little lady—your summer home," he said with a chuckle. "The others'll be along shortly. And are they in for a surprise!"

Jordan wished he would stop telling her what a surprise she was going to be. She was nervous enough without that.

She accepted Cookie's offered hand and climbed down from the van, then stood by the vehicle surveying the camp. Well, the professor had said "tents." He had warned in his letter that the camp was primitive.

What was it she had expected, she asked herself ruefully.

Somehow the professor's letter had not prepared her for the actual sight. Tents. In the middle of nowhere. Next to a river that liked to flood its banks. Her aunt and uncle's warnings all came rushing back to her.

She felt very foolish standing there in her linen suit and high-heeled shoes. Very foolish indeed.

Chapter Two

They seemed to emerge from the top of several large earthen mounds that occupied a sizable area near the river. Jordan counted ten men and one woman trudging across the field.

All of the crew were wearing shorts. All but two of the men were shirtless, and the woman was wearing what looked like a bathing suit top. Their scanty attire revealed bodies already toasted brown from weeks of working in the sun. Jordan felt very aware of both her clothing and her fair skin as the group approached the van in answer to Cookie's honked summons.

A tall, dark-haired man led the way and appeared to be in charge, which surprised Jordan for the man's broad forehead, high cheekbones, dark eyes and heavy, black hair bore the unmistakable stamp of American Indian ancestry. Nicolle was a French name.

His lack of a shirt revealed a smooth, broad chest and tautly muscled stomach and shoulders. He walked with long, purposeful strides, a stern scowl on his handsome face.

As he drew near, Jordan stepped forward and said, "Professor Nicolle?"

He nodded curtly. "Yes. And who are you? We aren't equipped for visitors, miss." He shot an angry look at the broadly smiling cook, apparently showing his displeasure at having such a person as Jordan brought to interrupt their work.

Jordan extended a small hand. "I'm Jordan Marshall."

The professor's scowl increased He looked as ferocious as any warrior in a western movie. Jordan took an involuntary step backward and withdrew her offered hand.

"But you're a woman," he said angrily.

"I never said I wasn't," Jordan said in a small voice. "Does it make a difference?"

"It makes a lot of difference," the angry professor continued. "For one thing, I certainly would have found out a whole lot more about you if I'd known that Jordan Marshall was a woman, and a very small one at that."

"And just what would you have wanted to know?" she asked, her own anger starting to grow. "Perhaps I can tell you now."

"For one thing, I would have wanted to know if you've had any previous camp life. But I don't need to ask. You've obviously never roughed it a day in your life. With a male, one can assume he's at least spent a night or two out-of-doors and is tough enough to make it through a hot, dirty summer full of back-breaking work. And one can assume a male is strong enough to lift a shovel full of dirt. I'll bet you've never been involved in any archaeological projects before—or ever done any museum work."

Jordan felt the color rising in her cheeks. "No, I have not," she said angrily. "I am here to gain experience. The announcement for the fellowship did not indicate that prior experience was a prerequisite."

"No, but from the paper you submitted, I assumed you'd worked with the Spiro artifacts. You sounded very knowledgeable and used many on-site observations. Where did you get all that information? That was supposed to be an original paper."

"I can assure you," she said icily, "that the work is my own. If it sounded like I had been there—well, I have, but not as a member of an archaeological project. And I don't think you have any right to exclude me from this project because I'm not a strong male with previous experience. If those were among your criteria for the fellowship, that should have been stated in the announcement calling for applicants."

Professor Nicolle glared down at her. He was obviously a man unaccustomed to being challenged.

If only she felt as brave as she was trying to sound, Jordan thought. He's right, of course. She had never spent the night out-of-doors in her life. And suddenly the primitiveness of the site and the prospect of spending a summer at hard, physical labor without the benefit of running water, air-conditioning, and electricity seemed grim indeed. Why had it sounded so glamorous back in Lincoln?

Judging from the looks of the assembled crew, working on a dig was anything but glamorous. They were sunbaked and dirty, although the one woman among them still managed to look quite beautiful in spite of her dusty arms and legs. Statuesque, her curvaceous figure was quite apparent in her hip-hugging shorts and her brief bathing suit top. Her olive complexion was enhanced by a deep tan, and her coal-black hair was pulled back in a flowing pony tail, exposing her high, patrician forehead and emphasizing her dark, Latin eyes.

The woman returned Jordan's appraising glance and moved to Professor Nicolle's side, putting a possessive hand on his arm. "What Paul means," she said in an oversweet voice that revealed a lilting Spanish accent, "is that this is a pretty strenuous life for the uninitiated. I don't know what you thought an archaeological dig was like, but it's not a place you come to in high-heeled shoes and a designer suit."

Darn those shoes, Jordan thought angrily. She would have changed them in Seneca.

"I'm sorry if my shoes and clothing upset you," she said, "but I came here directly from the Tulsa airport. You could hardly expect me to fly on a plane wearing cutoffs and a bikini top."

The woman's smile froze on her face, and she looked up at the professor with an irritated shrug.

Never had Jordan felt so unwanted. She was perilously close to tears. Only the knowledge that she could not possibly let that insufferable man see her cry gave her the strength to deny the waiting tears. Crying would only serve to confirm Professor Nicolle's opinion of her. He obviously considered her a weak, silly, incompetent girl. And what infuriated her the most was that was exactly how she viewed herself at this moment.

Maybe she should ask Cookie to drive her back to town. She could catch the bus to Tulsa tomorrow and be back in Lincoln by tomorrow evening. Only she did not have enough money for a bus ticket to Tulsa, much less a plane ticket to Lincoln.

If she left, she would have to wire her aunt and uncle for money, something they had precious little of with their retirement income. And she could almost hear the "I told you so" coming from her aunt's lips.

No. She would tough it out. And it was much more than not wanting to admit her aunt might have been right about the trip. As Jordan studied the handsome, arrogant man standing in front of her, she decided she did not want to give him the satisfaction of seeing her turn tail and run. He was obviously accustomed to intimidating people. Well, she was not going to give him that pleasure.

Maybe she should have investigated more thoroughly before accepting the fellowship. But she had not, and she was already here. She would have to make the best of it, in spite of this rude man. And surely the rest of the crew would not be as unfriendly as the professor.

With the small reserve of strength left in her weary body, she reached into the van and pulled out her suitcases and bedroll. Even her pale blue luggage looked out of place in this wild, primitive place.

"If you will show me to my tent, I'll remove my offensive clothing and put on something more acceptable to your dress code," Jordan announced.

The hot sun glared down on them. A radio in the open-sided kitchen tent was playing a popular love song. A cow could be heard lowing in a distant pasture. Sweat started to roll down the inside of Jordan's collar.

The suitcases were growing impossibly heavy as she stood waiting for Professor Nicolle to make his decision. Was he going to allow her to stay or was he going to order Cookie to take her back to town?

Jordan stood firmly, returning the professor's hostile stare as the rest of the group watched intently, their eyes darting from one antagonist to the other. Jordan realized what mismatched adversaries they must seem to the others—a tall, half-naked Indian with jet black hair and a small, fair woman with flowing hair the color of corn silk and clothing that looked like a fashion magazine.

Finally, Professor Nicolle shrugged and abruptly turned away. He walked in long, purposeful strides to one of the larger tents, its rolled-up sides revealing large tables covered with pieces of broken pottery.

The dark-haired woman flashed a brilliant smile for Jordan's benefit. "Well, it looks as though you are to stay," she said, extending a slender hand. "I'm Professor DeSilvestro—Yvonne. I'm second in command here. Welcome to our little dig."

She turned to a sandy-haired young man. "Dennis, why don't you double up with Carl and give her your tent. I suppose you'd better dismantle it and move it nearer mine to give her some privacy." With that, she turned and followed Professor Nicolle into the open tent.

The young man to whom Yvonne had given her instructions stepped forward and relieved Jordan of her suitcases, which she relinquished gratefully.

"Dennis Compton at your service," he said with a cocky grin. "If you'll give us fifteen minutes, we'd be delighted to move a tent for the first human being to ever stare down Paul Nicolle."

Several of the other young men grinned broadly and nodded in agreement. They introduced themselves as Sam Shaw from Tulsa and Wolf Birdsong from Anadarko—both students of Professor Nicolle's and here for the summer. Three others were also students of the professor's but were just here for a week or two. They explained that there would be many students drifting in and out over the summer, giving the project whatever time they could spare. And there were three of Professor DeSilvestro's students who had accompanied her from Peru to participate in the dig. Juan and Miguel spoke little English, it seemed. Edgar, a slender man with a broad, friendly smile, spoke hesitant but easily understandable English.

Jordan tried a few words of her college Spanish on the trio to which they replied in such a rapid flow of words that she begged, "*Mas despacio, por favor*. More slowly, please."

The friendliness of the young men who were to be her associates for the summer encouraged Jordan and helped compensate for her cool reception from Paul Nicolle.

She leaned against the van and watched Dennis, Sam, and Wolf quickly dismantle one of the tents. Its wooden slat floor was carried across the campsite to a small grove of locust trees, where a lone tent stood apart from the others. The dismantled tent was quickly erected over the slatted floor, and Jordan was ceremoniously escorted to her new home.

Dennis showed her how to tie back the tent flaps and roll up the side to allow for ventilation. And he pointed out a separate shower and latrine that had been erected for feminine use.

"Besides Professor DeSilvestro, we will occasionally have women come in to help," Dennis pointed out. "None that look like you, however," he said in a flirtatious tone, adding an intimate pat to the small of her back.

Jordan stepped away from his touch and turned her attention to Sam, who was short and stocky and had white ointment on his sunburned nose. He presented her with some coat hangers and showed her how to hang her clothes from the tent's ridgepole.

Wolf, who informed Jordan that he was a member of the Comanche tribe, and Dennis quickly moved in the tent's furnishings—an army cot with a rather lumpy mattress and two orange crates for storage. Jordan thanked them for their effort, and the three of them took off with a war whoop in a wild race to the river to join the other crew members in an afternoon swim.

In spite of the crudeness of the accommodations, Jordan soon got into the pioneering spirit. She unpacked her suitcases, hung her shirts on hangers from the ridgepole and pushed them to the back of the tent. She stacked her neatly folded shorts and jeans in a shelf of one of the upended orange crates.

She took time out from her settling in to replace her suit with a pair of red knit shorts and a pale pink T-shirt. She stored her traveling clothes and a few other garments for which she would obviously have little use in one of her empty suitcases and slid both cases under the cot.

Placing one of the crates near her bed, she put her clock and radio on top along with a tiny picture of her parents in a dainty silver frame, then arranged her cosmetics on the shelf below. On the crate's bottom she put the few magazines and books she had brought. She placed her shoes in a neat row under her bed.

Using the bed linen she had brought with her, she made up the cot with pale blue sheets and a colorful quilt. For a finishing touch she spread a small rag rug on the floor and stepped back to survey her domain. It pleased her.

"'Tain't much, but it's home," she said aloud. She would ask Cookie to get a can of spray paint for the orange crates next time he was in town—maybe a soft blue to match the sheets.

With a last look at her surprisingly homey dwelling, she strolled down to the river to watch the antics of the eight young men as they swam and splashed around in a deep pool the river had formed at the base of the sandstone bluff that dominated the opposite bank of the river. From this perspective, the intrusive highway construction was hidden from view.

Jordan realized her arrival on the scene had not gone unnoticed by the swimmers. Her shorts and knit shirt were certainly more revealing than her linen suit had been. A tiny gold chain circled her neck, and her white sandals—low-heeled this time—showed off her small feet and their carefully polished pink nails.

She had brushed the dust from her silvery hair until it shone, and it now fell in soft waves around her face and cascaded over her shoulders. Feeling much cooler and more at ease than when she had arrived at the encampment, she took a seat on a flat rock near the bank.

The boys called out for her to join them, but she smilingly shook her head no. She was content to sit on the rock and watch. A cool breeze stirred the leaves of the willow and cottonwood trees that shaded the clear water of the river and gently teased the tendrils of Jordan's hair.

As she looked around, she realized that this was a truly beautiful place with the imposing cliff and swiftly moving river thickly lined with trees and lush foliage. A mockingbird sat on a tree limb above her entertaining itself with an impressive repertoire of notes—melodious and otherwise.

She kicked off her sandals and dangled her toes in the clear, cold water. This was a nice place, she decided. She resolved to enjoy the beauty of the land and learn all she could while living and working here. She would not let one man ruin her summer, even if he was in charge.

And at that moment, the man himself—with Yvonne DeSilvestro at his side—appeared at the top of the slope that led to the river. The two professors strolled down the incline without looking in Jordan's direction. Yvonne paused on the bank to slip off her sneakers and pull off her shorts, revealing the bottom half to the bikini top she wore, then stepped out on a jutting rock and smiled back at Paul Nicolle.

It seemed to Jordan that the young men in the water were all stealing glances at Yvonne. Paul Nicolle, on the other hand, stared at the Peruvian professor with a frankly admiring look as she gracefully made a shallow dive into the cool, clear water.

Paul followed her onto the rock and poised for an instant on his toes, thigh muscles rippling, before he dived into the river. Yvonne was waiting for him in the center of the river pool when he surfaced. The exotic-looking Latin woman watched as Paul swam toward her with smooth, strong strokes, then threw a bold, deliberate glance in Jordan's direction, her coal-black eyes full of challenge. Jordan understood their message. Paul was hers.

Jordan felt a strange prickling sensation overtake the skin on her arms and neck. Why did she suddenly feel that woman was her enemy? Yvonne was more than welcome to the arrogant Indian archaeologist. Jordan found him insufferable.

Professor DeSilvestro, Jordan learned at dinner, was considered an expert on the prehistoric Incan culture of her native Peru. Paul Nicolle had worked on an archaeological excavation with her last summer near Lake Titicaca in southern Peru, and she was reciprocating by acting as a consultant on this dig and serving as second in command. Dennis told Jordan that the two professors had met while doing graduate work at Oxford University in England. He also informed Jordan that Nicolle was the toughest but the best professor he had ever had. Sam and Wolf agreed.

As Jordan watched the tall, handsome Indian man and the statuesque Latin woman, she could not help but think what an extraordinarily handsome couple they made.

Following his swim, Paul had changed into a pair of jeans and a buckskin vest worn over his shirtless chest. His straight, black hair was worn longer than current fashion and held in place by an intricately beaded headband. He wore an impressive turquoise ring with a large greenish stone, and a vividly beautiful blue turquoise nugget hung from his neck on a silver chain.

He was so unlike any man Jordan had ever met before that she found herself staring at him throughout the meal. There was a power about his physical presence that was both intimidating and stimulating. Jordan noticed how the crew members sitting at his table seemed to vie for his attention, while Yvonne sat regally next to him, her hand touching his arm at frequent intervals.

Following the meal, Paul lectured on their progress with the excavation to date and discussed the artifacts that had been uncovered. He outlined their work plan for the next day.

He looked in Jordan's direction and said, "And you, Miss Marshall, will work with me. I hope I can train you in a few rudimentary principles of archaeological procedure. I'd like to think that your presence on this project won't be a complete loss."

Jordan felt humiliated by his words, but she met his gaze, her chin held high.

For an instant, he stared into her eyes, unconsciously fingering the turquoise nugget on its silver chain. Abruptly, he dismissed the others, asking Jordan to remain.

The shadows from the kerosene lantern accentuated his high cheekbones and full, square jaw, giving his face a harsh, angry look. However, his voice was almost gentle as he said, "I hope I wasn't too rough on you this afternoon. I'm not going to pretend that I'm not very disappointed to have a fragile-looking, inexperienced young woman added to my crew. But I am to blame for not administering the fellowship more carefully. If you are determined to stay, I'd guess we'd both better try to make the best of it."

Having said his piece, he extended his hand to Jordan for a conciliatory handshake. As his large, strong hand engulfed hers, Jordan felt a shiver of sensation shoot up her arm. Abruptly, she pulled her hand away and moved to join the others, who were preparing to build a campfire and roast some marshmallows that Cookie had provided.

Paul watched as Jordan's petite form joined the others silhouetted by the growing campfire. The male members of the crew clustered about their new associate, the fire and marshmallows forgotten as they vied for the attention of the beautiful blonde.

Like bees to honey, Paul thought ruefully. The crew would never be the same—not with a young woman like that in their midst. His budding archaeologists already were turning into young bucks on the make.

Not that he disapproved of women students on digs. Quite the contrary. He'd had many fine female students in the past who worked hard and contributed greatly to excavations. They had been serious young women of an academic bent and not the Jordan Marshall sort. They hadn't shown up at a dig wearing designer suits and high-heeled sandals. None had manicured fingernails—and toenails. None had skin so fair it would burn unmercifully and were so physically unsuited for manual labor and primitive out-of-door living.

And none had eyes the color of Indian turquoise, he found himself irrelevantly thinking. She was attractive. He'd give her that.

It was her hair he noticed first. Claudia had hair like that. For a heart-stopping instant, Paul had looked across the compound and thought the small blond woman standing by Cookie was Claudia. Foolishness. Claudia lived in New York. She had spent a grand total of one day on a dig, and Paul was certain she had never gone back. And that was all a long time ago—during his Columbia University days. To think that the sight of a physically similar woman could bring those memories rushing back!

Paul put out the kerosene lamp and seated himself at a table in the darkness of the deserted tent. He would join the others later, he decided as he helped himself to another glass of ice tea from the jug Cookie had left on the table.

But he only toyed with the cool glass as he stared past the campfire and the youthful faces glowing in its dancing light and into the shadowed darkness beyond. That thoughts of Claudia could still hurt, he pondered. Why? Was it that she signified his loss of innocence, because his view of the world lost its rose-colored hue after Claudia left him? He didn't still love her. He was much better off with Yvonne, who was so perfectly suited to him. How lucky he was to have found the vibrant, intelligent Peruvian archaeologist. She not only understood, she also shared his passion for the world of archaeology. And she too traced her ancestry back to those who first inhabited this hemisphere. She was as proud of her Incan ancestry as he was of the Cherokee blood and that of other tribes he carried in his veins.

Yes. Yvonne and he were well suited. Not at all like Claudia and he had been. To think that he had once thought the spoiled daughter of a wealthy financier would actually marry him. That was before he learned he was part of a collection. Claudia collected exotic men back then. There had been the Turkish diplomat, the rabbinical student from Tel Aviv, the professional basketball player, and God knows how many others. But when it came time to marry, the spoiled young daughter of a fine old family had chosen one of her own kind. Had she stayed with that man, Paul wondered. Did she now reign over an elegant mansion and give galas to raise money for some symphony? Or had she grown bored with one man and moved on?

But she had once been his. Ever so briefly. A passionate, reckless, laughing blond vision who got under his skin and into his heart.

Such a time that had been! They played and drank and loved with a vengeance—he and Claudia. Never had he been so alive. Part of him even then had known it couldn't last, that it wasn't real—that she would move on when she was finished with him, that her feelings for her Cherokee lover were fascination not love. But the other part of him had made plans to buy her a ring and take her home to his mother.

She had hurt him terribly, but Paul had learned a lot from Claudia. He had learned to be cynical. And wary—ever so wary. But he hadn't laughed much since that time. He wondered if he ever would again. With a sigh, he shook his head to clear away the vision of days past and concentrated once again on the present problem presented by another small blond woman. He realized his immediate negative reaction to the young woman from Nebraska was because she reminded him of someone he didn't want to be reminded of. But that aside, there were plenty of other reasons for his displeasure over her arrival.

He knew Jordan Marshall's type. He'd seen if often enough in the past—frivolous young women who had seen a movie about archaeology and thought it sounded glamorous and exciting. A good way to have a summer's lark. Something to tell their sorority sisters about next fall. But Paul quickly had been able to dissuade such young women when he explained about the plumbing—or rather the lack of it—on dig sites. And he would point out the isolation of the sites—the distance to the nearest beauty shop and laundromat. He would discuss the disadvantages of living in hot, leaky tents and the problems associated with a lack of electricity—no hair drier or hot curlers. And he would explain about the dirt and the spiders. He would sometimes throw in a snake story for good measure, but it was usually unnecessary. The young woman in question would have already thanked him for his time and made a hasty exit from his office and the realm of archaeology.

But he hadn't had a chance to dissuade Jordan Marshall. He still felt as though he had been duped by her. If he had thought for one minute that the student applying for the fellowship was a woman, he would have at least made it a point to find out something about her previous experience and whether she was physically qualified to spend a summer at hard labor. Damn! What a waste. It was so hard to get funding for those fellowships. And he was so short-handed for what was probably the only summer this extremely important site would ever be worked. He had the distinct feeling that the young woman now exacting adolescent responses from his male students would be more of a liability than an asset to his summer's work. She wasn't big enough or strong enough to do any real work, and he feared she would provide a distinct distraction for the rest of the crew. He found himself wondering if she collected men. He would have been better off without anyone at all—precisely what he could be if a tarantula should share her bed with her.

Jordan was awakened the next morning by someone shaking her arm. As she opened eyes still heavy from sleep, she saw Yvonne DeSilvestro standing over her bed. The sun was already too bright, and Jordan flung a protective arm across her eyes.

"We don't serve breakfast in bed," Yvonne said sarcastically. "If you expect to get anything to eat, you'd better hurry. The others are already at breakfast.

"The little structure by the latrine is a shower of sorts," she continued. "If you pull the rope, the barrel tips and pours water on you. Or you can use the river like the men do.''

Jordan struggled to a sitting position and swung her feet slowly to the wooden plank floor. Yvonne stood with arms folded, watching her with dark, heavily lashed eyes. The older woman seemed to be appraising Jordan's slim legs and hips. Then she stared quite openly at Jordan's toussled mass of blond hair, fair skin, and turquoise-blue eyes. Jordan suppressed an urge to pull on a robe over her thin nightie and thanked Yvonne for awakening her.

Jordan watched as Yvonne pulled aside the tent flap and left, then she hastily gathered up a towel and some toilet articles.

The shower was a crude affair, consisting of three wooden partitions to provide privacy from the camp. The fourth side was open and overlooked the river. A wooden barrel was fastened to an overhead pully arrangement. When she pulled the rope, a torrent of cold water poured over her. She quickly lathered her hair and body, then once again pulled the rope to rinse off.

As she toweled her shivering body, Jordan wondered what Aunt Sarah would say if she could see her now, standing naked in the wilderness with a rascally blue jay for an audience.

She hurried back to her tent and quickly pulled on a pair of tan shorts and a yellow tube top that left her shoulders and arms bare. She ran a comb through her wet hair and twisted it in a knot at the nape of her neck, then took off at a half-trot for the meal tent.

Cookie brought her a hardy breakfast of eggs and toast served with a cheerful "good morning" and a friendly wink. Some of the others had already finished and were walking across the field toward the mounds, so Jordan gulped down a few bites of egg, took a few sips of coffee, and ate her toast on the way back to her tent to pick up a broad-brimmed hat and some sun screen.

She caught up with Paul as he neared the largest of the five mounds. "You start early," she said, resolving to be courteous in spite of his rude treatment of her the day before. "I'll have to set my alarm tomorrow."

"We try to be on the dig by seven and then take a break during the worst heat in the middle of the afternoon. I'm glad to see you have enough sense to wear a hat and use sun lotion on that skin of yours."

"Professor Nicolle, I'm twenty-six years old, so please don't treat me like a child. I know about sunburn. I realize I have fair skin. And we do have sun in Nebraska."

"Not like the sun here, Miss Marshall. And I shall try to remember your advanced age in the future and treat you with the deference you deserve."

Trying to keep control of her temper, Jordan followed Paul as they toured the site and he showed her the work that had already been accomplished in the two weeks they had been working. The area had been surveyed and metal rods had been driven into the center of each mound to serve as a reference point in recording the exact location of each unearthed object. In addition, a grid of strings had been stretched across the site from exactly spaced stakes to serve as a guide for the placement of trenches.

All the work done thus far had been concentrated on the largest of the mounds and a smaller one half eroded by the river. Shallow trenches had been dug to mark the perimeter of the area to be dug. And other trenches were being opened at right angles or parallel to the perimeter ones.

Sam and Miguel were using picks to open another trench. Yvonne and Edgar were in the deepest trench working with trowels and smaller digging implements.

Paul explained how they first used picks and shovels to open the trenches, then switched to smaller picks and trowels and finally to brushes and even spoons as each unearthed object was carefully uncovered, then photographed or sketched while still in place. The location of the find was then carefully recorded in a log so that its exact relationship to past and future finds may be reviewed. As Paul explained, it was important to know later if a piece of pottery or a tool or a weapon was used in dwelling or was found in a burial site or worship center. And it was important to know what other artifacts or skeletal remains were found with the find.

"Record-keeping is a big part of archaeology," he explained. "Many archaeological finds would be meaningless unless future researchers can know the exact level at which each was unearthed and its relationship to other artifacts."

Since this dig had been underway for only a few weeks, the finds made thus far had been limited to arrowheads and pottery shards from Plains Indian culture, Paul told her. The diggers were just now reaching levels that held artifacts from pre-Indian cultures left by people who inhabited the site long before the Plains Indians ever camped with their ponies in this sheltered meadow beside the tree-lined river.

"We know this is a very ancient site," Paul explained, "because of the artifacts that have been exposed by the river eroding away the mounds. The site was first called to my attention by the farmer who owns this land. He brought me a human skull and some animal bone tools that he had found sticking out of the bank over there," he said pointing to the most eroded mound.

As he explained the work to her, Jordan began to see another side of Paul Nicolle, one that in some ways contradicted the stern, arrogant man she had met the day before. She could understand why the others said he was an excellent teacher. Jordan found herself listening intently to his fascinating explanations. He had named the people whose past he was trying to unravel the Fourche Maline People after the river by which they had once lived. And when he spoke of them, it was as though he was speaking of old friends. Jordan realized that even if she did not like Paul Nicolle as a person, when it came to archaeology, he showed a sensitivity she greatly admired. He was, she decided, a most remarkable man.

However, she realized it was more than his knowledge and his ability as a teacher that intrigued her. There was a virility about the man that Jordan found somewhat overwhelming. He seemed to exude a masculine strength that was both compelling and intimidating. When their arms brushed against one another in the close confines of the trenches, her flesh reacted in an amazing fashion. A discernible warmth radiated from the point of contact in a most distracting manner. And she found it impossible to concentrate on his words—no matter how informative—if she watched his lips. He had a sensual, full mouth set in an incredibly strong jaw, but Jordan forced herself to concentrate instead on his eyes or to examine whatever aspect of the site he was pointing out. For she didn't want to miss anything he said. She truly wanted to learn. So much knowledge awaited her this summer. The prospect thrilled her.

"Have you done any carbon dating yet?" Jordan asked.

"No," he answered. "We haven't found any charcoal yet at the lower strata. But we will. I think some people are going to be very surprised at how old this site is."

"Tell me about the Fourche Maline People themselves," Jordan said. "What kinds of the tools did they manufacture? Did they use bronze? Have there been any signs of agriculture or domesticated animals?"

Paul actually laughed. "Hey, hold on a minute. We don't know any of those answers yet, but you're asking the right questions."

He took her arm and led her toward the mound where the first discoveries had been uncovered by the eroding river. Jordan marveled that she had finally drawn a kind word from the ungracious professor, and the smile that had momentarily crossed his face softened its hard planes. He was, perhaps, the most handsome man she had ever met, which made the feel of his hand on her bare skin all the more disturbing. She was acutely aware of each of his fingers as they lightly curled themselves around her upper arm.

There was no need for him to touch her like that. She could climb up and down these mounds as well as he could. Did he think she was too weak or clumsy to manage on her own? Yet, she did not pull away. And it maddened Jordan to find herself responding to a man she did not even like.

"This is a very small operation," Paul explained as he propelled her up the side of the four-foot mound. "The dig I worked on last summer had six archaeologists representing different areas of expertise and about fifty native diggers. But on a dig like this one, everyone has to be both digger and supervisor.

"Of course, a project like the one in Peru," he continued, "will go on for years and eventually a whole city will be unearthed. I suspect all that will ever be found out about the Fourche Maline People will have to be discovered this summer. I'm sure you noticed the waiting highway. It seems we are holding up progress with our excavation, and I'm not sure we'll have any more time than just this summer—if we're allowed that long. I had to go to court to obtain just these few months' reprieve for the site."

"But aren't there laws against destroying an archaeological site before it's explored?" Jordan asked in amazement.

"The state's antiquity laws are rather weak, I'm afraid," he said. "I just wish we had more funding and a larger crew so we could take better advantage of the time we do have."

"Weren't you tempted to return to the project in Peru where you could get more done?" Jordan asked. "This site must seem rather unimportant after Inca ruins?"

"I'm interested in all of man's prehistory, wherever it is found," he explained, his tone revealing the enthusiasm he felt for his chosen field. He was a man who lived for his work, Jordan decided. There was a passion about his explanations which eloquently bespoke of how much he cared.

"I have a special interest in the prehistory of this region," he continued. "My area of expertise is the Caddoan civilization. The Coddoans were a federation of people who lived throughout the region that is now Texas, Louisiana, and the eastern part of Oklahoma. The people who built the Spiro Mounds were their ancestors. And if my hunch is right, the Fourche Maline People were the predecessors of the Spiro inhabitants. If that proves to be the case, I'd like to know why these people developed and flourished into the magnificent Spiro culture. And I'd eventually like to discover why that culture diminished, leaving in its place bands of fierce warriors who had lost most of the artisan skills and refinements of the Spiro culture."

Paul explained that the bluff dominating the opposite side of the river was a flint outcropping known as

Medicine Bluff. It had served for thousands of years as a source of precious flint for Indian and pre-Indian people since they had first learned to make tools and weapons by chipping away layers of the incredibly hard, even-grained gray rock and had learned to make fire by striking flint against metal. Flint became so important to their way of life, Paul told her, that sources of flint such as Medicine Bluff were incorporated into legends and were often considered sacred places.

The flint cliff, the deep pooling of the river at this bending, the broad flat valley floor protected by the surrounding hills—all these things had made this place a site of human habitation for many thousands of years, and as with many archaeological sites, the remains of that habitation were layered one on top of the other. As they toured the trenches and he continued his orientation, Paul pointed out some of the layers that had already been unearthed. The deeper a site was dug, he pointed out, the further back in time the archaeological journey.

"With the advent of the Plains Indian culture," Paul said as they crossed the field separating the largest mound from the smaller one by the river, "this site no longer supported a permanent village as it previously had but became a regular stopover for their nomadic wanderings. Legend has it that Medicine Bluff was a favored place for the old to be brought to die. I've heard they made their peace with the Great Spirit from atop the bluff—right up there where the highway department plans to put its approach to the bridge they will build over the river. A bridge support will destroy the smallest mound, and the others will be covered by the earth work necessary to elevate the roadbed on the approach to the bridge," he said, pointing out the pathway of the proposed highway with an outstretched arm.

"It really doesn't seem right for all this to be destroyed," Jordan said, "not when there is so much to learn from it. It represents so many chapters in mankind's story."

"Well, you'd find a lot of agreement on that from several different quarters," Paul said, "but for different reasons. The state's archaeologists want it preserved for further study. But there are Indian groups in the state who want the highway department *and* the archaeologists to leave the site alone. They think tampering with this place in any way is an offense to the ancient spirits and a sacrilege to those who have been buried here over the ages."

"And offending the spirits doesn't bother you?" Jordan asked.

"That's one of the things I came to terms with a long time ago," he said as he looked in the direction of the gray stone cliff. "I decided my people needed a history more than they needed to preserve old burial grounds."

Jordan was entranced by the enigmatic professor who, with his beaded headband, rawhide vest, and turquoise necklace, seemed firmly rooted in the world of his ancestors, yet bore prestigious academic degrees and taught at a twentieth-century university. And she was thoroughly fascinated by his explanation of the Fourche Maline site and its saga of human habitation. Here were the layered remains of communities that existed thousands of years ago by this same lovely river with its sparkling-clear rushing water, its tree-lined banks basking under a sky so brightly blue it hurt her eyes—and she was listening to a man who was as intrigued as she was by the unraveled mysteries of these ancient people.

What wonderful puzzles were waiting to be solved! And she was going to be a part of it. She was going to have the opportunity to learn from a man who not only was a renowned scholar but who traced his heritage to the people who had lived in this land since dimmest antiquity.

For regardless of what she thought of him personally, Jordan respected his knowledge. She wanted him to go on talking—to keep on sharing that knowledge with her. She wanted to hear his words and learn from him.

Paul had paused for a minute and was staring across the river, but Jordan knew he was not looking at the bluff. He was seeing a vision of what used to be.

"I am honored to be here," Jordan said simply.

Paul turned and stared down at her. For an instant her eyes held his, then he abruptly turned away. His fingers absently trailed to the turquoise nugget that rested against his broad chest, and his features hardened into a stern mask.

"You are a fool to be here," he said. "I should send you home before you ruin that pale skin in this sun and grow calluses on those soft hands. You're not cut out for this, Miss Marshall."

"But what about Professor DeSilvestro?" Jordan asked, her conciliatory feelings of just a minute before changing once again to dislike. "She's a woman and obviously seems to survive archaeological life well enough."

"There are many fine woman archaeologists, and she's one of the finest," he said, his admiration for the woman apparent in his voice. "She, like many other women who have succeeded in the field, literally grew up at excavation sites. Yvonne spent all her summers with her father working at digs. Don't let her glamorous looks fool you. She's remarkably tough. In fact, she's a remarkable woman."

Jordan knew that he was implying that she herself was the exact opposite of the beautiful, accomplished—and tough—Peruvian professor.

"Maybe I'm tougher than I look," Jordan said softly. "Don't I even get a chance to find out?"

"If you left now, I might be able to get someone to take your place. Later in the summer that would probably not be the case." He turned and stared down at her. "If only you were just a little bigger," he said, "and your skin not quite so fair. You look like something out of the proverbial ivory tower—a pale, fragile princess, who should be embroidering by the window and awaiting her prince's return, not a woman shoveling dirt in the wilderness."

"Are you asking me to leave?" she demanded to know.

His eyes were black and unfathomable as he returned her challenging gaze. Again his fingers trailed to the ornament he wore around his neck.

"No," he said firmly. "I have no right, as you so eloquently pointed out last night. But I want to make sure you understand what you're getting yourself into. You may be a featherweight, but you will have to do as much work as those strapping lads over there."

"I wouldn't have it any other way," she announced. And she meant it. No matter how hard she had to work, she wanted to stay. She wanted to learn from this mysterious man with his quicksilver moods and his tremendous knowledge of ancient civilizations. She desperately hoped that she was equal to the task. Keeping up with Aunt Sarah's chores and planting Uncle Joe's garden would seem easy after the physical labor that would be expected of her this summer.

"So be it," he said with a tone of finality.

Jordan turned to start back to the larger mound where the others were working, but he surprised her by grabbing her hand. He turned it over, exposing her palm.

"Do you have gloves?" he asked.

Jordan shook her head no.

"I'll have Cookie get you some next time he goes to town for supplies, and I will expect you to wear them whenever you are working. You won't be a bit of good to me with sore hands. And don't take off that hat," he said sternly. "After lunch, put on a long-sleeved shirt. That ridiculous garment you are wearing exposes entirely too much of your skin."

Having completed his inspection of her hand, he released it and they turned toward the largest mound, ready to rejoin the others. Yvonne was standing a few yards away, hands on slim hips, watching them with narrowed eyes.

"If you're through with the novice," she said to Paul in a voice that matched her haughty stance, "I'm ready for you to look at the pottery shards we've unearthed before I lift them from the ground. Juan has already photographed them."

Paul nodded in agreement, then scrambled down the side of the mound and reached up to give Yvonne a hand. As she took it, she threw Jordan a triumphant look over her shoulder.

Jordan watched as the two professors walked across the basin formed by the cluster of raised earthen mounds. Both had hair so black that it took a deep bluish sheen in the bright sunlight. Their heads were almost touching as Paul leaned near to better hear Yvonne's words. Their brown, muscular legs were in perfect stride as Paul's hand touched first the small of Yvonne's back, then trailed over the provocative roundness of her derriere.

Unconsciously, Jordan's fingers went first to her waist, then smoothed lightly over her own firm hips.

Chapter Three

After Paul had inspected the pottery shards, he finished touring the site with Jordan.

"We usually work in pairs," he explained to her. "Two sets of eyes are better than one in order to make sure nothing of importance is overlooked, and it helps make the time pass more quickly. We sometimes trade off during the day, but if a pair has something exciting going, they'll stay with it until it's recorded, sketched, or photographed and taken from the ground."

Leaving Jordan in Dennis's charge, Paul went to help Yvonne with some cataloging. Dennis was delighted to share his trench with "Lady Jordan," as he insisted on calling her.

Jordan had already determined that Dennis was a dedicated flirt, and there was definitely admiration in his gaze as he watched her hop down into the waist-deep trench. She found herself wishing she had on more clothing than the shorts and halter top she had worn in hopes of staying cool. Dennis was taking obvious pleasure in every inch of bare flesh.

She adopted a very businesslike tone in questioning him about his progress.

He explained that he was unearthing the remains of a dwelling that once stood where they were now working. The structure had been supported by wooden posts driven deep into the ground, and although the posts themselves had long since rotted away, there was evidence of the holes they had once occupied. The dirt that filled in the holes as the wood rotted was less densely packed than the surrounding earth. Dennis was carefully scooping the dirt from the holes with a battered tablespoon. Eventually, he informed Jordan, he hoped to use the post holes to help him determine the size and shape of the structure they had once supported. Such information would help the crew determine the location of future trenches.

"We would like to find the family trash heap, for example," he explained. "You'd be surprised what you can find out about the way people lived by what they threw away. And I'd like to find the place where they cooked their food. If I could find some charred wood, we'd be able to carbon date this level of the site. I found some quail bones yesterday. If they were left from someone's dinner, I may be getting close."

Jordan was fascinated. To think they were able to find about the meals eaten by a family who had lived right here on this spot thousands of years ago. She found herself wanting to learn more about this family. How many children did they have? Did they grow crops or just hunt? Did they keep dogs and other domesticated animals? What else did they eat besides quail? How long did they live here?

Jordan worked closely with Dennis throughout the morning, skimming off layers of dirt a quarter of an inch at a time and putting it in baskets. When the baskets were full, they carried them to a large wooden sifter hung from a tripod taller than Jordan. Each basket of dirt was carefully sifted through large wooden frames covered on the bottom with wire mesh that allowed only the fine dirt to fall through, leaving the larger debris in the frame. They then carried the frame to the river to wash away the dirt from the remaining pieces, which were carefully examined to make certain what appeared to be pebbles and rocks was not really something of significance such as a piece of pottery or a spearhead.

Since the sun was not yet directly overhead, the walls of the trench provided some shade, and Jordan periodically rubbed sun screen onto her shoulders, arms, and legs—and she kept the broad-brimmed hat firmly on her head. She hoped she could baby her fair skin into a tan. It would be one less thing for Professor Nicolle to bully her about. She wished she could grow a few inches taller while she was at it and add a little strength to her underdeveloped muscles. She was very aware that most of the lifting of baskets and frames was being done by Dennis, although she went through the motions of holding up her side.

Dennis did not seem to mind, however. He was chatty and friendly—and his shoulder or knee brushed against hers far more often than necessary. His hand frequently touched hers as they labored away with their flat trowels and spoons.

He was very good-looking with curly blond hair almost as light as her own. His skin, however, was nut brown from long exposure to the sun. He was a football player, he told Jordan proudly, on the famous University of Oklahoma football team. And she could well believe it. He had a characteristic football player's build with a thick neck and massive shoulders and thighs.

Dennis had a cocky way about him that was both infuriating and amusing. He obviously took it for granted that he and Jordan would soon become romantically involved.

"Your lips are made for kissing," he told her as they got ready to hoist another basket of dirt from the trench. "And I can hardly wait to get my hands around that tiny waist of yours. Professor Nicolle may be disappointed that you're not a fellow or the size of an Amazon, but I'm delighted with your size and sex."

"You assume too much," Jordan told him firmly.

"Resistance is futile, milady," he insisted. "I'm irresistible. And you're the answer to my prayers. When I realized I was going to have to spend an entire summer without a woman, I almost found myself another dig."

"There's Professor DeSilvestro," Jordan said. "You can't deny that she's a woman."

"Ah, yes. The Dragon Lady. I'll admit the prospect of an older woman is a challenging one. But in case you haven't noticed, the lady is taken. And I need ten hours of A for the summer's work. I doubt if Professor Nicolle would give it to me if I tried to romance his lady."

"I've noticed," Jordan confessed, "but I didn't know if their relationship was a serious one."

She wondered what Dennis would think when he found out that she too would fall into his "older woman" category—and was divorced. He would probably become even more forward in his advances. But Jordan did not want to think about that problem right now any more than she wanted to think about the romantic attachment of the two professors. For some reason, she found Dennis's confirmation of the relationship between Paul and Yvonne strangely disquieting.

To change the direction of their conversation, Jordan asked, "Why do you need an A so badly?"

"I've decided to become an academic All-American, since a second-string fullback can never be a regular All-American," he told her with his characteristic cockiness punctuated by a quite endearing boyish grin.

"I had no idea I was sitting in a ditch with someone so intelligent," Jordan said in a teasing tone as she crouched over her work trying to determine if the object she was uncovering was a rock or something of importance.

"Ah, yes. Intelligence is just one of my many attributes," he said as his hand strayed to her bare thigh.

Jordan drew back from his touch and lost her balance. Before she realized what had happened, she had toppled from her crouched position and fell against him.

He quickly put his arms around her and said in a laughing voice, "See there? I'm positively irresistible. You're already throwing yourself at me."

In spite of his blatant advance, Jordan did not take the outrageous young man too seriously and laughed with him, while half-heartedly trying to extract herself from his grasp.

At this moment a shadow fell across the trench, and she realized Paul was standing on the edge of the trench looking down at their antics.

Jordan quickly righted herself. She could feel her cheeks redden under the broad brim of her hat. What must he be thinking of me now, she thought, seeing me in the arms of some boy I just met.

She retrieved her dropped trowel and began to scrape away a thin layer of soil the way Dennis had shown her.

The shadow remained. A jay screeched overhead. The ever-present sound of rushing water filled the air. Juan and Edgar were talking rapidly in Spanish on the other side of the mound. But the silence surrounding Jordan was ominous.

At last she heard Paul swear softly under his breath, and sunlight once again fell across the exposed red earth of the trench.

Jordan looked at Dennis, who seemed unconcerned about the whole episode. "What must he think of us?" she asked.

Dennis winked and said, "Probably thinks it's love at first sight. That fate has brought us together. That being inside the bosom of old Mother Earth has brought out primeval urges."

"But he misunderstood," Jordan said.

"So what? Maybe we were providing him with a vision of things to come," he said as his fingers once again began to inch themselves toward her bare thigh.

"I think we'd better concentrate on our work," Jordan announced in her firmest voice.

Dennis saluted and returned to his scraping.

The rest of the morning passed pleasantly enough. As they worked, Dennis told her about the classes he had taken from Professor Nicolle and the two previous Nicolle digs on which he had worked.

"Don't let Nicolle get you down," he warned Jordan. "He's gruff and a slave driver, but he's the finest professor I've ever had. He's the reason I've changed my major. My dad still hasn't gotten over it. I was supposed to become a lawyer and enter the family firm. He still can't believe that I'm considering working for an advanced degree in archaeology rather than going to law school."

"Does Professor Nicolle have many female students?" Jordan wanted to know.

"A few. But he doesn't encourage them, as you've already discovered. Digs are tough, and most women don't have what it takes."

"He doesn't seem to mind that Yvonne DeSilvestro is a female," Jordan said with a touch of sarcasm.

"Well, Yvonne may look like a movie star, but she's tough as nails," he said with admiration in his voice.

"So I've been told. How does he know that I'm not tough too?"

"Milady Jordan, when he saw you in your little high-heeled sandals and your prettily polished finger and toenails—when he saw that you were no bigger than a doll and had skin like a cosmetics commercial—when he took a whiff of your cologne—well, you sure didn't seem very tough. And you still don't," he said with an appraising glance. "Not tough at all. Just soft and feminine and touchable. You've got a lot to prove, and it won't be easy."

His voice was sympathetic as he said, "I've got a feeling Nicolle is going to be kind of hard on you, Jordan. Because of the highway, he's under a lot of pressure to get this site excavated quickly, and I think he feels that you put one over on him—that you should have somehow called attention to the fact that you're female when you applied for the fellowship."

"Frankly, it never occurred to me. And I still don't think it has any relevance. Archaeology is no longer considered to be an all-male pursuit. And, from what you say, if I had told him I was a woman, he would never have accepted my application."

He shrugged. "You're probably right. Well, Lady Jordan, are you tough? Are you going to be able to survive a summer of dirt, sun, very hard physical labor, and a resentful professor who doesn't want you here?"

She looked down at the chipped polish on her fingers and the dirt caked under the nails. Already her body ached from being so long in a cramped position.

"I don't know," she said honestly. "I really don't know. But I'm going to try. I don't like Professor Nicolle, but I respect his knowledge and would like to learn from him."

"Yeah, I know what you mean," Dennis said, serious for a brief minute before nudging her with his elbow and saying, "Say, I'd like to teach you a thing or two myself. Between the learned professor and me, you should have a very educational summer."

After her scanty breakfast, Jordan was feeling very hungry long before Cookie rang the bell signaling that it was time for lunch.

As she and Dennis approached the meal tent, Jordan was aware that Paul was watching them. She purposely separated herself from Dennis and took a seat at the table with the three Peruvian students.

She soon discovered that Edgar was as gregarious as the other two were shy. Jordan and Edgar soon became engaged in a lively conversation about South American history, something with which she had more than a passing acquaintance since she had taken two courses in the subject.

Before long, Edgar was telling her of his girlfriend back home in Lima, and it became apparent to Jordan that Edgar was a very homesick—and lovesick—young man.

"We are to be married at Christmastime," he told Jordan proudly. "She is a wonderful girl—small and beautiful like you, only her hair is as shiny and as black as a raven's wing."

Jordan could tell that it eased his loneliness to be able to talk to her about his Margarita. For some reason she was able to put him at ease, and he did not seem to be embarrassed to be telling her of his love for a woman. He bent his head close to hers. His words were just for her ears. He obviously did not want any of the male members of the crew to know of his loneliness.

Jordan formed an instant fondness for the friendly young Peruvian and, in spite of his present pain, envied him. It must be wonderful to feel that deeply about another human being. Edgar's eyes fairly glowed with love as he spoke of his intended. Jordan supposed that she had once felt that way about Clayton, but she could not remember the feeling. Maybe it never had really been there.

As they returned from carrying their food trays to the kitchen tent, Jordan impulsively reached over and touched Edgar's arm. "Your Margarita is a very lucky woman," she told him. "It must be wonderful to have a man love you as much as you love her."

He gently reached out and touched her cheek. "Ah, lovely Jordan, you will awaken love in the eyes of some man. He will look at that sweet face and those incredible eyes the color of Indian turquoise, and his heart will open up just as mine has for Margarita. It will happen. You will see."

Jordan was strangely touched by Edgar's words. She felt good about having him for a friend. After experiencing the hostility of Professor Nicolle and spending the morning fending off Dennis, it was comforting to know there was a man here who wanted to be her friend. She knew she would be able to confide in Edgar just as he had confided in her.

She nodded a greeting to Paul as she left the meal tent in the company of Edgar and the other two Peruvian students. She felt somewhat pleased that the professor would see the other crew members did not seem to object to her presence on the archaeological project.

A layer of gray clouds had managed, over the course of the morning, to overcast the sky, and Paul decided the crew should work straight through the afternoon to take advantage of the cooler temperatures. They would stop earlier in the evening rather than take a midafternoon break during the heat of the day.

But in spite of the overcast sky, Jordan grew warm and uncomfortable. It was hot in the airless trench. She could well imagine how unpleasant it would be when the temperatures soared to one hundred and above.

Periodically, she and Dennis would take the dirt they had removed to be sifted, then wash the residue in the river. Jordan began to look forward to the wades in the

river, enjoying both the cooling waters on her bare legs
and the chance to stretch her aching muscles.

Paul spoke to her only once during the afternoon,
telling her to go put on some jeans and a long-sleeved
shirt.

"You're getting sunburned," he told her gruffly.

Surprised, Jordan glanced down at her arms and
shoulders. "Oh, I think I'm just a little flushed with the
heat. There's not enough sun to worry about today."

Paul grabbed her arm as she turned to walk away
from him. "As I have already pointed out to you, this is
Oklahoma, not Nebraska. The sun can be treacherous,
especially on days like today. You don't realize how
much of the sun's ultraviolet rays you are soaking up."

He pressed his fingers on her bare shoulder. When
he removed them, white imprints remained aptly dem-
onstrating the overexposure her skin had already suffered. He repeated the gesture on the other shoulder.

Jordan found his physical closeness disturbing. And
his fingers felt hot on her skin. She felt his eyes looking
at her face, but could not bring herself to look up and
meet them.

"You're right," she stammered. "I'll go change my
clothes."

"And don't take off your hat. I've already told
Cookie to get some gloves for you."

At the mention of gloves, he grabbed one of her
hands. The day's work had taken its toll. The remnants
of her manicure looked pathetic on her dirty, split fingernails. He turned her hand over and stared at the be-
ginnings of blisters already forming on her soft palm.

"And you're still planning to stick it out?" he quer-
ied, his voice implying that her wounded hands bore
out the truth of his previous warnings.

"It's not the first time I've had blisters," Jordan said
angrily.

He idly traced a finger across the damaged skin on her palm. Jordan felt the need to withdraw her hand from his grasp, but she was mesmerized by his touch. How strange that sensations from his feather-light strokes danced their way up her arms and brought a strange but altogether pleasant tingling to her breasts. And as she stared at the broad expanse of his muscular chest, its brown skin naked and moist, she wondered how it would feel to trail her own fingers across his skin.

The flush from her sunburned shoulders and arms seemed to surge upward to her neck and face. Her mind became a jumble of confused thoughts. She did not like him. He did not like her. How was it possible for her to be responding to the physical closeness and to the touch of this offensive man?

Suddenly ashamed, she hastily pulled her small hand from the grasp of his large one. "I appreciate your concern for my welfare," she said in what was supposed to be a sarcastic tone, and without looking at him, hurried off to her tent to change clothes.

Paul's second warning about the sun had come too late. In spite of a cooling swim in the river, by the time she sat down to dinner Jordan felt as though her skin was on fire. The fabric of her jeans and shirt seemed to be scraping her raw skin from her body, yet she was too embarrassed to wear something that exposed her burned shoulders and legs to the cool evening air—and to the critical eyes of Paul Nicolle.

She felt feverish and exhausted. Not only was she sunburned, her muscles ached unmercifully. She picked at her food and thirstily drank several large glasses of ice tea. Concern was apparent in Cookie's eyes when she took her tray of scarcely touched food back to the kitchen tent and asked for yet another glass of iced tea.

"It's going to be rough until you get used to things," he said sympathetically.

More than anything, Jordan wanted to drag herself to her tent and fall across her cot, but she forced herself to sit through the evening's lecture and ensuing discussion.

When the campfire was lit and Edgar had hurried off to fetch his guitar, Jordan announced that she was tired and left the others to their camaraderie.

With the light of the moon and the glow of the campfire providing her only illumination, Jordan lowered the front tent flaps for privacy and left the side and back flaps partially open to the night air. Carefully she removed her shirt and jeans, then lay down across the cot without even pulling back the quilt. The idea of anything touching her skin was unthinkable.

There was no position of comfort. No matter how she tried, the muscles in her arms and legs and back cried out protest. If she lay on her back, her sunburned shoulders hurt too much. Yet, if she lay on her stomach, she could not tolerate the pressure on the raw skin of her thighs and knees.

She fell for a time into an exhausted, feverish sleep, vaguely aware from time to time of Edgar's pure voice singing a folk song in Spanish with the voices of Juan, Miguel, and Yvonne joining him in the chorus.

After a time, however, sleep would no longer come. She felt even more feverish than before, and the ache in her muscles brought involuntary groans to her lips with even the tiniest movement.

How will I ever be able to work tomorrow, she kept asking herself. *I won't be able to move, much less work.* Yet, the humiliation of begging out of work on only the second day at the dig was unthinkable.

The camp had grown quiet but for the nighttime chorus of a thousand chirping insects. Through a gap in the tent flaps, Jordan could see that the campfire was nothing but glowing embers, and the lantern in the meal tent had been put out. A light came from Sam and Dennis's tent for a time, but as she watched through the narrow opening in the tent flaps, it too dimmed and died, leaving only the silvery light from a hovering moon.

Jordan felt helpless and alone. There was no fussing aunt to call the doctor. There was not even a telephone. She was ill and lonely and too proud to ask for help.

She shifted her weight for the hundredth time but found no relief. The movement brought only pain to her sore muscles and her burned skin. Timidly, she tried rolling over on her stomach, but the tender skin on her knees would not allow such a maneuver. A groan escaped from her lips and tears from her eyes.

She knew that comfort would come only with sleep, but when she closed her eyes, she saw an intensely glowing sun radiating heat to her burning body. If only she could relieve the heat in her skin, she might once again achieve the release that sleep provided. She concentrated on coolness, thinking of the river, of cooling breezes, of ice and snow.

Then there was coolness. At first she thought it was a dream—that sensation of cool wetness on her overheated skin. She concentrated on staying in the dream, on keeping the coolness there, grateful for the relief it brought her. A sigh of pleasure escaped from her lips.

But it was not a dream. Slowly, she realized the coolness was from wet cloths that covered her shoulders and legs. She sensed someone removing one of the cloths from her right knee and heard it being dipped into water, then rung out. She felt it being reapplied. Then the process was repeated for her other knee, then each shoulder. The wet compresses seemed to pull the heat from her afflicted skin.

Such blessed relief. So welcome, it was almost erotic.

Then she remembered with a start where she was and how she was dressed, or rather undressed. She wasn't even wearing a bra and was clad only in a pair of bikini panties.

Reluctantly, she opened her eyes. A dark figure hovered over her, silently ministering to her feverish body. Thin moonlight penetrated the interior of the tent through an open flap, but she did not need its eerie light to recognize the form of Paul Nicolle. She struggled to her elbows and looked down at her exposed breasts, then fell back on her pillow with a groan.

She attempted to grab a corner of the quilt and wrap it around herself, but a firm hand prevented her.

"This is no time for modesty," he told her in a husky whisper. "As tempting as it might be, I'll not ravish you. But something has to be done about your sunburn. I know you're in pain. These wet soaks will help take the heat from your skin and make you more comfortable. And here are some aspirins to relieve your aching muscles."

"How did you know..."

"How did I know that your muscles ached?" He finished her question for her. "It showed with every move you made."

He gently put his arm around her back, careful of the burned skin on her shoulders, and eased her to a sitting position, then gave her two aspirins and a cup of water. She was acutely aware of her full, naked breasts.

After she had dutifully swallowed the pills, he produced another cup. "What's this?" she asked.

"Wine. Drink it. It'll help you sleep."

As she held the tin cup with both hands and sipped at it, he continued to freshen the wet soaks covering her sunburned shoulders and legs. Jordan was amazed at how much relief they provided.

It did not take long for the wine to have the desired effect. It allowed her exhaustion to overrule her discomfort and soon her eyelids grew heavy.

Sensing her drowsiness, Paul helped her lie back onto her pillow. "You go on to sleep. I'll stay for a time and keep the soaks from drying out."

She looked up at his large form silhouetted by the moonlight. "I'll go home tomorrow if you want me to," she said, surprised at how regretfully the words came. "I've caused you a great deal of trouble. And I'm not as strong as I thought I was."

His features were hidden in shadows and his voice was noncommittal as he said, "We'll talk about that tomorrow. You'd better try to get some sleep now."

"I will. And thank you. You've been very kind—only..."

"Only what?" he demanded.

"Only I wish you would tell me that you don't have very good night vision. I can't believe I'm lying here like this with a man looking at me."

"Sorry," he replied. "I've got Indian blood, remember? I can spot a flea on a hawk at four hundred paces at midnight on a moonless night. I promised I wouldn't ravish you, but I didn't promise I wouldn't look."

She closed her eyes and flung an arm across her face. A heated flush, which was not the result of a merciless sun swept over her body. She was intensely conscious of his gaze on her body. It was as though she could feel his look. The ravishment was with his eyes.

He could see her bare legs, her scantily clad hips barely covered by a few inches of white lace, the curve of her body where it dipped in to form her slim waist and then surged outward again until her breasts mounded their fullness. She knew he could see the whiteness of those breasts with their sensitive nipples growing firm and erect just from his look.

She should roll over. Or pull the covers over her na-
kedness. She should not allow this man to stand there
like that staring at her.

Maybe it was the wine. Or the fever. But she felt
languid and not at all ashamed. She was going to float
into a sleep while this man feasted his eyes on her
body.

She was glad she had removed her bra. She was glad
her breasts were bare. She wanted him to look upon
her.

Chapter Four

Paul did not go immediately to his tent after leaving Jordan. Instead, he walked down by the river and seated himself on the large flat rock at its edge. He liked it here. The river soothed him. It had been flowing here long before the first men visited its banks and refreshed themselves with its clear running waters. The river was timeless. It always had been here to quench man's thirst and cool his flesh. Steadfastness. An admirable quality. One needed steadfastness in rivers and other things.

She would leave soon, Paul assured himself. Jordan Marshall would take her burned and aching body and exit from his life. If she didn't leave tomorrow, it would be soon after. Such women always leave.

She was bright enough. He had to admit that. Her questions today had been intelligent and insightful. And he had pulled her Spiro paper out of her folder and reexamined it. It was good. Damned good. He regretted his crack that questioned her authorship of the paper. As he had read it again, he could see her personality coming through—her inquisitiveness and her insistence on speculating about the personal emotions and lives of those who once lived at the Spiro site. Not too professional, but something of which he himself was often guilty.

And she had tried to do her share today, Paul had to admit. She'd pushed herself hard. But now she was so sunburned and exhausted, she wouldn't be able to work a lick tomorrow.

She certainly had made quite an impact on his crew. He had known she would. Yvonne was gorgeous, but she intimidated them. Jordan didn't intimidate, she just tantalized. It was all the guys could do to keep from staring at her. And when she singled out one of them for conversation and a smile, he seemed to grow an inch or two and puff out his chest a bit. But that was okay. Women like Jordan made a man feel good about himself—more manly, more attractive—which was okay as long as a fellow realized it was a game with her. Then he didn't get hurt.

Dennis had looked like a little boy who'd just had his first taste of candy when he saw her climbing down to share his trench. And he didn't waste any time making his move. Or maybe it was the other way around. Maybe Jordan put the move on Dennis. Whatever. It wasn't archaeology they were pursuing when he made his rounds.

And Edgar. Poor Edgar. At least Dennis wouldn't get hurt. He was a womanizer from day one. But Edgar was an innocent. Edgar was like Paul himself was when he first met Claudia. Dazzled. And so utterly vulnerable.

Paul reached down and scooped a handful of pebbles from the water's edge. One by one, he tossed them into the moving water. When did one get over being vulnerable, he wondered. When did one acquire a strong enough coat of armor to resist the likes of Jordan Marshall?

He knew when he closed his eyes in search of sleep that the sight of her moonlight-bathed body would haunt him. He had wanted to do more than tend her sunburn. He hadn't wanted to leave her tent.

He uttered an oath under his breath, then stood and kicked off his shoes. The water was cold as his body sliced into it. Paul hoped it was cold enough to calm him.

The camp was still quiet when Jordan awoke to the first thin light of dawn. She had managed to sleep for several hours, but her aching muscles pulled her back to wakefulness.

As she lay on her narrow cot listening to the first tentative chirpings of the birds and the ever-present sound of rushing water, her thoughts kept returning to what had happened in this tent only hours before.

Had it really happened? Had Paul Nicolle really come here and ministered to her nearly naked body? Or was it just a feverish dream?

But the evidence of what had transpired was still here for her to see. The metal cup from which she had sipped his wine was on the orange crate beside her bed. And the cloths he had used to cool her sunburned skin still covered her body. They fell away as Jordan painfully eased herself to a sitting position.

She sat on the side of her cot still clad only in lacy panties, and remembered. She looked down at herself to see what he had seen, once again experiencing the erotic glow she had felt when his eyes had looked upon her body.

Such memories both disturbed and excited her. She could not deny that she was physically attracted to the handsome professor. Even now, as she thought of his hands applying the cooling cloths to her sunburned body, she felt light-headed and confused.

Sounds of utensils striking metal drifted with exaggerated clarity across the crisp morning air as Cookie started breakfast in his canvas kitchen and brought her thoughts back to the morning. Overruling her protesting body, Jordan forced herself to gather up her toilet articles and wrap her body in a robe. Painfully she made her way to the shower.

The cold water felt soothing on her hot skin, and she lingered under the shower's stream. When she returned to her tent, she rubbed moisturizing lotion into her skin, hoping to prevent some of the peeling she knew was to come. She dressed in her oldest, softest blue jeans and a blue cotton long-sleeved shirt, adding a red bandana to protect the back of her neck.

She stared at her face in the mirror, grateful that she had kept her hat on yesterday. At least the skin on her face didn't look like it belonged on a boiled lobster. Feeling a little silly, she found herself taking extra care with her makeup, putting on a discrete touch of rouge, applying a layer of pink lipgloss and adding mascara to her lashes. She completed her makeup with a light application of eye shadow.

And since she was early this morning, she took the time to brush her hair until it was soft and shining, then pulled it back in a pony tail. After adding a wide-brimmed hat, she surveyed her appearance as best she could in the small cosmetic mirror and decided no one would be able to tell how sunburned she was and how terribly her arms and shoulders and legs ached.

But as she made her way to the kitchen tent to pick up her breakfast tray, she was aware her awkward gait might betray the complaining muscles in her calves and thighs. Painfully, she attempted to adjust her steps to a more normal appearing stride.

Paul was standing just inside the tent. Jordan felt very timid at the sight of him and felt the skin on her face making an attempt to match the rest of her body as a flush spread upward from her neck to her cheeks.

"How do you feel?" he asked in a polite tone that in no way suggested the intimacy of the night before.

"Better, I guess. I'd hate to think how I'd feel if you hadn't come to my aid. Thank you. And I promise I'll be more careful of your Oklahoma sun in the future."

"At least you had enough sense to keep your hat on yesterday," he said gruffly as he looked down into her face. "Go eat your breakfast, then I'd like to talk to you."

Stung by his harsh manner, Jordan got her food tray from Cookie. Yvonne entered the tent bearing her empty tray and stacked it on the table with the other dirty dishes. She nodded at Jordan, then fell in step with Paul. Jordan watched them walk side by side toward the mounds.

She had thought Paul might have been waiting to inquire how she was feeling, but obviously he had been waiting for Yvonne. Well, why shouldn't he? After all, they were apparently engaged to be married.

Paul's interest in Jordan the night before had been that of the person in charge administering aid to one of his charges. Jordan felt foolish for allowing herself to think it might have been something more. Perhaps he had been somewhat titillated by her unclothed state, but he would have given the same help if it had been one of the other crew members in need.

It was not like her to allow a man's physical attractiveness to take on so much significance. Paul's handsome face and fine body did not make him a nicer person. No, indeed.

Jordan was in no shape to work. It was difficult for her even to ease her body down into the three-foot trench, mush less lift a shovel or box of earth. But she was determined to get through the day somehow.

As she and Dennis returned from their first trip to the river with a tray of washed diggings, Paul called her over to the shade of an elm tree where he had set up a small folding table and some camp stools. He was busy making entries in the log book as Jordan arrived.

Hoping her physical discomfort was not too apparent, she sank onto a stool.

Paul continued to write in the log book for several minutes before looking up and acknowledging her presence. Jordan had a sense of what was coming and was determined not to be intimidated by him. She met his look full on, her eyes offering an unspoken challenge.

"You're in no condition to work," he said. "Do you really think it's worth it for you to punish yourself so?"

"Am I being asked to leave?" she demanded, her eyes flashing.

"No. I told you I wouldn't do that. But I'm advising you to reconsider your decision to stay on. You're obviously not cut out for a summer out-of-doors at hard labor."

"How do you know I'm not?" Jordan demanded. "After I get over this sunburn, I'll be fine."

The line of Paul's mouth hardened, and he tipped his stool slightly as he leaned back against the tree trunk and crossed his brown, muscular arms across his bare chest in a gesture that conveyed his exasperation with her. "I have eyes, Miss Marshall," he said in a tone one would use in speaking to a obstinate child. "And it isn't just your size. You obviously are about as tough as a cream puff. I don't know what misguided, romanticized notion of life on an archaeological dig brought you here, but movies and novels have tended to paint a far prettier picture of an archaeologist's life than really exists. And this is not Egypt or Rome. We are not unearthing the tombs and palaces of pharaohs or Caesars. There is not buried treasure here. We're digging up people's leavings—their trash heaps, their abandoned dwellings, their graves—in an effort to discover something about those who walked this land before us. And basically, they were simple folk. They didn't build cities of gold or erect pyramids. Those who work on archaeological excavations must have a thirst to find out things that most people don't care about. It's an intellectual hunger, not a summer's vacation. And the only payment is the satisfaction that comes from knowing you've added to man's body of knowledge—that scholars will know a tiny bit more about their species because of what we find here."

Jordan rose from her stool, her sore muscles forgotten for the moment. "Although I know you'll never believe me," she said, looking down into his proud, almost cruel face, "but I knew all that before I left Lincoln. Now if you'll excuse me, I'll get back to work."

With her back straight and her head high, she crossed the grassy knoll separating the spreading elm from the mounds. A cream puff indeed! She had worked hard all of her life. Did he think she had servants back home who waited on her hand and foot? Did he think she had never scrubbed a floor and weeded a garden until her body ached? Did he think she had never bent over her desk studying until her shoulders and neck became so cramped she could hardly move?

He will not drive me away from here, she promised herself. *I want to learn about this place as much as he does.*

Pharaohs and Caesars! What did he take her for—some sort of uneducated child? She knew there wasn't buried treasure in Oklahoma!

But as furious as she was with his condescending manner, Jordan soon began to wonder if she should have heeded his advice. Every move was agony for her. Her body ached as it never had from weeding Uncle Joe's garden. And each movement chafed her sunburned skin as it rubbed against the fabric of her clothing. Only her stubborn desire to prove Paul Nicolle wrong gave her the strength to continue.

Dennis helped her in every way he could, assisting her in and out of the trench and carrying far more than his share of the load when they lifted the trays of earth from the trench and carried them first to the sifter, then to wash them in the river.

After lunch, as they were taking their first tray of the afternoon down the riverbank, Jordan slipped on a wet rock and sent herself, Dennis, and the tray full of sifted diggings tumbling down the bank into the river.

"Well, I hope the find of the century wasn't in that tray," said Dennis laughingly as he knelt beside her in the shallow water at the river's edge. "Are you okay?"

"Oh, yes. I'm fine," Jordan said as she rubbed a scraped elbow. "What's another pain or two when your body is already one big ouch."

She was sitting half in and half out of the water. "Come on and join me," she said pulling Dennis down beside her, "and give me a few minutes to catch my breath. Maybe Simon Legree over there won't notice," she said, indicating the table under the elm where Paul had been working since lunch.

Dennis sprawled beside Jordan with his long hairy legs immersed in the clear, cool water next to her jean-clad ones. "Here, let me see that elbow," he insisted.

With a great deal of show, the affable young giant probed up and down her arm, examining it as though he were a physician. He rotated it several times, then bent it back and forth. After wiggling each of her fingers, he gently probed her neck, then moved over her shoulder until the heel of his palm was brushing against her breast.

"Hey, *Doctor* Compton," she said, trying to keep the smile from her face. "That's not the part of me that's hurt."

By this time, several of the others had joined them and were standing in a semicircle, the river water lapping around their bare legs.

"They're playing doctor," Wolf called over his shoulder to Sam, who came splashing through the water to join them, his nose bearing its usual layer of protective ointment.

"My turn! My turn!" Sam called out. "I'm thinking about changing my major to premed any day now."

"No way," Dennis said, throwing his arm around Jordan's shoulders. "The lady is *my* patient."

Jordan shook her head at their nonsense and handed Dennis a small round pebble washed to a perfect black oval by the river. "Here's your fee, Doc. Now, we'd best get back to work before the chief witch doctor over there 'operates' on us." she said, tilting her head in Paul's direction.

Jordan groaned as Dennis pulled her to her feet. Her wet jeans felt as though they weighed more than she did, but she shook off as best she could and climbed up the bank. Dennis followed with the empty tray. They left Sam and Wolf engaged in a mock battle to see which of them would get to play doctor with Jordan next.

A midafternoon rain shower spared Jordan from further labor, but only after she helped the others scurry around covering the trenches with heavy planks, then stake heavy sheets of plastic over the planks.

"Do we have to do this every time it rains?" Jordan asked as she struggled to pull the plastic taut while Dennis drove in the stakes.

"Yes, indeed," he answered. "Fortunately, it doesn't rain often, but when it does, it usually pours. Professor Nicolle is worried that in this sandy soil, it wouldn't take much to flood the trenches and cave them in."

The rain began to come in sheets just as the last stake

was driven. The others all raced for cover, but Jordan did not have the energy to follow their example. She trudged alone through the stinging rain.

When she reached her tent, she let the flaps down, but her bed had already gotten wet. She stripped off her soaked clothing and hung them over the ridgepool, then dried off and put on her robe.

Fortunately only the quilt on her bed seemed to be rain soaked. She pulled it back and draped it over the end of the narrow cot and crawled beneath the sheets, grateful to the rain for presenting her this rest.

The rain had ended and it was almost dark when she was awakened by Edgar's voice outside the tent. "Jordan, are you all right?" he was saying.

She sat up and retied her robe. "Yes, I'm okay," she called. "Come on in."

He pushed open the front flap and entered with a tray of food. "We missed you at dinner. Are you going to be able to attend the evening lecture?"

"Oh my," she said, pushing a lock of damp hair from her face. "I'm glad you woke me up. I wouldn't want Professor Nicolle to have something else to get upset with me about. Do I have time to eat this?"

"Yes. Some are still lingering over their meal, and the professors are sorting the day's finds and logging them in. You have plenty of time. I told Professor Nicolle I would take you a tray and check on you."

"Good. Sit here beside me and talk to me while I eat," she said, making room for him on the bed beside her. "You're awfully nice to take care of me like this."

"I decided your nap was more important than eating dinner on time," he said in his careful English. "I was thankful that the rain came so you could stop early. This was probably your worst day. Your body will begin to adapt."

"I hope so. I know I can prevent more sunburn by

being careful, but I don't know if my body will ever get used to conditions here. Professor Nicolle said I was a cream puff. I sure hope he's wrong."

"A cream puff? I do not understand," Edgar said.

As Jordan ate her meat loaf and creamed potatoes, she tried to explain why one might be called a cream puff.

"I think he is wrong," Edgar said gravely. "I think perhaps you are more like a flower on a slender stem—fragile, yet able to bend in the wind and weather the storm."

Edgar waited for her outside the tent while she hastily slipped into a pair of dry jeans and a long-sleeved mauve sweater. She brushed her still damp hair and twisted it into a knot on the back of her neck.

They walked together toward the pair of larger tents. They could see the others gathering in the open-sided meal tent. Jordan waited while Edgar put her tray in the kitchen tent, and then, before joining the others, she stood on tiptoe and kissed him softly on the cheek.

"You are a good friend, Edgar."

With his hands on her shoulders, he leaned down and kissed her forehead. "Yes. We are friends. Being the friend of such a lovely, feminine one as you helps ease the loneliness for my beloved. For that, I thank you."

Jordan linked her arm through his, and they slipped into the main tent. Paul seemed to have been waiting for them. As soon as they were seated, he began going over the day's activities. He had Wolf show some pottery shards he had unearthed, then discussed identification techniques and passed around samples of Plains Indian and Pre-Caddoan pottery along with some striking photographs of pottery from the Spiro Mounds.

Jordan was enthralled. So much could be learned about prehistoric people by the study of their pottery.

Their legends and religious beliefs were often revealed by the designs painted on the sides of the graceful containers. The complexity of their culture was demonstrated by the skill with which the pottery was made and the various uses for which it was created. Some of the pottery had been made for purely domestic purposes, others for storage of agricultural products and some for ceremonial uses.

When Paul was finished, Yvonne showed some illustrations of the pottery discovered in various Inca ruins. Her remarks indicated she considered the pottery found in North American sites inconsequential when compared to the state of the art during the Inca civilization.

While they listened to Yvonne, rain began to fall again—a gentler rain this time sounding like grains of rice falling softly on the canvas roof. As Yvonne finished, Sam stood and announced, "No campfire tonight. Anyone for a game of poker?"

Although Jordan was invited to play, she was sure no one would mind if she declined. She excused herself and prepared to make a dash for her tent, not wanting to get another set of clothing and shoes wet.

Dennis was suddenly at her side saying, "You'll get your feet muddy, milady," he warned.

"So I will, but since no one thought to build a sidewalk to my tent, I guess I have no choice."

"Ah, but you do. Chivalry is not dead," he said mischievously and scooped her into his arms and took off for her tent at a fairly brisk trot. Jordan felt a little foolish and knew the others were watching them, but she was firmly ensconced in Dennis's burly arms, and she had to admit he was going to get her to the shelter of her tent faster than her still aching muscles could have managed.

Very shortly he deposited her on her cot, then knelt

beside her. Jordan could barely see his face as he leaned close and asked, "Will there be anything else, Lady Jordan?"

"No, kind sir. That will be all," she said, entering into his game.

But before he left her, he swiftly wrapped his arms about her and planted a kiss firmly on her mouth, catching her quite by surprise. His tongue made a deft entry between her startled lips.

Before she could collect herself enough to push him away, he released her and whispered, "The first of many. Hope you feel better tomorrow." With that he disappeared into the night.

She lay back on her pillow. Dennis could be a problem, she realized. However, she couldn't help but like the presumptuous young man. He certainly did love women. *All* women.

In spite of her nap this afternoon, Jordan knew she would have no trouble sleeping. After her restlessness of last night, and the exhaustion brought about by the day's work, she was ready once again for the healing that sleep would offer her body. She lit her lantern long enough to get ready for bed and read a few pages in a magazine until her eyes grew heavy. She wanted to be very certain the dark would bring sleep when she doused the light—and not thoughts of Paul Nicolle.

When Jordan woke the next morning, she realized a third complaint had added itself to her body's list of discomforts. Her muscles still ached, but not nearly so badly as the day before. Her shoulders and legs were still tender and feverish from her sunburn. And she was now absolutely ravenous.

She had eaten very little the day before, her stomach was reminding her. And the incredibly tantalizing aromas of bacon cooking and coffee brewing wafted their way to her nostrils on the crisp morning air and provided all the incentive she needed to propel herself out of bed and into her clothes.

As she left her own tent and headed across the compound toward the meal tent, Jordan realized the camp had an early morning visitor. A bright yellow station wagon bearing the name and logo of a civil engineering firm was parked near the grouping of larger tents.

Cookie winked his approval as Jordan requested two eggs and a generous serving of bacon. She gulped down a glass of orange juice while waiting for him to fill her tray.

As she entered the meal tent, she saw Paul engaged in an intense conversation with a young man dressed in Levi's, western shirt, and cowboy boots. His clothing, slender frame, and reddish hair offered a marked contrast to the muscular, dark-haired professor who was dressed only in cut-off jeans and his customary rawhide vest. Several documents were scattered on the table between them, and the two men took little notice of the arrival of the crew as they filed in with their breakfast trays.

Very shortly, however, Paul rose and introduced the visitor to the group.

"This is Larry Jarvis of the Jarvis Engineering Firm of Tulsa," Paul said somewhat stiffly. "His firm has a contract with the state to build the bridge over the Fourche Maline."

The highway engineer nodded to the group, then leaving the table cluttered with unrolled plans and scattered papers, he followed his host to the next tent for a breakfast tray. Their conference apparently was unfinished.

When the two men returned with their breakfast, they sat down at the table where Jordan and two of the Peruvian students were sitting. Paul introduced the trio to the engineer. Paul ate his breakfast in silence. The two Peruvians spoke little English, so Jordan assumed the responsibility of conversing with the visitor at their breakfast table.

She found the young engineer an engaging, soft-spoken man with a sad, almost tired look about his hazel eyes. Jordan soon discovered that Larry had assumed the reins of his family's civil engineering firm following his father's heart attack. He had dropped out of graduate school in order to keep the company operating during his father's illness.

"I just found out about the delay on the bridge last week," Larry said "I had no idea there had been a change of plans. The highway department led me to believe I could begin heavy blasting of the bluff area by July first and sink the first bridge pilings on this side of the river before the end of the summer. I was stunned when I learned of the archaeological excavation."

Paul added little to the conversation. Although the two men were cordial to one another, Jordan realized there was a definite conflict of interest represented by their two professions. Each man had an entirely different perspective of the Fourche Maline site.

Jordan knew from Paul's lectures to the group that there was a history of conflict between road builders and archaeologists. It was the law in most states that archaeological excavations take precedence over roads, bridges, pipelines, dams, or any project that would cover an archaeological site and render it inaccessible to future excavation. Oklahoma, like other states, maintained a state archaeological survey whose job it was to survey any land to be covered with roadbeds, major construction, or lakes. The survey determined first if any archaeological sites were present, then assumed the responsibility for deciding if the sites were important enough to be explored before the proposed construction was allowed.

Paul had explained to the group that, in actual practice, such surveys were often ignored. Usually, if there were no immediate plans for the exploration of a site, the proposed construction would continue on schedule. But it was possible for archaeological exploration to hold up construction, and the archaeological surveys did offer a legal means for archaeologists to delay damns or roads for limited periods of time—provided funding could be obtained and proposed digs gotten under way.

When Paul had learned the plans for a north-south turnpike to link Tulsa with Shreveport, Louisiana, threatened the undeveloped site on the Fourche Maline River, he was already aware of the site's potential. He was able to obtain enough funding for a modest excavation during the summer months, and the archaeological survey office required the state highway department to delay the segment of the new highway that threatened the site.

Jordan wondered if Larry had come to survey the "enemy" camp, or if he was trying to determine the earliest possible date he could begin construction.

Very shortly the crew members began returning their trays to Cookie and heading across the field toward the mound area. Jordan excused herself and rose to leave. Larry immediately got to his feet—a polite gesture that somehow seemed out of place in their tent dining hall.

"Please sit down and finish your breakfast," Jordan admonished. "We don't bother with gallant manners around here."

"Yes," Paul agreed with a note of sarcasm in his voice. "We attempt to treat Jordan as just one of the boys."

Jordan left without comment, uncertain what was meant by Paul's remark. Was he making fun of her? Or was he indirectly referring to the aid he rendered to her sunburned body two nights ago—a time when he was quite aware that she was not "just one of the boys."

The rest of the crew was busily at work when Paul brought the highway engineer over to the excavation area for a tour. They stopped at the trench where Jordan was attempting to extract a large rock from firmly packed soil that had been its home for centuries. Larry knelt down beside the trench and visited with her for a few minutes about her work. He asked several questions about what she expected to find, and Jordan answered as best she could. Paul listened to their conversation without comment.

"You don't look like an archaeologist," Larry said good-naturedly as he watched her work.

"Looks can be deceiving," Jordan said tersely without looking at Paul.

"I'm sure they can," Larry agreed. "But this looks like an awfully rough life for a young lady like you."

Shading her eyes from the sun, Jordan looked up into his friendly, smiling face and realized he meant no harm by his remarks—that he was just making conversation.

But when she looked past him and saw the smug look on Paul's face, she found it infuriating. Paul's lifted eyebrows and the shrug of his broad shoulders seemed to say, "See? I'm not the only one who thinks you don't belong here."

Jordan stood and angrily jabbed her trowel in the sod beside the trench.

"Look, Mr. Jarvis," she said, "I've heard this all before. I realize all you big, strong men who equate size with ability would be more comfortable if I were working at a typewriter or at a kitchen sink, but I'd rather be here, thank you!"

"Looks like I touched a nerve," Larry said apologetically. "Sorry. I'm sure you'll do just fine."

The hurt look in the man's eyes made Jordan immediately regret her outburst. She watched the two men as they walked toward the next mound and considered following after them. Perhaps she owed the engineer an apology.

But Larry and Paul were soon engrossed in a conversation with Yvonne. The woman professor stood next to Paul, her arm lightly around his waist, as they talked to their visitor.

When at last Cookie's bell announced the evening meal and the end of her day's labor, Jordan was surprised to see Larry Jarvis's yellow station wagon once again parked by the dining tent.

As she walked across the field separating the sleeping tents from the larger ones, Jordan could see the highway engineer sitting just inside the shade of the dining tent, his booted feet jutting out in front of him as he used the edge of a table for a backrest.

He waved when he spotted her and immediately stood and started walking in her direction.

"Hi, there," Jordan called. "What's the matter? Didn't you get enough of Tent City, U.S.A., this morning? If you're looking for Professor Nicolle, he should be along shortly."

"Actually," he said as he fell in step with her, "I came to see you."

"Me?" Jordan said in surprise. "Whatever for?"

"Well, I realized I sounded a little chauvinistic this morning, and I wanted to apologize."

"That's very nice of you," Jordan said. "And I apologize for being so short with you. You couldn't possibly have known you were rubbing a little salt in the wound."

They stopped outside the tent, and Larry extended his hand to her. "Friends?" he said rather tentatively, as though he was afraid she might refuse him.

"Sure," Jordan said as she shook hands with him.

"And now that we're officially friends, would it be okay if I asked you out? It would have to be just for a movie and a hamburger. There really isn't very much to do around here," he said apologetically as though it would be quite understandable if she elected not to go out with him.

"Sure, I'd love to," Jordan said impulsively. "Maybe some Friday or Saturday night. We're not supposed to leave during the week."

This seemed to satisfy him. He shook hands with her again, somewhat awkwardly, his shy grin making his face quite boyish and erasing the wistful look in his hazel eyes, and was on his way.

As Jordan waved after the departing station wagon, she wondered if she should have accepted his invitation. On other occasions, she had thought men were shy and sweet, only to find out otherwise—especially after those apparently shy, sweet men discovered she was not as young as she seemed and had once been married.

Maybe she could just go out with him a time or two—and not mention her divorce. Thus far she had not told anyone at the dig that she had been married—not because she was ashamed of the fact but because too many times since her divorce, she had seen men's attitudes toward her change dramatically when they learned she was a divorcee. Suddenly they seemed to view her as a sex-starved *femme fatale* just waiting for the next man to take her to bed. She decided that for the time being she would not mention her divorce to Larry or to the members of the dig crew—except perhaps Edgar. Keeping it to herself could head off problems, or in the case of the flirtatious Dennis, keep an existing problem from growing worse.

A nighttime rain shower presented Jordan with a clean, wet world as she emerged from her tent the next morning. With two showers in three days, the river was higher than it had been when she first arrived, and its more urgent sound filled the air and provided a background for the bird chorus that was busy celebrating the new day.

Jordan took a deep breath of the fresh air. She was feeling much better. Her muscles were growing accustomed to the rigorous labor and her sunburn was healing, although her skin was starting the ugly process of peeling.

As she strolled across the open space that separated the sleeping tents from the working tents, Paul emerged from his tent and fell into step with her, offering a somewhat neutral "good morning."

In spite of intentions to the contrary, Jordan found herself affected by his nearness. Her pulse quickened and her palms grew moist. Part of her response, she realized, was brought about because of the power the man had over her. She still half expected him to send her home, and her grade for an entire summer's work depended on his opinion of the knowledge she acquired while she was here and of the contribution she was able to make to the project. It was the same sort of nervousness she felt when she was around one of her professors in a more academic setting. But with Paul, it was something more. There was also her awareness of the man himself. He was unlike any man she had ever met before, and she experienced an unwelcome physical attraction whenever he was near.

Like many who bear the blood of two races in their veins, Paul's appearance seemed to combine the best

of both his Caucasian and Indian ancestry. His skin was
no darker than a summer's tan, but it was weathered
beyond his years and bore the leathery look of one who
had spent much of his life out of doors. An open rawhide vest revealed a smooth, bare chest that was—like
that of most men of Indian ancestry—devoid of hair.
His broad forehead was accentuated by the beaded
band he wore to keep his hair out of his eyes as he bent
over his work.

His widely set eyes dominated a face whose features
had an almost brutal strength. His strong, square jaw
and high cheekbones were pure Indian. But his aquiline
nose and prominent chin would have suited a bust on a
Roman coin. His movements were as graceful and as
wary as a predator stalking its next kill. Jordan found
she both feared him and was attracted to him—a combination that dismayed and confused her.

Jordan offered a tentative comment about the weather for lack of anything better to say.

But there was no answering small talk from the professor. "I observed you yesterday with the other crew
members," he said in an accusatory tone, "especially
with Dennis and Edgar."

Jordan stopped and looked up at him, not understanding the intent of his remark. "Oh? Is there something the matter?" she asked.

He crossed his arms across his chest, a gesture which
only served to emphasize the musculature in his fore-
arms. "I don't know what sort of game you're used to
playing, Miss Marshall, but I don't want any conflict to
develop among the male members of this crew over
the favors of the only female student."

"Do you think I'm trying to cause trouble?" she demanded, unable to believe what she was hearing.

"I think you're playing a game and seeing how many
of the fellows you can get to fall for you. You were even

flirting with that highway engineer! Dennis and Edgar have obviously already succumbed to your charms, and no doubt, you could have similar success with the others. I'm just trying to avoid trouble. An archaeological dig is no place for a promiscuous female. That sort of thing can only be dangerous—and the outcome of this project depends on a harmoniously working crew. Therefore, I must ask you to curtail such behavior—or leave."

It was a long moment before Jordan could trust herself to answer.

"If I ever cause that sort of 'trouble,'" Jordan said at last, "I can promise you that I'll leave of my own accord. In the meantime, you have no right to make an accusation like that! No right at all!"

"Perhaps," he acknowledged, "but I shall remember your promise."

Jordan watched as he continued on to the main tent without her. She realized she was trembling with rage and her fingernails were digging painfully into her palms. How could he be so quick to accuse—and so unfairly? Promiscuous! Just because she made friends easily and some of the crew members liked to flirt a little. Professor Nicolle had obviously chosen to believe the worst about her. Or was he just trying to drive her away with insults?

She felt defeated. Was she to have an entire summer of torment at the hands of this man? Of one thing she was certain. She would never allow him to know how angry he made her—and how his physical closeness made her so acutely aware of her own body.

Maybe it was just stubbornness, but the more difficult Paul made things for her, the more she wanted to stay. She vowed once again that she would not give him the satisfaction of driving her away. She wanted very much to stay here on the bank of this beautiful river and make a contribution to this excavation. She could and would work just as hard as the rest of the crew and be just as serious about her work. And she wanted to learn. How strange that she had such a yearning for knowledge, and the man who could teach her so much wanted her to leave.

She wondered if she would ever be able to win the admiration of the harsh professor. Probably not. Things had not gone well for them from the moment they met. But she could show him how determined she was and that she could be as tough as the rest of them—even Yvonne DeSilvestro.

Chapter Five

Jordan came to realize over the next few days that the beautiful Peruvian professor was as harsh a taskmaster and as exacting as Paul. Both professors seemed tireless and expected the same degree of dedication and hard work from their students.

But in spite of her undeniable professionalism, Yvonne often belittled the Fourche Maline site. She seemed to believe that all North American sites were inconsequential when compared to the glorious Inca ruins of South America.

Jordan wondered why Yvonne had bothered to travel all the way to Oklahoma if she did not think the site worthy of her attention. She asked Edgar about it as they began the third day of working as a team. They had been assigned to work in the only trench that had been started in the smallest of the cluster of mounds and the one most eroded by the river.

"Professor DeSilvestro is very ambitious," said Edgar. "She will be considered for promotion next year, and if it is approved, she will be the youngest full, tenured professor at the university. I think this trip was a necessary part of her preparations for consideration by the tenure committee. All of her previous work has been in Peru. She needs to branch out and add non-South American sites to her resume."

"But why not the Middle East or someplace more exotic?" Jordan asked. "She obviously doesn't care for North American sites."

"I imagine that has something to do with Professor Nicolle," he answered as he prepared to lift a large rock from the trench. "There was some talk of Egypt, but I guess the opportunity to work with someone of Nicolle's credentials was too tempting for her."

"Were you disappointed in her decision to come here?" Jordan asked as she scraped away at an unusual-looking rock.

"Not really. When you are a novice such as I am, there is much to be learned no matter what sort of site it is. And regardless of how enamored Professor De-Silvestro is with Inca ruins, there are far more sites in Peru on a caliber with this one than there are magnificent remains of great civilizations. I think as much prehistory should be explored as possible so we can have an idea of how all people lived, not just the small percentage who built large cities and made gold jewelry."

"I agree," Jordan said as she continued digging around the long, narrow rock with a battered tablespoon. "But you and I aren't planning to be famous. I'm sure that Yvonne aspires to be internationally known, and that must enter into her decision when she selects her next project."

"Yes, but the Middle East did not have Paul Nicolle. I think the glamour of the Fourche Maline is a certain half-Cherokee professor," he said with a grin and raised his dark eyebrows in a knowing way.

"Well, they certainly do make a handsome couple," said Jordan in a voice that caused Edgar to pause and look into her face.

"A little pensiveness I hear? No?"

"Oh, heavens no," Jordan denied. "I'm just concen-

trating on this rock. It's unlike anything I've yet uncovered."

She took a brush from their box of implements and
began dusting away the loose dirt, then carefully
scraped away more packed earth from the slender,
cylindrical-shaped object. It was longer than she had at
first thought and bowed out at the ends. It looked
like...

But no. Wait and see. Don't get too excited yet, she
told herself.

She was excited though. Edgar sensed it and knelt
besider her, watching intently.

"Oh, Edgar, is this what I think it is?"

"We'll know soon," he said. "You're doing fine.
Just keep on as you are now."

All conversation between them stopped. There was
the sound of her scraping, and the sound of her breathing. All other sounds came from outside the narrow
trench—the rushing river, the voices of the others
drifting to them from the larger mounds, the familiar
lowing of neighboring cattle, and the distant barking of
a dog.

Then Jordan was sure. "Oh, Edgar! It is. Look. It
is."

Before them, still half-buried in the red clay, was a
bone—a human bone. It was a tibia, the shin bone of
an adult human being.

Jordan sat back on her haunches and surveyed it.
The first human remains. There was no doubt about it.
Her excitement left her breathless.

They smiled at one another, then Edgar solemnly
put out his hand in a formal, congratulatory handshake.
And without another word, the two of them attacked
the surrounding floor of the trench. Carefully, but
swiftly, they scraped away the dirt in search of the rest
of the skeleton.

First the tip of a pelvis. The end of a rib. Edgar located the unmistakable roundness of a human skull.

Jordan was elated. She could not tell if the beads of moisture rolling off her face were sweat or tears of excitement. Maybe both.

"I think we'd better get Professor Nicolle," Jordan said.

"Yes," Edgar agreed. "But you go tell him. It's your find."

"It's *our* find," Jordan corrected. "Let's go together."

Like two excited children, they scrambled from the trench and crossed the small valley separating them from the main mound and the center of the morning's activities. Arm in arm, they fairly danced up the side in search of the professor. When Paul heard them calling, he stood and peered at them with a frown. Only his chest and shoulders were visible with the rest of his body concealed in the deep trench.

For once Jordan was unperturbed by Paul's harsh expression. Let him think what he wants, she decided recklessly, as she recalled their conversation a few days earlier concerning her relationships with Edgar and Dennis. She refused to refrain from physically touching her friends because of Professor Nicolle's suspicious mind. With her arm still entwined with Edgar's, she said, "We need to show you something."

Without a word, he vaulted from the trench and followed after them.

"Is he ever going to be surprised!" Jordan whispered to Edgar. "He thinks we're acting silly. I can tell by the way he looks."

"I think we are acting silly," Edgar admitted with a laugh. "But the professor will forgive us when he sees Ernest."

"Sees who?" Jordan asked.

"Ernest. We've been working in Ernest," he said obviously pleased with his pun.

"What a perfect name," Jordan said in delight. "Yes. Just wait until *he* sees Ernest." She had to cover her mouth to stifle a giggle.

Jordan and Edgar reached the side of their trench. They stood looking down, feeling like two proud parents who had just given birth as they waited for Paul to join them.

Jordan looked up into Paul's face, wanting to see his reaction to their find. He stood next to her, his arm very near hers as he peered intently into the trench below them. His lips parted slightly and a small "ah" escaped—the sound of pleasure. Jordan felt like clapping her hands, but she restrained herself.

Then Paul was all movement. He jumped down into the trench and touched each one of the exposed bones in turn as though making sure it was not an illusion. "As many times as this has happened," he said, "I never get over the awe of discovering a burial site. By our intruding on this most private of all human sacraments, we discover so much about them. Let's just hope this is a burial ground and not an isolated body."

He touched each of the bones again, reverently. "So much to do. So much to learn."

He stood and looked up at them, shading his eyes from the glare of the late afternoon sun. "You've done well. If you wish, you two may concentrate your efforts in this area. I'll help you as much as I can."

Jordan's heart fairly soared. He said they had done well.

She and Edgar joined him in the trench and listened carefully while he explained to them the next steps they needed to take and at what point they should extend the trench and in what directions. For the first time since Jordan had arrived at the Fourche Maline,

Paul was not telling her why she should leave, but was giving her a long-term assignment. For the first time she felt like she really belonged.

When the dinner bell sounded, Jordan uttered a small groan. "Does that mean we don't get to work anymore right now?"

Paul looked at her, his face softened by a half-smile. "You mean you'd rather work than eat?"

She met his gaze. How dark his eyes were, and so perfectly framed by his high cheekbones and heavy, well-formed brows. "Yes, as a matter of fact, right now I would. But I guess Ernest will still be here tomorrow."

"Ernest?" Paul said. "Ah, yes. I named the first skeleton I ever unearthed. I called him Grandfather. He taught me much, just as Ernest will teach you."

Edgar was busy gathering up the tools and storing them for the night. He climbed out of the trench, then looked down at them. "Hey, are you two coming, or are you just going to sit there admiring Ernest? I leave you now. I must go tell Professor DeSilvestro of our wonderful discovery."

They were alone. Paul was very close. Their thighs were almost touching as they knelt by the skeleton in the close confines of the trench. His intense eyes held her with a force she did not understand. She was not sure if she wanted to flee from his gaze or remain its prisoner.

But it was Paul who looked away first. He stood, his fingers straying to the ever-present turquoise nugget that hung against his bare chest. Such a magnificent chest, Jordan thought admiringly, with its smooth expanse of brown skin stretched across his muscular frame. The nugget on its silver chain belonged against such a chest as that.

They both stood, their bodies acting in unison. Paul

put his hands around her waist and lifted her out of the trench as though she were a doll. Each of his fingers left an imprint of sensation on her flesh.

Paul sprang like a panther from the trench and stood beside her. Once again his eyes seemed to draw hers into their depths. He reached out and pushed a stray lock of hair from her forehead. "You have beautiful hair," he said.

There were no more words as they crossed the grassy field side by side.

Edgar had already told the others. Everyone clustered around Jordan and Paul as they entered the main tent. Questions filled the air.

Paul held up his hands to quiet the barrage and with a broad smile announced that it was true—the first human remains of the excavation had been unearthed. He told them he was hopeful they were on the verge of unearthing an entire burial ground.

"The diligent and careful work of Jordan and Edgar has more than paid off," he said, putting an arm around Jordan's shoulders as a means of drawing their attention to her. "They did a splendid job of uncovering the skeleton. Everything is in place. They disturbed nothing. We'll all go have a look after dinner, and I'll answer your questions then."

Jordan was euphoric with Paul's praise. Gone was the arrogant professor whose main interest in her seemed to be convincing her to leave. He had praised her—and in front of the entire crew.

His dark eyes shone with excitement. He was moist and warm where his bare skin pressed against Jordan's arm. The turquoise nugget rested against a chest that was streaked with sweat and fresh earth. Jordan found the combination of turquoise and earth symbolic of the man who was Paul Nicolle. How proud she felt standing there beside him.

Suddenly, however, his arm dropped from her shoulders, and he rushed across the tent to greet Yvonne, who had just come in with Edgar.

"You've heard?" he asked in an excited voice that almost seemed out of character for him.

Yvonne greeted him with a dazzling smile, her white teeth contrasting beautifully with her smooth, bronzed skin. "Yes, Edgar told me," she said as she opened her arms to him for a congratulatory embrace. "What good luck. Now perhaps we can really begin to get someplace with this project, I was beginning to think we might be wrong—that the site was just a regularly used camp ground and not a village at all."

Their arms slipped easily around one another's waists as they turned to go pick up their meal trays in the kitchen tent. They continued to talk animatedly to one another as they strolled away.

The others, anxious to investigate the aromas wafting their way from Cookie's kitchen, followed the two professors. Jordan was momentarily left alone, and she made no move to join the hungry crew.

Her excitement had suddenly left her like wind leaving the sails of a ship entering the doldrums. And she understood that the rise and fall of her moods seemed dependent on the attention, or lack of it, that Paul paid her. Jordan realized she was infatuated with a man who cared nothing for her. He was obviously in love with the sophisticated and beautiful Yvonne, a woman who was his intellectual equal and obviously a far more suitable companion for him than Jordan could ever hope to be.

It almost seemed as though Paul and Yvonne were meant to be man and wife. They were both extremely respected in their shared field of archaeology. Their lives together would be a fascinating journey through prehistory.

Even in their physical appearance, the two professors could not be more suitably matched. They were both tall and bold-looking with their long, muscular legs and purposeful strides. Their olive complexions, blue-black hair, and wide-set, dark eyes blended perfectly. And Jordan could almost imagine their full, sensuous mouths merging in a passionate kiss.

When she thought of Yvonne's exotic beauty and magnificently statuesque body, Jordan felt small and drab. A man like Paul would have eyes only for a woman like Yvonne. She was his professional, educational, and physical match. Together they would make impressive waves in the world of archaeology. Like other famous husband-and-wife archaeological teams of the past, their accomplishments would make archaeological history.

And after all, Jordan reasoned, her own feelings for the handsome, half-Indian professor were purely physical. She was dreadfully attracted to him, but that was the sort of feeling that would pass. It wasn't as though she were afflicted with some sort of lifelong condition. In two more months, she would return to Nebraska, and her tumultuous feelings for Paul would fade like the heat of summer.

It would be difficult until then, Jordan realized, but she could manage. She was not a stranger to difficult turnings in her life. And she would survive Professor Paul Nicolle. But he must never know the effect he had on her. Her pride demanded that he never discover that every time he came near her, Jordan's heart skipped a beat or two and her breathing became more difficult. She must make certain he'd never realize how her thoughts became a confused jumble whenever she saw him—so confused that she tended to misinterpret his actions.

Paul's behavior toward her had never been anything

but proper. He had touched her only in the course of his duties as director of this excavation. He had tended her sunburn. His arm had brushed against hers a few times, but only when they had been working side by side. And tonight he had put a paternalistic arm around her shoulders to show her he was proud of her work, a gesture she had seen him use with the male students on other occasions. If her skin remembered his touch as though it were imprinted on her body, it was the result of a schoolgirl's crush on a teacher, and she was too old for that sort of nonsense.

But even now she could still feel where his arm had rested across her shoulders. There was a pathway of tingling warmth.

She put her hands up to her shoulders and tried to rub the sensation away. It was a problem, she admitted. But she would manage, she told herself once again. And he must never know.

The others were already starting to bring their food-laden trays into the tent and were selecting places at the half-dozen tables. Jordan hurried off to get her own tray, although she was not sure if she still wanted to eat.

It was as if Cookie anticipated that this would be a special night. The meal of fried steak, mashed potatoes and gravy, and fresh vegetables was a favorite with the male members of the crew. Jordan was still picking at her salad when most of them were going back for second helpings.

Cookie brought in a large platter of fried okra and insisted that Jordan have some.

"I don't like okra," she protested.

"But I bet you've never had it fried before," Cookie said good-naturedly. "Folks in this part of the country are the only ones who know how okra's supposed to be fixed. And you eat those tomatoes too. I picked them myself right out of my cousin's garden."

Not wishing to hurt his feelings, Jordan tentatively tasted the okra, which had been sliced, rolled in corn meal, and fried to a golden brown.

"Why, it's really good," she told him and took another bite.

Cookie watched her long enough to make sure she was really enjoying the okra, then put two slices of a surprisingly red tomato on her plate before returning to his kitchen.

Jordan discovered she was hungrier than she had realized and ate with a growing appetite. And soon she found the good spirits of the rest of the crew infectious and was drawn into their conversation, which consisted mostly of talk about the skeleton with much speculation as to how old it would prove to be and whether more like it would be found.

Like Paul, everyone was hopeful the skeleton would prove to be the first of many and that they would be able to unearth a major burial ground that had been used for many generations. Such a discovery would tell them much about the Fourche Maline People. Jordan knew from her university classes that burial customs were usually very revealing of a culture, giving valuable indications of religious practices from the manner of burial—such as the position of the body, the direction it was facing, its relationship to other bodies, and what possessions were interred with it. Very often people were buried with objects that held great significance in their earthly life and were intended to accompany them into their afterlife.

Although Paul and Yvonne entered into the lively conversation, they would often lean their heads close and share words intended only for one another. Jordan tried not to watch them and was determined to enjoy the evening along with the rest of the enthusiastic crew members.

Their after-dinner lecture was conducted atop the small mound nearest the river. The setting sun cast the trench in a deep shadow, and Paul used a flashlight to illuminate the skeleton as the crew lined the trench's edge and listened intently to his discussion of the skeleton's burial position and its possible antiquity. He instructed Jordan and Edgar about what they should look for as they proceeded with the unearthing process and assigned Sam and Dennis the job of opening another trench at right angles to the existing one.

Yvonne offered a few remarks concerning her estimation of the age and sex of the skeleton. For once she had nothing disparaging to add about this excavation site. While she spoke, Dennis managed to maneuver his way to Jordan's side.

"How about a midnight stroll by the river?" he asked in a suggestive whisper.

"By midnight I'll be sound asleep," she whispered. "Now, hush and listen to Professor DeSilvestro," she instructed with a friendly pat on Dennis's arm and a glance in Paul's direction. Would he think she was flirting again when he saw her touching Dennis, she wondered. But Paul's face was in the shadows. His expression was hidden from her.

When Yvonne finished, Paul announced that a celebration in honor of the dig's first major find was in order. "Cookie has a cooler of beer waiting," he told them as he hoisted himself from the trench.

With a war whoop that made Jordan's ears ring, Dennis led the pack of eager young men across the grassy field, leaving Jordan standing with Yvonne and Paul. Feeling very awkward at being left alone with the two professors, Jordan hesitated a moment, then started walking after the others. Paul and Yvonne were outlining future trench openings for the small mound and did not seem to notice her departure.

The building of a campfire was already under way by the time Jordan reached the tent compound. Sam offered her a beer and announced that he was going to "dress" for the occasion. He disappeared in his tent and when he emerged, the ever-present white ointment had been removed from his nose and an orange-and-blue striped necktie was neatly tied over his "Ski Colorado" T-shirt. He then assumed the chore of passing out beer to everyone and when the fire was lit, started the singing with a rousing round of "Boomer Sooner," the University of Oklahoma fight song. Dennis and Wolf played the part of cheerleaders, and their antics soon had everyone holding their sides.

When Yvonne and Paul joined the circle around the campfire, Yvonne asked Edgar to get his guitar. He quickly obliged, and soon he and Juan and Miguel were entertaining with a nonsensical but lively song about a donkey who insisted on climbing Peru's mountains backward and came to no good "end." Yvonne interpreted the words to the song as the three Peruvian students sang, and she taught the rest of them the simple chorus which recommended one know when he gets to the top because mountains, like gossip, always have another side.

Then, at Yvonne's insistence, Edgar sang a hauntingly beautiful Peruvian love song. Jordan could understand enough of the words to realize the song promised a love as strong as the mountains, a love as pure as the snows, a love that would flow through a lifetime just as the mountain streams flow to the sea. Yvonne joined Edgar on each chorus, their voices blending in a sweet harmony that made the lovely melody all the more poignant.

As Jordan looked around the campfire, she could tell the others were just as caught up in the magic of the moment as she was. Even those who did not understand the words of the song seemed spellbound by its beauty.

It was that wonderful twilight time when the western sky still glimmered softly with the fading sunset and night's first stars appeared like tiny pinholes of light in a vast, black canopy. The fire crackled and popped as it cast a golden glow on the faces of those encircling it. And a feeling of fellowship enveloped them like a warm blanket.

Jordan looked around her, memorizing the look and feel of this night, enjoying these people who were now her friends but would pass out of her life at summer's end. She wanted to remember them always.

For this brief period in time this group was joined in a common cause. Their isolation from the rest of the world only served to join them more closely together and enhance the feeling of camaraderie that they shared one with another. Jordan was glad none of the "temporaries," who often drifted in to help for a day or two, were here tonight. This was a special time that should be shared by just the regular crew—a time none of them would ever forget.

She had not noticed Wolf slipping off to his tent to fetch his drum, but when its beat began, it seemed a natural thing, blending with the eternal sound of the river and the nighttime chirping of a thousand insects.

After his tom-tom had set the mood, Wolf's chant began. It was low and gutteral, composed of words Jordan could not understand, yet somehow seemed full of meaning—mysterious words from a strange language that spoke of another time, another world that now existed only in his song.

And as Wolf sang the ancient words, Paul rose and began to twist his body slowly in a dance that was primitive, yet captivatingly beautiful.

It was a dance unlike any Jordan had ever seen before, slow and methodical, executed with an economy of movement that seemed to concentrate and strengthen each fluid gesture, each precise step of his bare feet, each bending and twisting of his magnificent body.

Jordan felt as though she had been transported to another age. The rising moon, the flickering fire, the beat of the tom-tom, the tall Indian whose glistening skin and dark eyes reflected the fire's radiant glow were from long ago.

His dance was majestic, a ritual performed in remembrance of times past, of those who came before, of the old ways. The dance, the chant, the beat of the drum— all seemed to symbolize a noble people whose time had passed, whose grandeur had faded. The faces of the two Indians emitted such fierce pride. And sadness too.

Gradually, however, the beat of Wolf's drum changed. It began to quicken and demand another dance. Paul's movements responded to its command.

Now his body leapt and twisted and strained with an intensity that was pagan and wild. His hands held invisible weapons. His uplifted arms beseeched the ancient spirits to bring him victory.

Even Paul's face changed. Gone was the twentieth-century professor. He now wore the face of a warrior.

But once again the beat changed. Its wildness stopped abruptly and was replaced by a repetitive, almost sedate pattern. Paul stopped in front of Jordan and grabbed her hands.

Before she realized what was happening, Paul had pulled her to her feet and, without any word of explanation, guided her to his side. Holding her hands, with their arms crossed in front of them, he wordlessly taught her the shuffling, sideways step of a line dance. Together, they danced their way around the fire just inside the circle formed by the seated crew.

Her small hands were lost inside his large ones. The

nearness of his body and the aura of warmth that arose from his sweating skin brought tightness to Jordan's chest and a quickening to her heart.

Paul had allowed her to enter his other world, and Jordan was proud of the honor he had paid her. They danced as one, swaying in unison as they performed the methodical steps to the persistent beat of Wolf's tom-tom.

Slowly the others began to join them in the simple dance until all were united in a line that snaked its way around the ever-changing campfire, and they formed a circle that not only joined them one with another, but seemed to join them with other generations who had walked this land before them.

Jordan was certain that even the Fourche Maline People, all those thousands of years ago, must have danced a similar dance on the banks of this timeless river, moving their bodies in unison to the beat of a drum just as she and her comrades were doing now. She sensed that the others felt as she did—that they were linking hands not just with one another, but with the ancients.

It was a mystical moment. It was much more than *knowing* she was part of a continuum that linked all human life—past, present, and future. Tonight, at this moment, she *felt* it.

Jordan was not ready for the dance to end. She did not want to relinquish the circle of hands, but Wolf's chant ceased and his drum grew softer and softer until it was still and the night was returned to the insects and the crackling fire and the rushing water.

She did not realize there were tears streaming down her cheeks until she felt Paul's eyes upon them. She wanted to say something to him, to explain why she had been so moved, but suddenly she was embarrassed and turned away.

As the others helped themselves to another round of beer, and Dennis challenged Wolf to a match of Indian wrestling, Jordan slipped away and made her way to the river. She knelt on the bank by the widened pool they used for swimming and bathed her flushed face in the cooling water, scooping it up with her hands and patting it on her hot skin.

Jordan realized it was more than embarrassment, or the heat of the fire, or the exertion of the dance that brought this feeling of warmth to her body. It was because she had been linked physically and emotionally with Paul during that moving and beautiful experience. And now that it was over, she felt disoriented—even a little dizzy.

Why did that man have such an effect on her? She must learn to control herself better than this, Jordan reminded herself as she scooped up more of the wonderfully cool water.

The sounds of merriment drifted across the night air. She could hear Edgar challenging Dennis, who apparently had already beaten Wolf at their match of strength. Dennis could probably beat them all, she thought, except perhaps Paul.

Someone was strumming Edgar's guitar. The fire crackled and popped as another log was thrown on it. She could even hear the "snap" as someone pulled a tab from a can of beer. But she did not hear Paul's steps coming down the steep path to this quiet, secluded place. Suddenly, however, she sensed that he was standing behind her.

She waited, not daring even to breathe.

He touched her hair. At first, it was just a fluttering of fingers teasing a stray tendril, then it was a hand firmly burying itself deeply in masses of soft, blond hair.

Her body swayed slightly, then leaned back just

enough to make contact with his legs. She closed her eyes, unable to bear the agony of his nearness, yet fearful that he would leave.

His hand continued to experience the fullness of her thick hair, which had long since fallen from its clasp and hung in shimmering waves down her shoulders. She knew it shone silver in the moonlight. She knew he was admiring the way it looked.

On the edges of her consciousness, Jordan knew that she should take some sort of initiative—that she should say something or get up and return to the campfire. She was aware that her muteness and her passive acceptance of his hand caressing her hair communicated a message to him, a message that was forbidden.

But she was mesmerized by the touching of his hand to her hair and his legs against her back, by his overwhelming presence and by the knowledge that she was alone with him. The part of her mind which demanded that she correct the situation seemed far away, not really a part of her at all, but something outside of herself—just an annoying irritant like an gnat fluttering in the face of a dozing sunbather.

A voice deep within her sounded an alarm, but it was so far away it seemed intended for another being.

But when he released her hair and pulled her roughly to her feet, the voice grew nearer and more insistent.

She was facing him now and started to tell him that she had come here to bathe her face in the water and was going back to join the others, but before the words left her lips, his mouth was on hers. Her words were muffled and useless.

Instinctively, she raised her arms to form a wedge between them, but he crushed her body to his, firmly capturing her arms and rendering her helpless. And as she attempted to draw her face away from his mouth, he put a hand firmly behind her head and his tongue thrust its way between her lips, ruthlessly invading her mouth.

The alarm was sounding clearly now, but it was difficult for Jordan to think. How could she decide what to do when his body was pressed against her like that? And his tongue was rapidly becoming the center of her universe as it probed and teased and cajoled her own tongue until it too became an aggressor.

Knowing he had rendered her powerless, he relaxed his grip long enough to allow her arms to slip upward and lock themselves around his neck. Now his hands were free to roam up and down her body, feeling the smallness of her waist and the swell of her hips, stroking their way up and down her arched back.

Desire coursed through her veins. Desire became the life force of her body. Her mind closed itself to warnings, and she strained against him, wanting to feel the proof that his desire matched her own.

A groan formed itself deep in his throat as she rubbed her body against his. She could feel him. She knew. He wanted her and was going to make love to her here on the banks of the river.

Wolf—or someone—was playing the drum again, and Paul's tongue began to probe in cadence to the primitive beat. Jordan responded by twisting and turning her hips as though she were trying to become a part of him, to merge with him.

Now his mouth was at her neck. His hand was on her breasts. Any earlier thoughts she had of resisting him had long since been pushed from her brain by the insistent need of her aching body. Jordan wanted this man more than she had wanted anyone, or anything, before. Every part of her body seemed to cry out for him, to beg him to possess her.

When, at last, he lowered her to the riverbank, she was a willing victim for his lust. She pulled his face back to hers, unable to be without his mouth for even an instant.

He jerked the front of her blouse open and ripped a strap free from her bra, freeing one full, straining breast. Only then did her mouth relinquish his tongue for another, greater need. He lowered his mouth over her nipple, and she arched her back upward, relishing the exquisite flash of sensation as his teeth teased her nipple to erection.

There had been no words between them. But Jordan needed words too. She tried to say something, to tell him no man had ever filled her with such desire, to tell him she felt as though she had never known a man before— but his hungry mouth on her breast was too distracting and made all hope of coherent speech impossible.

His hand traveled downward and pulled open the zipper of her jeans. Then his tongue moved from her breast to her belly, tickling the soft, sensitive skin there as his hand buried itself hard between her thighs, cupping his fingers around her. Jordan lifted herself to fit even more firmly against his hand, pushing against him, wanting him so, gasping with her need of him.

But still she felt the need for words. Shouldn't something be said to express feelings? Shouldn't one of them say something?

It was Yvonne's words, however, that broke the silence, stabbing into Jordan's passion like a sliver of ice. Yvonne was at the top of the bank calling out into the darkness.

"Paul? Are you down there?"

Pebbles were dislodged as Yvonne started down the path. Paul disappeared into the darkness.

Hastily, Jordan sat up and drew her blouse over her exposed breast.

"Paul?" Yvonne called insistently. "Is that you down there?"

"No, it's just me," Jordan called in a strained voice that sounded unfamiliar—like the voice of another. Frantically, she tried to rearrange her clothes.

Yvonne made her way down to the small clearing. "What are you doing down here all by yourself?" she demanded of Jordan.

"I was hot," Jordan explained wearily. "I just wanted to splash a little water on my face."

"It's taken you long enough. We thought you'd gone on to bed. Have you seen Paul?"

"Yes, he was here," Jordan said, grateful for the darkness as she clutched at the front of her blouse and hoped Yvonne would come no closer. "But he walked on down the river."

"I see," Yvonne said in a voice that indicated she apparently "saw" a great deal.

As Yvonne turned and left, Jordan hugged her knees to her chest in an effort to calm her trembling body. The consummate desire she had felt only minutes before had all but seeped from her body, leaving in its place a sense of humiliation and a hardening resolve never to let anything like this happen again.

Obviously Paul was infected with the same infatuation that she was. That a mutual physical attraction existed between them had been only too apparent. But it could lead no place. Paul was committed to a life with Yvonne. Jordan was nothing but an interloper, a role of which she was not proud.

Jordan found some satisfaction, however, in knowing that Paul had carnal thoughts of her—that the attraction had not been one-sided. But that only salved her pride. And it was not going to make preventing future episodes any easier.

Almost academically she wondered if she and Paul had made love, how she would feel right now. Would she be filled with regret? Would they have doused the fire that burned within them and ridded themselves of its curse?

Or would the fire only burn with greater vengeance?

Not wanting to face the others in her disheveled state, Jordan decided to follow the river for a short distance until she was directly behind her and Yvonne's tents, then cut up the bank and enter her tent from the rear. From what Yvonne had said, the other crew members thought she had gone to bed, so it would not matter if she did not return to the campfire.

The male students were still continuing with their revelry. Their songs had changed from college fight songs and love songs to ones of a somewhat ribald nature. The words carried quite clearly across the still night air. Jordan wondered if they had run out of beer yet. There certainly were going to be some headaches at the trenches tomorrow, but they seemed to be having a good time tonight.

The short journey from the riverbank to the back of her tent was more difficult than Jordan anticipated. There was no path, and the underbrush was a tangle of briers that caught on her clothes and pulled at her hair.

Yvonne's tent was just ahead, and her own tent just the other side of it, but Jordan was forced to stop and free her hair from the clinging briers one last time. She could see Yvonne crossing the clearing, walking briskly toward her tent.

Jordan stepped deeper into the shadows, not wanting to have to explain why she was lurking in the underbrush outside Yvonne's tent. And she certainly did not want Yvonne to see that there were buttons missing from her blouse.

Jordan began to back away as quietly as she could. She would have to retrace her steps to the river, then come up the bank on the other side of her own tent. She felt like a thief sneaking around like this.

She was startled to hear Yvonne's voice addressing someone in the tent. "Well, where have you been?" Yvonne demanded of the unseen presence.

Jordan already knew whose voice would answer.

"Waiting for you," Paul said in a half-whisper.

Jordan turned and headed toward the river. Quietly. They must not know she was out here. They would think she was spying on them.

Still, she could hear Yvonne's voice. "What is the matter, Paul darling? Would the little tramp down by the river not give you her favors? She passes them out to everyone else, you know."

Jordan tripped on a rock and fell to her knees. Pain shot up her leg, but she ignored it and struggled to her feet, desperately wanting to get away from the sound of Yvonne's voice.

Chapter Six

When finally Jordan was able to crawl into her narrow cot, safe at last in her own tent, she knew that sleep would be a long time in coming. The day had been a roller coaster ride of emotional highs and lows. She had soared to such wonderful heights with the exciting archaeological find, with the glorious fellowship by the campfire, and with her passionate encounter with Paul by the river. But those highs had been followed by such abrupt plummetings that, in spite of the good things that had occurred this day, Jordan felt miserable and exhausted.

Even though she knew it would be ethically wrong for her to leave the excavation this far into the summer, Jordan even considered getting up and packing her bags. She could have Cookie drive her to town before breakfast in the morning before any of the others were up. She would not have to see Paul ever again.

But it was too late for her to be replaced, and Jordan knew how desperately every member of the understaffed crew was needed, especially if anything meaningful was to come out of the project before it was destroyed by the highway and its bridge. And in spite of Paul's early misgivings about her ability to contribute to the project, Jordan knew she had indeed contributed. No one could deny that she made up in determination and hard work what she lacked in size and physical strength. Jordan now felt a deep sense of commitment not only to the project itself, but to the other crew members who would have to assume her share of the work load if she left.

As disasterous as her relationship with Paul Nicolle had been, the rest of her experiences on the banks of the Fourche Maline had been some of the most meaningful of her life. She had never felt so intimately part of a group and enjoyed such close camaraderie.

She would stay. She would see the summer through. There would be more good times. She supposed there would also be other bad times. And somehow she would learn to control her feelings for Paul.

Those terribly intense feelings for the half-Indian professor were such a puzzle for Jordan. She had never experienced such a deep physical attraction before. She supposed that was a strange admission for a twenty-six-year-old woman who had once been married to be making to herself, but Clayton had never aroused such passion in her. No one had until now. Maybe she had been too young before.

But Jordan knew it was more than a matter of age. Even if she had been meeting Clayton for the first time at this point in her life, she was certain he would not have brought the intense, frightening feelings that Paul unleashed within her.

And was it merely lust she felt for Paul? Was it lust she felt when he praised her for her work? Was it lust that had made her proud to be at his side during the evening's festivities?

Paul had quarreled with Yvonne, their angry whispers filling her small tent. Yvonne was furious that he had chosen Jordan to be his partner for the line dance.

"Can you not imagine how that made me feel in front of the others?" she accused.

"Why should it make you feel any way at all," he tried to explain. "I've done the line dance with you before. It was a new experience for Jordan. I thought she'd enjoy it. It meant nothing."

But even as he spoke the words, Paul mentally questioned their truth. Meant nothing? Then why had he forgotten Yvonne was watching? Or any of the others for that matter? For a time, no one else mattered for him except that small blond woman with the name like a faraway river. They had been transported together to another time. Jordan felt it too. He had seen it in her face. He would never forget the look on her face!

"My, the little student from the north really likes the fellows," Yvonne said sarcastically. "She even makes a play for her professor...or is that the way it's done with American university students and their professors? Do you often have little romances with your students, Paul darling? Just what was going on down by the riverside? Did I interrupt something? What is it your students call it...'fooling around,' I believe? Did I interrupt you fooling around with Jordan Marshall?"

Paul had left. He didn't want to argue with Yvonne. And her words had too much truth in them for comfort. He had been way out of line in his behavior toward Jordan.

Jordan. The name no longer sounded masculine to him. It was *her* name. It sounded like the whispering of the wind through the branches, like the water rushing against the rocks. He heard it all around him. He could not escape its sound.

Why in the world had he followed her down to the river? If he had been thinking at all, he would have realized it could only have ended badly. But he hadn't wanted the spell to end. He had wanted the dance and the primitive beat of the drum to go on and on. He wanted to keep that fair woman at his side, her vivid eyes and silvery hair reflecting the glow of the fire, her heartbeat coursing through his veins where their bodies touched.

He walked. First around the mounds, then along the river. Brambles crawled at his bare arms, but he scarcely noticed. It was like before, he thought in agony. Only worse. Once before a woman with pale hair had shown him about passion. She· had been like a beautiful butterfly, unable to stay in any one place for very long. But while she perched on his soul, he had known he was alive. He had experienced life more fully than he ever had before or since. Until tonight.

Tonight he had fallen once again into a chasm of vulnerability. But he had promised himself he wasn't going to allow that to happen again. He was going to be objective. He was going to choose wisely. He was not going to let his heart rule his head. He was not going to get hurt!

Did he have some sort of fatal attraction for women who could never really return the adoration he felt for them? Was it a sickness with him? For he knew Jordan was just like the other woman. Like Claudia. And it wasn't just their vitality or their beauty. It was the way they looked at life. It was a game with them. A big happy game. Men were part of the game. Collections of them.

And like the butterfly, they would fly away. Always.

The next Saturday morning Jordan was surprised to look up from her labors and see Larry Jarvis approaching the trench where she and Miguel, one of the Peruvian students, were working with one of three weekend "temporaries" from the state archaeological society. Jordan excused herself and scrambled from the trench.

"You busy tonight?" he asked all in a rush, as though he wanted to get a dreaded chore over with at once.

Jordan would have liked nothing better than to do some laundry and catch up on her sleep that evening, but she realized how much courage the reticent young man had used in asking her out. And she could probably get Cookie to make a trip into town the next day so she could make her weekly visit to the laundromat.

"Well, it just so happens that the annual Diggers' Ball was cancelled, and I am free," Jordan said with a grin as she wiped away the dirt on her nose with the back of her glove.

"It is? I mean, you will? Gee, that's great!" Larry said enthusiastically. "But all I can promise you is an outdated movie and the greasiest hamburger in the west."

"That's okay," Jordan said. "I'm really quite weary of caviar and chamber music. Hamburgers and a movie will be a delightful change of pace."

She met him by the main tent at eight o'clock wearing her last pair of clean jeans and a V-neck cotton sweater. She had washed her hair and brushed it dry, leaving it loose over her shoulders.

"You're beautiful," Larry said in lieu of a greeting.

"So are you," Jordan said as she took in his new-looking western-style shirt and carefully polished cowboy boots.

The hamburgers *were* greasy. And the movie mediocre. But Jordan enjoyed being with the slender young man with sad, hazel eyes. Over their hamburgers and after-movie drinks, she discovered that Larry too was divorced. He had a two-year-old son for whom he was desperately lonely. And, Jordan suspected, he was still in love with his wife. Jordan listened to him sympathetically, feeling grateful that her own divorce had not been so traumatic.

In spite of her earlier intentions to the contrary, Jordan found herself telling Larry of her own failed marriage. He seemed to feel he had found a kindred spirit with whom to share his loneliness.

It was after midnight when Larry dropped her off at the sleeping archaeological encampment. Jordan thanked him rather formally for a nice evening, and yes, she would enjoy going out with him again sometime.

The crew usually worked until midafternoon on Saturday, then took the rest of Saturday and all day Sunday off from their labors. Sometimes Sam or Dennis or Wolf would leave to spend Sundays with their families. The rest of the crew went into town on Saturdays to wash their clothes at the laundromat and have milk shakes at the old-fashioned drugstore that had occupied the same site on Seneca's main street since statehood, so the elderly druggist had informed them. A couple of times they had driven over to Wilburton to go to a Saturday night movie. Sunday was used to write letters, catch up on reading, and allow oneself the luxury of a nap.

For the first time, however, Paul had given the whole crew the entire weekend off. The excavation was to be manned on Saturday and Sunday by professionals and amateurs from the Oklahoma Archaeological Society, whose members began to arrive Friday afternoon in an assortment of vans and campers, and set up their camp on the other side of the mounds from the tent village.

Yvonne had a speaking engagement in Oklahoma City for the second weekend in a row. This time she had taken the three Peruvian students with her to tour the state's capital city. They planned to visit the capitol building, the Cowboy Hall of Fame, and the city zoo. Edgar confided in Jordan that he hoped he would have a chance to buy some Indian jewelry for Margarita during the weekend—or perhaps something "western."

Dennis had left for a party weekend in Dallas. He had invited Jordan to go with him, but she knew he would have been surprised had she accepted.

The relationship between Dennis and Jordan had become a funny, predictable game. He continuously flirted with Jordan, and she never took him seriously. Jordan had developed an almost big-sisterly fondness for the likable young man. They enjoyed each other's company, and their little game was the foundation on which a nice friendship had been built.

Jordan had no doubt that Dennis would be willing to carry their friendship to a more physical level, but unlike many young men she had known, he goodnaturedly accepted her decision that they be friends and nothing more. Jordan found herself wondering if those other forward young men she had dated would have been willing to settle for friendship when she rejected their sexual advances. Perhaps she had been too hasty in assuming they had only one-track minds.

Dennis informed Jordan that other than the women he had gone out with, she was the only one with whom he had ever formed a close friendship. And he had never worked side by side on a job with a woman. Jordan knew he had learned to respect her even if he did keep up his constant barrage of "lover-boy" antics. It was just a comfortable and harmless habit he had fallen into. Jordan usually did not even bother to respond to his outrageous suggestions, such as "Let's fly to Paris tomorrow and get married" or "If you make love with me, I'll give up profanity and beer." The rest of the crew seemed to realize his antics were just a game, but on more than one occasion, Dennis's silliness had brought a scowl of disapproval to Paul's face.

Thursday evening, Dennis had driven Jordan into

Seneca. She washed some clothes at the laundromat while Dennis picked up the mail and some supplies. On the drive back, he again asked her to accompany him to Dallas. But this time his invitation was a serious one.

"I really mean it. We'll get separate rooms. I'd love to show you 'Big D,' and I promise I'll behave. I'd love to 'do' Dallas with you on my arm."

"You wouldn't be nearly so adorable if you behaved," she told him as she mussed his curly, blond hair. "I'd love to, but I really can't afford to go—and no, I will not allow you to pay my expenses."

"But I hate to go off and leave you here with the old fogies from the archaeological society."

"I'll be fine. It will be nice to just do nothing for a change," Jordan assured him.

At the last minute even Paul decided to leave for the weekend, leaving the head of the archaeological society in charge.

By late afternoon on Friday the rest of the regular crew had vacated the premises. Jordan fixed herself a sandwich in Cookie's deserted kitchen and helped herself to an apple, then headed for the river with a book under her arm.

She slipped out of her shorts and dove into the refreshingly cool river, then paddled around the clear water. But she soon became bored. There was none of the playful splashing and dunking that she was used to.

She dried off and stretched out on the large, flat rock that jutted out of the bank and prepared to enjoy the pleasant rays of the late afternoon sun. Her skin had long since healed from her sunburn, and she had carefully nursed her body to its present uniform tan that made her skin the color of ripe apricots and provided an arresting contrast with her hair, which was now several shades lighter than her skin.

Although there was little time for primping and

makeup, Jordan fairly glowed with good health, and she was well pleased with the face that looked out at her each morning from her mirror.

Outdoor life had not only tanned her skin, it had firmed her muscles and increased her physical stamina far beyond what it had ever been before. And she had a zestful feel for life that she recognized as another fringe benefit of living among the trees and wild things on the banks of this beautiful, crystal-clear river. She felt completely in touch with her environment, and this gave her a sense of well-being that showed in the way she walked and in her ready smile and sparkling eyes. Except for the uncomfortable presence of Paul, she felt good about the summer and was glad she had been daring enough to come on the dig.

Jordan found the work rewarding, and the knowledge she was acquiring fascinated her beyond any academic discipline she had yet tackled. She found herself wishing she could pursue her study of archaeology when she returned to Nebraska next fall. How wonderful it would be to earn a doctorate in the field when she completed the work on her master's degree. But that was a luxury she could not afford. In less than a year she would have earned her master's and a teacher's certificate. She hoped to get a teaching position at a community college or perhaps a high school. She was anxious to move out of her aunt and uncle's home and get on with her life.

One could pursue a career in archaeology only with a doctorate and that took time and money. She had no money, and she did not want to live with her aunt and uncle any longer. She loved them, but living with them made her feel like she was already into middle age. The main concern in Aunt Sarah's life was the state of the wax on her kitchen floor, and Uncle Joe seemed to think mostly about his arthritic joints. Jordan knew there had to be more to life than her family's simple existence.

Jordan ate her sandwich and decided to save her apple for later. She had planned to read but began to feel a little sleepy and decided to be lazy for a change.

Pillowing her head on her folded towel, she laid back on the flat, sun-warmed rock. Since there were no staring male eyes, Jordan had worn only a brief bikini in the interest of evening up her tan, and the sun felt delicious on her moist, warm skin. She spread her hair in a fan about her head to allow it to dry and closed her eyes.

At first, she could not decide what had awakened her. She lay there with closed eyes, realizing she had been dozing and knowing that something had caused her to wake up. Then she realized something was touching her hair. When she opened her eyes, she saw Paul's face.

"You really do have beautiful hair," he said. He was sitting beside her on the rock.

"You seem to enjoy sneaking up on me," she said as she hastily scrambled to a sitting position and grabbed her towel with the intent of covering her scantily clad body.

But Paul grabbed her arm. "Don't," he said. "You look beautiful. You should be proud of your body."

"I am in the habit of covering it better than this when there are others around," she said as she pulled her arm away and wrapped her towel sarong-style around her torso as she warily remembered the last time they were alone by the river. "I thought I was going to be alone," she told him.

"And I thought you'd gone to Dallas with Dennis. It sounded as though he had big plans for the weekend."

Jordan thought she detected a note of disapproval in his voice, but his intensely brown eyes were unread-

able. He was wearing slacks and a sports shirt. It was
the first time Jordan had seen him dressed in street
clothes. Somehow, his dig attire of jeans or cut-off
shorts and his buckskin vest over a bare, brown chest
seemed to suit him better. This Paul Nicolle was terribly handsome, however. The conventionalness of his
clothing only served to accentuate his unusual good
looks.

Gone was the beaded headband, and his muscular
chest was hidden from view. But the cut of his thick
black hair, his dramatic features and the ever-present
turquoise nugget just visible in the V of his open shirt
collar were even more striking when set against ordi-
nary attire.

"Dennis likes to talk," Jordan said, wishing she had
a larger towel with which to cover herself. Paul's casual
perusal of her tan legs and bare shoulders made her
very self-conscious. And she was terribly aware of his
nearness. His hand was almost touching her thigh, and
his face was very close to hers as he spoke.

"What's the matter?" he asked sarcastically. "You
and Dennis have a fight? I'm sure one of the other
fellows would have been glad to take you along if you'd
batted those big, blue eyes in their direction."

Jordan did not like the implication in his voice. "I
never intended to go with Dennis or anyone else," she
told him sharply. "Why did you come back anyway?
Surely it wasn't to check to see if I was off for weekend
of fun and games in Dallas."

"I left my briefcase," he said. "I've been down talking to a landowner about a site on the Kiameche River
that should be investigated next summer if I can get
funding. I decided to swing back through and take
some of my work with me."

"And where are you off to now?" Jordan asked, not
sure if she wanted him to linger or to hurry and be

gone. "I don't think I heard you mention your weekend plans."

"I'm going to Tahlequah. My mother lives there."

"Is it far?" Jordan asked.

"Just a couple of hours," he said, seeming in no hurry to leave.

"Did you grow up in that town—in Tahlequah?" Jordan asked, trying to imagine a little-boy version of the virile man who sat so near.

"Yes. For the most part. And both sets of grandparents lived there. The town has a large Cherokee population. It's the old capital of the Cherokee Nation, and a lot of tribal functions are still held there," Paul said as his fingers idly strayed to the turquoise nugget.

Jordan looked into his vividly dark eyes and studied the handsome face that seemed to bring together the most striking characteristics of two races. "If you are Cherokee," she asked, "how is it that you came to have a French name?"

"A mixture of French-and-Indian blood is common in Oklahoma," he explained. "The first white settlers in the state were French. I am a descendant of Jean Pierre Nicolle, who ran one of the first permanent trading posts west of the Mississippi and married a Cherokee woman. She bore a grand total of eleven children so there are lots of Nicolles around. I've got cousins in politics, publishing, banking. One's even a ballerina. And one of my second or third cousins was a bank robber," he said with a hint of a smile softening the sculptured lines of his handsome face.

The chill of evening was beginning to settle over the riverbank. Jordan was enjoying her conversation with Paul, but an involuntary shiver shook her body. She rubbed her hands over her bare shoulders and arms in an attempt to warm them.

The gesture seemed to spur Paul into mobility. He

rose and offered Jordan a hand. "What are you going to do now?" he asked as he pulled her to her feet.

"Wash my hair. Write a few letters," she said, feeling a tingling wave of warmth emitting from the large hand that was still holding hers.

His touch was disturbing. Suddenly she could no longer look into his eyes, and she felt awkward and ill at ease. Withdrawing her hand from his, she gathered up her book and uneaten apple.

"Why didn't you go with Dennis?" he asked in a challenging tone. "There certainly isn't much for you to do around here this weekend."

"I'll manage. I don't mind being by myself," she said as she tightened her towel sarong more firmly around her body.

Paul stood looking down at her, his wide-set eyes unfathomable pools of darkness. Once again his fingers trailed to the ornament at his throat. The sinking sun set his face in stark relief, giving it the look of chiseled granite—an impressive face. Jordan found herself wondering what it would be like to outline his features with her fingertips, to trace his square jaw, his broad forehead, his full sensuous mouth. Did Yvonne admire his appearance, Jordan wondered. Did she ever take his face in her hands and kiss it passionately?

But of course she did. What a silly thought. Jordan was sure the gorgeous woman professor did that and much more to Paul. Much more.

The realization of where her thoughts were taking her brought a flush of color to Jordan's tanned cheeks. She hastened up the riverbank. Paul followed her, and she was aware of his eyes on the back of her bare legs.

She paused at the top of the bank and turned to tell him good-bye, but before the words had left her mouth, Paul announced, "Pack your bag. You're coming with me."

"I beg your pardon," Jordan said, certain she had not heard him correctly.

"I'm not leaving you here by yourself," he said firmly, his voice indicating that he was not willing to negotiate his decision.

"I won't be alone," Jordan protested. "The society members are close by."

"They are over on the other side of the mounds," he pointed out. "I would be lax in my responsibility if I went off and left a female student alone in the wilderness for two nights."

"I assure you, I can manage just fine," she told him, irritated by his authoritarian manner. "You needn't bother yourself about me."

"And what if some local yokel decided to come out here and attack you?" he asked, his tone brutal and taunting. "What would you do about that?"

Jordan gasped at his words and took an involuntary step backward.

"Or what if some passing hunter caught a glimpse of you in that next-to-nothing bathing suit while you were dozing by the river, and was out there just waiting for darkness to come back and have his kicks?" Paul said with a sweep of his hand taking in the shadowy trees that surrounded the camp. "I stood there for a long time and watched you. And no one from the society was around. I could have been a rapist, you know."

Thoroughly confused by his onslaught, Jordan stammered, "I could always scream for help, I suppose. But I'm sure I'd be perfectly safe. There's never been any sort of threat before."

"That could be because you've been surrounded by a group of brawny men. I've seen the way some of those fellows in Seneca have stared at you when we've gone into town. Now, go get your things and be quick about it. I'm running late the way it is."

The terseness of his invitation aggravated Jordan. She had never noticed any men in Seneca staring at her. And she was certain he was exaggerating the danger. Apparently he considered looking after her a mere duty. She could almost read his thoughts. He was probably thinking that she had been nothing but a bother to him from the day she arrived. Well, she could look after herself even if she had to stay awake all night, or take a bedroll over and join the state society folks. No way was she going to tag along with Paul to his mother's house like some child in need of tending.

But before she had a chance to inform him, "Thanks, but no thanks," he had taken off in long, determined strides and was heading for her tent. By the time Jordan caught up with him, he had already pulled a suitcase from under her bed and had grabbed a handfull of freshly laundered underwear from the orange-crate shelf.

"Which of these things will you be needing?" he said, indicating the confusion of pink and blue and lace that was dangling from his fingers.

"Since you seem to know everything, you decide," Jordan said haughtily as she took a seat on the end of the cot.

She watched as he counted out two pair of panties and two matching bras. Then he pulled a pair of shorts from a neatly folded stack and jerked a pink T-shirt from its hanger. He added a pair of jeans and her bathrobe and gown.

"Where's the stuff you had on when you arrived here?" he demanded.

"Under the bed in the other suitcase," she said, her voice a study of cool indifference.

Paul pulled the larger suitcase from under her cot and removed the navy skirt, the ivory-colored blouse, and the high-heeled sandals.

After folding the clothing and packing it in the smaller of her two suitcases, he stood in the middle of the tent surveying her small supply of cosmetics. His physical presence was overwhelming in the limited confines of the tent. The look on his face was determined, almost fierce. Jordan wondered if she would have the courage to go against him.

He packed her toothbrush and toothpaste, a hairbrush, and a tube of lip gloss. Then he looked at her. "What else?" he said harshly, obviously angered by her lack of cooperation.

"Not a thing," she said, "since I'm not going anyplace."

"The hell you're not," he said roughly. "I'll give you two minutes to dress and finish packing this thing, or I'll take you with me just the way your are."

"You wouldn't dare," she taunted, furious with his overbearing attitude. He had no right to order her about like this.

She jumped as he slammed her suitcase shut. He jerked it from the bed and marched off toward his car. Jordan watched him put her suitcase in the backseat, then turn and head back toward the tent. One look at his hostile face, and her heart began to beat wildly. She steeled herself for the scene she was certain would follow. Paul Nicolle was used to being obeyed, and she had no intention of allowing him to bully her into taking a trip she did not want to take and one on which she knew she would not be welcome. Frantically, she mentally rehearsed the words of her continued refusal.

But there were no words between them. He unceremoniously scooped her from the cot and tucked her under his arm like a sack of dirty laundry.

"Put me down," she demanded with as much authority as she could muster from her embarrassingly undignified positon. She had never been so humiliated in her life! How dare he treat her like this. "Put me down," she implored once again, this time with an hysterical note creeping into her voice.

Her towel sarong had fallen away, and Jordan felt unclothed, ridiculous, angry, and more than a little bit afraid. She realized how helpless she truly was. Suddenly his talk of rape seemed more than a remote possibility. Was it Paul himself who was the threat?

She began to beat against his leg with her fists. "You put me down this instant!" she said in a voice that was choked with sobs of frustration and fear.

"Not until you agree to come with me without a struggle," he said, sounding unruffled and completely in control.

"You're nothing but a bully," Jordan sputtered. "A great big, horrible bully!"

"Sometimes one has to resort to unsavory tactics when dealing with unreasonable females," he said calmly.

"Unreasonable females!" Jordan shrieked, her fear changing to rage. "I wouldn't go with you if my life depended on it."

"I rest my case," he said as he swung her easily to her feet. They were standing beside the open door of his car. "Your life may very well depend on your coming with me, and yet you insist you're not about to do that. I'd say a little bullying is in order under those circumstances."

Jordan felt very exposed and vulnerable. Her bare skin was chilled, but she resisted the urge to cover her bareness with crossed arms. She stood as tall as her small frame would allow and tilted her chin defiantly.

"I have never been so poorly treated in my life," she told him. "What makes you think I'd go off with a man who treated me the way you have?"

But even as she spoke the words, Jordan was aware

of the falling darkness. There would be no cheerful lanterns hanging from the tent posts. There would be no campfire to bring warmth and light to the tent compound. But most of all, there would be no other people here—not for two days and two nights. Suddenly she realized just how alone she would be. True, the society people might hear a call for help, provided she was able to call for help or the wind was not blowing too hard for them to hear. And she probably would have been too embarrassed to drag a bedroll over to their campsite and intrude on their group.

She was intensely aware of Paul's gaze as she looked around the deserted camp. For two nights she would be alone. Maybe she should have gone to Dallas with Dennis.

"You would be very alone," Paul said gently, as though he was reading her thoughts.

"I suppose I would," Jordan said miserably. "But I don't want to go uninvited to your mother's house and intrude on your weekend. And I don't appreciate the way you treated me. Maybe I'll just go over and stay at the society camp."

"It's my home also to which I'm inviting you. And you would not listen to my warnings or heed my advice, so I resorted to more physical means. I'm sorry I upset you, but I really do want you to go with me. That way I'll know you're safe. Now, are you going to change your clothes or travel to Tahlequah in a bikini? Make up your mind, because I can assure you I'm not driving away from here without you."

Jordan felt just as she had that first day at the camp when she stood facing the overbearing professor and sensed his strong disapproval of her. Only that day she had won the right to stay. Today she was not to be allowed the same privilege.

She felt her defiance crumbling. He was probably

right. It would have been foolish to stay here alone. She was all for equal rights, but one also had to use common sense. And women were more vulnerable than men in some instances. Camping alone in the wilderness was one of those instances.

Reluctantly, she turned and marched across the grassy compound, feeling very much like a chastised child.

The first part of their journey was a silent one. Jordan stared out the window at the passing countryside. She was a captive passenger and felt no compunction to break the silence with entertaining small talk.

It was Paul who finally spoke as they drove among the lengthening shadows and wound their way through a small mountain range.

"They're called the Winding Stair Mountains," he announced, his voice abruptly breaking the silence. "It's really quite lovely here, especially in the fall when the foliage turns."

As the car wound its way over hairpin turns, there was just enough remnant sunlight for Jordan to make out wooded hills and outcroppings of boulders starkly silhouetted against the darkening sky. Paul pulled off at a scenic turnout and got out of the car. Jordan hesitated, then followed and went to stand beside him. Together, they watched the sun setting itself over the miles of lush forests that were interrupted only by sandstone ridges made golden by the sky's reflected glory. The sunset was streaking the western sky with shades of orange and gold and pink in a blending no artist could hope to imitate. And there was a peace across the land that infiltrated Jordan's body and calmed her. Once again, she felt at harmony with nature—a part of the panorama that spread before her.

In the distance a majestic hawk made easy, soaring

circles in the glowing sky. Jordan soared with him for a time, then turned to the man who stood beside her.

"Thank you for showing this to me," she said simply.

He looked down at her and nodded, his face less determined than before, but nevertheless dominated by an unreadable look in his dark eyes—a look that left Jordan wondering what he really thought of her.

At times, she was certain he considered her a foolish, immature girl. Other times, she was not so sure.

The second leg of the short journey was more companionable. Paul told her about his trip to Kiameche and his hopes that the site could be excavated the following summer since the Fourche Maline site would have been destroyed by then.

"But will you be here to work on it?" Jordan asked. "I understood that you might be working in South America next summer."

"That's a possibility," he said. "But even so, the site should be worked. One of the other professors can supervise."

It was shortly after nine o'clock when Paul parked the car in front of a handsome two-story white house on the outskirts of Tahlequah. As Jordan pushed open the car door, the front door of the house opened and a tall, dark-haired woman emerged and waited for them on the top step of the wide porch.

Hannah Nicolle responded graciously when her son introduced her to Jordan and was warm in her welcome although Jordan could detect a puzzled quirk to her eyebrows as she looked from Jordan to Paul and back again.

Before showing Jordan to her room, Hannah Nicolle gave Jordan a tour of her historic home, which had been built in the 1850s by her great-great-grandfather, who had been chief of the Cherokee Nation at the time. It had been added onto and updated by subsequent generations and had been continuously occupied by Hannah's family.

Hannah briefly shared some of the history of the more interesting pieces of furniture and family portraits and completely changed Jordan's image of life in Indian Territory before Oklahoma became a state.

"Oh, but this part of the state was quite different from the western part," Hannah quickly explained. "The area around here was settled by the Five Civilized Tribes, who built houses and towns. The western part of Oklahoma was populated by tribes who had a more nomadic culture and resisted the white man's ways far longer than we Cherokee. But I like to think we have used the best of both worlds," Hannah said with pride. "We have kept our legends and our crafts, but we quickly took to formal education and permanent homes. There are many fine old homes such as this one that belonged to early-day Cherokees—and I might add that they educated their daughters as well as their sons. My great-grandmother was one of the first graduates of the Cherokee Female Seminary, which was started in the 1840s by the wife of a Presbyterian missionary. But enough of my history lesson. I'm sure you must be famished. Since it's so late, we'll have a light supper in the kitchen and celebrate your visit in a grander fashion tomorrow night."

She showed Jordan to her room—one dominated by a glorious canopied bed. Jordan quickly freshened up and joined the two Nicolles in the kitchen where Hannah was warming open-faced ham sandwiches in the oven.

Jordan did not realize how hungry she was until she started eating. She allowed Hannah to place a second sandwich on her plate. For some reason, Jordan felt quite at home in Hannah's kitchen with its happy clutter of cookbooks and cooking utensils. It presented a contrast to the almost antiseptic appearance of Aunt Sarah's kitchen where nothing was ever left out on the counters and you had to look twice to realize you weren't in an operating room.

As the three of them visited over their meal, Jordan learned that Hannah was a curator at the Five Civilized Tribes Museum. Her father had been a leader in Cherokee affairs. Hannah's own mother was white.

"Paul got his love of history from my mother," Hannah explained. "She was a well-known historian. Her textbook on the history of Oklahoma is still used in some state schools."

Jordan had formed an immediate regard for the youthful-looking half-Cherokee woman and admired the comfortable relationship between the widowed woman and her son. From their conversation, Jordan realized Yvonne had been here several times. Jordan knew Hannah must wonder why Paul had brought home one of his students with no prior notice, but other than her initial puzzled glance in Paul's direction when they first arrived, Hannah acted as though it was the most common thing in the world to have an unannounced stranger as a weekend guest in her home. Jordan was grateful for the woman's hospitality. She could well understand why Paul had not been concerned about his mother's reaction to an unplanned guest.

After a cup of coffee, Jordan left mother and son and went upstairs. She was very tired, and she thought Paul would like to have some time alone with his mother.

Jordan spent a few minutes delighting in the magnificent bed before falling asleep. It was so high off the floor, that a tiny footstool was provided for the bed's occupant to step up on. With its brocade canopy and ornately carved posts, the bed seemed fit for a princess.

Snuggling under smooth sheets, Jordan admitted to herself that she was glad she had come. It was delightful to be sleeping in this magnificent bed after a bath in a real bathtub. And Paul's mother was awfully nice.

She was awakened the next morning by a sharp rapping on her door. Momentarily confused by her unfamiliar surroundings, she quickly remembered why she was lying beneath a brocade canopy rather than a canvas roof.

The rapping sound repeated itself, and this time the door opened and Paul stuck his head in the room. "Breakfast in fifteen minutes," he announced.

Jordan grabbed the sheet and covered her bare shoulders. "I don't remember saying 'Come in,'" she said primly.

Paul ignored her remark and strolled into the room. "Just because we aren't working the dig doesn't mean I'm going to let you sleep all day," he announced. "There are roads to be driven and places to be visited. Get yourself out of that big bed and come eat breakfast."

Through all his bravado Jordan could detect a mischievous twinkle in his dark eyes, something she would not have thought possible of the normally stern professor.

Entering into his game, she said with mock animosity, "Well, how can a lady get out of bed and dress herself when a gentleman has improperly entered her bedroom and denied her of her privacy?"

"I wouldn't be seeing anything I haven't already seen before," he said over his shoulder as he started out the door.

He quickly closed the door behind him, avoiding the pillow Jordan had sent sailing in his direction.

Jordan climbed down from the bed and caught a glimpse of herself in the bureau mirror. She was wearing a rather foolish grin, which she promptly removed, cautioning herself not to misinterpret Paul's light-hearted mood. She was still a trespasser in his weekend in spite of his mother's hospitality.

A trespasser. That was certainly what Yvonne DeSilvestro would think of Jordan if she learned about this impromptu journey. She would think Jordan was making a play for her man.

Well, Professor DeSilvestro had nothing to worry about, Jordan thought soberly. She fully realized Paul would trifle with her sexually if given the chance, but other than his interest in her as his student, his feelings for her went no deeper. She was here in his home because he felt responsible for her safety. And she must not place any importance on his seemingly playful mood, she decided as she picked up the pillow from the floor and made the bed.

She slipped on a pair of jeans and searched for something other than the pink T-shirt Paul had thrown into her suitcase. But there was only the shirt she had on yesterday and the dressy crepe blouse. Reluctantly, she pulled the pink shirt over her head and studied her reflection in the mirror. The shirt was too tight, she decided, and stretched the knit fabric until it was less clinging, but there was no way she could prevent it from emphasizing the feminine fullness of her bust.

With a shrug, she tucked the shirt into her jeans and added a belt to her waist and a thin gold chain to her neck. She applied a touch of makeup and brushed her hair until it shone like spun gold, then pulled it back in a simple twist before joining Paul in the kitchen for breakfast.

"Mother's already left for the museum," Paul explained. "Saturday's a big day for them during the tourist season. Come sit down, and I'll get you something to eat."

"Oh, I can manage myself," Jordan protested.

But Paul insisted on cooking her a breakfast of scrambled eggs and bacon, then putting on the airs of a snobbish waiter in an expensive restaurant as he served her, revealing a fun-loving side of himself Jordan had not dreamed existed. He reminded her more of Dennis than the uncompromising professor whose students sometimes called him a slave driver behind his back.

As she ate her breakfast and drank a second cup of coffee, Paul explained the city of Tahlequah was located in a very historic region of the state.

"I'm going to take you on a guided tour," he announced, "and we'd better get started if we're going to get back in time for the pageant and powwow."

"What pageant and powwow?" she asked.

"You'll find out later," he said as he wisked her plate and cup from the table.

Soon they were in his car heading west. Their first stop was a log fort that looked like a set from a Hollywood movie. Fort Gibson, Jordan learned from Paul, was the oldest military post in the state. It was built in 1824, and many illustrious figures such as Zachery Taylor, Jefferson Davis, and Sam Houston once served there.

"The removal of the Cherokee and other eastern tribes to Oklahoma had already begun by 1824," Paul told her. "Fort Gibson was built to help supervise those Indians and as another outpost in the continuing war with the Plains tribes. The post was used until after the Civil War, and many of the troopers who were killed in the Indian wars and the Civil War are buried in a small national cemetery near here."

They drove the short distance to the small cemetery, which occupied a gentle hill and was shaded by a grove of large trees. Jordan was filled with a sense of history as she strolled with Paul among the old markers, reading the names of young men who had been caught up in their nation's wars and lost the right to live out their lives. The beauty of their final resting place and the intervening years did not diminish the tragedy of their deaths for Jordan. She thought of all the love and joy they never experienced, of all the children they never sired. It was a sad place.

A circle of graves ringed the flagpole, and Jordan paused in front of these, her brow creasing in puzzlement as she read an inscription on one of the stones.

TALAHINA R.
WIFE OF GEN. SAM HOUSTON

"What's this?" Jordan asked as Paul strolled up behind her. "I wrote a paper on Sam Houston once. He had a wife in Tennessee, and then later married a woman in Texas, but he was never married to a woman in Indian Territory."

"Ah, but he was," Paul said. "White historians have chosen to ignore the existence of such a woman in Houston's life, and the Houston family denied that he married while he lived in Indian Territory, but he was indeed married to a Cherokee woman for three and a half years."

"Don't you mean he lived with her?" Jordan asked. "He didn't actually marry her, did he?"

"Yes, he did. Her name was really Tiana Rogers. Talahina is a Choctaw name. She was the daughter of a prominent Cherokee family that had befriended Houston during the years he spent among the Cherokee as a youngster in Tennessee. The tribe had moved to Oklahoma, and when a scandal over his first marriage forced his resignation as governor of Tennessee, he headed straight for Indian Territory and Tiana."

Jordan was entranced by Paul's tale. She looked

down at the tombstone of this forgotten woman who history had all but overlooked.

"And they actually got married?" Jordan persisted.

"Yes, in a Cherokee ceremony at the Rogers's home in Mays county. Of course, the missionaries didn't recognize the marriage, but according to Cherokee law, Houston and Tiana were man and wife. And Houston was a citizen of the Cherokee Nation at that time."

"How fascinating!" Jordan said. "What was Tiana like?"

"It is said that she was tall and beautiful," Paul said, "and Houston was supposed to have had a discerning eye for the ladies, so I'm sure she was as lovely as legend has remembered her. They had known each other when they were children and apparently had been lovers in their youth."

"What happened to their marriage?" asked Jordan. "Why did it end?"

"Destiny called," Paul said with a shrug. "Houston saw the Texas struggle for independence from Mexico as his vehicle back into public life. Legend has it that he begged Tiana to go with him to Texas, and even sent messages back to her imploring her to join him, but she remained in Indian Territory. She died a few years later."

Paul showed her another tombstone marked Sam Houston Benge. "Some say he was their son," he told Jordan.

Before leaving the cemetery, Jordan and Paul strolled back by Tiana's grave, their feet making crunching sounds on the gravel of the well-tended path.

Filled with the mystery of the legendary Cherokee woman, Jordan pondered aloud, "I wonder if Tiana ever regretted not going to Texas with Houston."

"No one knows. But maybe she wanted a home for her child among her people. Houston was a wanderer. Like archaeologists. Some of us seem to have been born to chase dreams," Paul said in a wistful tone.

"My father is a wanderer," Jordan said. "And that's what he does—chase after dreams. I guess that's why my mother often said that a home doesn't have to be the same four walls year after year. A home is wherever a family and love reside."

Paul had a puzzled, searching look in his eyes as his gaze left the gravestone of Sam Houston's Cherokee wife and traveled to Jordan's face. For an instant, his intense, dark eyes held her vivid blue ones. Then, fingering the nugget at the end of his silver neck chain, he abruptly turned and started for the gate.

Beware, Paul told himself. *She's not what she seems at this minute.* He reminded himself of her relationship with Dennis. And the way Edgar had obviously fallen head over heels in love with her. And as if that wasn't enough, that highway engineer—Jarvis—had been hanging around her like a lovesick puppy.

But this afternoon was so perfect. She was so eager to see and experience everything. She had quite amazed him at times with her grasp of the history of this region. Jordan had the makings of a true scholar. And Paul delighted in answering her questions and in just being with her. She was so vibrant, so full of life, so beautiful.

He had been wrong about her ability to contribute to the work at the excavation. She worked hard and her enthusiasm was infectious. On more than one occasion he had seen her get everyone going when work was lagging. The lady was gutsy and a whole lot tougher than she looked. Yes, he had been dead wrong in that regard.

Could he possibly be wrong about some other facets of Jordan Marshall? When he looked down into her blue-green eyes, he wanted to be. He wanted their time together to go on and on. He wanted to keep her all to himself and not return her to that camp full of men.

And he wanted to do more than brush against her

arm as they walked. He felt like such an adolescent doing that. Stealing touches! But he was filled with the need to touch her. His fingers ached with the need of it.

Watch out, old man, he told himself. *Remember, you're older and wiser now. You have no need of this nonsense. You have intellectually selected Yvonne—the one woman in the world most suited to you and the life you have chosen.*

But he reached out and touched the small of Jordan's back in what he hoped seemed like a helpful gesture as they climbed the small hill that separated them from his car. Yesterday Jordan had been crawling in and out of ditches almost as deep as she was tall, but today he was using a gentle slope as an excuse to make physical contact with her.

Chapter Seven

From Fort Gibson they took a leisurely drive to Green-lief Lake—a jewel of a lake nestled among rolling, tree-dotted hills—and had lunch at a lakeside café.

Then Paul drove to the small town of Sallisaw, where they stopped at the Sequoyah Memorial, which had been built to honor the inventor of the Cherokee alphabet, and visited the tiny log cabin that had been built by the famous Cherokee in 1841.

"The Cherokee were the first tribe to have an alphabet and a written langauge," Paul explained. "This made educating the tribe far easier, and as a result we were able to have books in our own language and our own newspaper."

Jordan sensed Paul's pride in his tribeman's accomplishments as she surveyed with him the simple log cabin that had once been the home of the illustrious Sequoyah.

The cabin contrasted greatly with the next home Paul showed her. They toured the George Murrell home, which was located south of Tahlequah. Murrell was a famous Cherokee leader, and his home, like that of Paul's mother, demonstrated the style of living adopted by many of the more prosperous Cherokees. Built in 1844, the colonial-style mansion had been completely restored with many of the original furnishings and paintings. Paul told Jordan that Murrell had earned the rank of major while fighting for the South during the Civil War.

Throughout the day, most of their conversation had revolved around history. Jordan was surprised to discover that Paul's undergraduate major had also been American history. He was, of course, extremely knowledgeable about the history of his state. But their conversation often strayed far outside the borders of Oklahoma, and Jordan could tell Paul was impressed with her understanding of the events that had shaped the nation's history.

Paul seemed to be enjoying his role as tour guide. They stopped at each roadside historical marker, and Paul had tales to go with most of them. He was as fascinated as Jordan was with the little asides that never appeared in history books but made the people who created the history seem far more real.

And Paul was behaving in a most gallant fashion. He helped her in and out of his car at each stop and was constantly touching her elbow or back as he guided her through the various historical sites they visited. Jordan decided he was trying to make up for his bullish behavior of yesterday. It was silly, of course. She could get around as well as he. But such pleasure those small touches brought! His attentiveness and his touch were like a drug for her. She felt flushed and excited. She felt wonderful!

She knew she was being foolish, and that she should calm herself. But she chose not to analyze away the joy of the afternoon. She could be calm another day. Today might be the only day in her life she had this fascinating man all to herself.

They returned to Paul's home in the late afternoon after a drive through the town of Tahlequah itself, including a visit to the stately building that had once served as capitol of the Cherokee Nation.

Hannah was busy in the kitchen and refused Jordan's offer of help.

"You go freshen up, dear," she told Jordan. "Dinner will be ready in about half an hour. Paul wants us to eat early so you won't be late to the pageant."

Jordan took a quick shower, still euphoric from her joyous afternoon with Paul. She put on her navy skirt and ivory-colored blouse. The necklace and earrings she usually wore with this outfit were still back in her tent. When she studied her reflection in the mirror, she was somewhat disappointed by the drabness of her appearance. By way of compensation, she added a bit more lipstick and eye shadow than usual, left her hair loose over her shoulders, and slipped into her high-heeled sandals. She had no stockings, but her legs were so tan, none were really needed.

"My, how lovely you look," Hannah said as Jordan entered the dining room.

Hannah was removing a fourth place setting of china from the table and explained that Paul's younger brother had hoped to join them for dinner but had called saying he couldn't make it.

"I told him to come late if he could," Hannah said. "Paul and Frank haven't seen each other in several months."

Paul entered from the kitchen wearing a shirt embroidered with an Indian motif and a braided leather headband over his heavy black hair. His eyes were full of admiration when he looked at Jordan.

"You are pretty as a grubby archaeologist, but you're beautiful as a stylish young woman—only you were wearing some jewelry with that blouse when you arrived that first day."

"You have a good memory," Jordan said with a touch of sarcasm. "You were so angry, I didn't think you noticed anything other than my size and sex."

"I noticed more than you think," he said in mock seriousness, his frank perusal of her silk-covered breasts causing her to blush. "And since I did your packing, I guess it's up to me to find something to complete your outfit this evening."

He seated Jordan at the table and, asking his mother to accompany him, left Jordan alone in the room.

Very shortly, they returned with a handsome silver-and-turquoise necklace that Hannah fastened around Jordan's neck as a loan for the evening.

"How lovely the turquoise looks with your eyes," Hannah exclaimed. "Paul, have you noticed that Jordan's eyes are just the color of turquoise?"

Paul did not respond to his mother's question. He seated her in a chair at one end of the elegantly set table.

"Since you cooked the dinner," he told Hannah, "I'll serve it."

Another surprise, Jordan thought. She had never known a man who was willing to serve a meal to two women. She found herself thinking of her aunt and uncle, who never once in the years Jordan had lived with them had ever slipped out of their rigidly defined roles. Even though her uncle was now retired, it never would have occurred to him to assist with preparing or serving a meal—nor would her aunt have allowed it. Yet Jordan had never met a more masculine man than the one who was now serving her dinner.

The meal was a delicious one of curried chicken with a green salad and French bread. Jordan complimented Hannah on the lovely dinner.

"I'm glad you enjoyed it," Hannah said graciously. "And I'm delighted Paul brought you for this visit. I hope he brings you again."

As Paul removed their dessert plates from the table, his younger brother Frank arrived and joined them over coffee. Frank was a more youthful, slightly smaller, and somewhat unkempt version of his other brother, except that the intense look on Frank's handsome face gave him an almost hostile appearance. Jordan immediately sensed an animosity between the two brothers, and in spite of Hannah's skillful attempts to steer the conversation to safer topics, the brothers were soon caught up in an argument over the Fourche Maline project.

Frank obviously believed his brother was desecrating sacred Indian grounds by excavating the Fourche Maline site and thought his brother should be using his influence as a college professor to prevent the proposed highway's destruction of the riverside mounds and Medicine Bluff.

"You have no respect for your own heritage," Frank said hotly. "That highway is being built on land that has been a sacred place to our people since the time of our most ancient legends. You say you care about unraveling our people's history, but I think all you care about is getting your precious artifacts out of the ground and getting written up in archaeological journals as the University of Oklahoma's brilliant young Cherokee archaeologist. Well, you can be a white man's professor, but I choose to be an Indian. *I* am proud of my heritage and don't attempt to deny it like my esteemed older brother!"

The angry young Indian rose to his feet, knocking his chair over in the process, and stared down at his brother. Paul pushed back his own chair and started to rise and face him, but his mother's hand on his arm caused him to pause.

"Frank, Paul," she said tersely, "we have a guest in our home."

Frank put his black, wide-brimmed hat firmly on his head and stormed from the room. Paul uttered an oath. And Jordan stared down at her empty coffee cup, embarrassed to have been witness to a family quarrel.

The three of them silently stared out the dining room window as Frank backed his battered brown van out of the driveway and roared down the street.

"When is he ever going to grow up and live in the real world?" Paul asked his mother as the brown van rounded a corner on two wheels and disappeared from view. Paul's tone was almost accusative, as though he thought his mother should be doing something to remedy her younger son's behavior.

Hannah calmly patted Paul's hand. "I remember the times you accused your father and me of 'selling out to the white man.' Give him time, Paul. He'll be all right," she said reassuringly.

"It's something native Americans have to come to terms with," Hannah explained to Jordan. "They have to figure out where they fit into a world that for many years tried to destroy their culture. They have to decide just how 'Indian' they want to be—especially the ones like Paul and Frank who are part white. Many of our young people attempt to give up modern ways and return to a time that no longer exists. For many native American youths, that period is a painful part of their maturation process. Paul went through it also—not to the extent that Frank is, but at one time, he joined a colony of native Americans who gave up all modern ways and were attempting to live as their forebearers had. They built hogans and tried to grow their own food."

"What happened?" Jordan asked.

"One of the young women died in childbirth," Paul interrupted, his dark eyes closing for an instant with the impact of remembered pain. "She wouldn't have bled to death if she had delivered in a hospital."

"It took a tragedy like that," Hannah continued, "to make them realize they had to find a balance. Today's native Americans try to preserve their art, their legends, and as many of the traditions as they can. But this is the twentieth century, and this is the United States of America, and to deny advances made in medicine and health care, in transportation and food production, in sanitation and in a hundred other things—well, it's something young Indians like Frank have to come to terms with."

Hannah poured herself another cup of coffee, then took a sip before continuing. "My younger son seethes with the injustices of four hundred years," she said with an understanding smile. "But one of these days, he'll come home, take a shower, and concentrate on his fine artistic talent. He has an artist's ability and responsibility to immortalize all those traditions he cares so much about—just as Paul has a responsibility to use his analytical mind and love of history to find the roots of those traditions and bring understanding of the past to native Americans. Frank just hasn't figured this out yet, but he will," she said confidently.

Paul lifted his wineglass in a toast to his mother. "As always, you are incredibly wise. I salute you—and thank you. Sometimes I get so mad at him I could thrash him soundly. But you're right. I'll hang in there and wait for him to find things out for himself."

Hannah acknowledged Paul's toast with a loving smile, then proceeded to hurry them on their way.

"It's getting dark," she warned. "You two had best hurry on to the pageant, or you'll be late."

Tsa-La-gi, or "Trail of Tears," was performed in an outdoor amphitheater and depicted the history of the Cherokee Tribe from 1838 to 1907, including the tragic removal of the Cherokee people by the U.S. government from their tribal lands in the southeastern United States and their forced march to Indian Territory in the winter of 1838. During that march, more than five thousand of the Cherokees died of cold and starvation.

Watching the moving performances by the Indian performers brought Jordan a greater respect for the Cherokee people. Their tribes had survived so much. It was not difficult to understand how young Indians like Paul's brother became embittered when they thought of the past.

After the pageant Paul provided a quick change of pace by taking Jordan to a powwow that was being held in a park across the road from his mother's two-story home. The powwow was opened to all tribes, Paul explained as they joined the ring of spectators on the edge of a large viewing area.

Many of the Indian spectators had brought along their lawn chairs and picnic baskets. Others were stretched out on blankets. There were small children in the laps of grandmothers, teenagers holding hands, sleeping babies in the arms of their mothers, and young boys ignoring the dances and playing tag among the trees. The entire area was illuminated by bonfires and had a festive atmosphere that contrasted markedly with the dramatic pageant Jordan had witnessed earlier.

The dancers all wore colorful, authentic costumes whose designs represented various aspects of traditional religious beliefs and legends. And the dances they performed represented a wide range of ceremonial occasions, Paul explained.

"Nowadays," Paul told her, "we don't dance the Buffalo Dance to ask the Great Spirit for a successful hunt, but rather to keep our culture alive and remember the old ways."

Jordan watched the young men in masks made of buffalo scalps and horns twist and turn their lean bodies around the bonfire as they raised their shields and spears heavenward.

"They'll never go on a buffalo hunt," Paul said of the youthful dancers. "In fact, the oldest man here never went on a buffalo hunt, but the animal is so much a part of the history and traditions of the Plains tribes that they still perform the dance in remembrance of the mighty hunters and herds that once roamed this land.

Jordan watched war dances, rain dances, dances asking the spirits to bring a good corn crop, and even a dance performed with live rattlesnakes.

When the group of elderly chanters and drummers changed their beat to a slower, more sedate tempo, Paul rose and pulled Jordan to her feet.

"Remember the steps?" he asked as they joined a circle of dancers to perform the line dance he had taught her to the beat of Wolf's drum.

Jordan felt rather strange shuffling around the fire in a circle composed almost exclusively of Indians, but the smiling faces that passed in front of her as she danced her way around the ring were friendly and encouraging. Obviously no one minded the presence of a blond stranger in their midst.

During a break in the dances, Paul bought Jordan some fry bread from a young Indian woman dressed in jeans and a T-shirt decorated with a picture of a popular rock group. She was also selling soda pop and candy bars from her tailgate concession stand.

"The fry bread's made of cornmeal," Paul said with a grin, "and guaranteed to give your non-Indian stomach trouble if you eat the whole piece. The recipe was contrived in the days before leavening, and it will sit in your stomach like a brick."

"Thanks for the warning," Jordan said gaily, thoroughly enjoying herself.

She nibbled cautiously on the bread as she listened to Paul converse with a group of elderly men, some of whom Jordan recognized as being among the drummers and chanters who provided the accompaniment for the dancers. Soon, however, the conversation shifted from English to the Cherokee tongue, and Jordan once again felt very much the outsider. She strolled over to a trash receptacle to dispose of the remainder of her fry bread.

It was darker here away from the bonfires, but when a movement among a cluster of parked vehicles caught Jordan's eye, there was enough light for her to recognize the battered brown van Frank Nicolle parked in his mother's driveway earlier in the evening. Jordan realized that Paul's younger brother was sitting in the open back door of the van, a can of beer in his hand.

Jordan glanced back to where Paul was still engrossed in a lively conversation with the tribal elders and strolled in the direction of the solitary figure of Paul's younger brother. Perhaps the "angry young man" would be more approachable when he wasn't arguing with his older brother.

But Jordan was startled to hear a familiar voice coming from the darkened interior of the open van. Quickly, she stepped out of sight behind a parked pickup truck.

Yvonne DeSilvestro was inside Frank Nicolle's van! That was her voice!

How could that be, Jordan asked herself. Yvonne had gone to Oklahoma City for the weekend. She had a speaking engagement. Jordan had seen her drive off in the university van along with the three Peruvian students. Why would she be here? And what in the world could she be doing hidden away in the back of Frank's van?

I must be mistaken, Jordan decided. But then she heard it again—the cultured, lilting accent of the Peruvian archaeologist. There was no mistaking that distinctive voice.

Jordan quickly dropped back into the shadows and returned to Paul's side. She did not mention the incident to him, fearful that it would sound as though she were implying that something improper was going on between his brother and his fiancee.

Was there? Jordan wondered. Was Yvonne trying to make a conquest of both Nicolle brothers? It did seem very strange for her to come to Tahlequah and visit the younger—rather than the older—Nicolle brother.

Paul took her arm protectively as they crossed the grassy field separating the park from the road in front of his house. Her footing was made difficult by her high-heeled sandals, but this time she was not embarrassed by their presence on her feet. After all, Paul had packed them himself. Tonight, apparently, he had not wanted her to look like a grubby archaeology student. Had he planned for them to have this night together when he was angrily throwing her possessions in her suitcase, Jordan wondered, or had it just happened? Whatever the reason, she was grateful. Except for the disturbing intrusion of Paul's brother—and of Yvonne—into this day, it had been one of the most delightful she had ever spent.

Hannah was sitting in the porch swing waiting for them. They sat with her in the darkness listening to the beat of the tom-toms and watching the silhouetted shapes of the dancers as they passed in front of flickering fires. Paul slipped a glass of wine into Jordan's hand, and she sipped at it as she listened to mother and son gossip about relatives and friends.

Jordan felt the wine relaxing her. It had been a full day, and she realized that she was tired. She leaned her head against the high back of the wicker settee and allowed her eyes to close, feeling pleasantly languid and contented.

The next thing she knew, Paul's strong arms were carrying her up the stairs. She must have fallen asleep. How silly of her. He should have awakened her. She could have gotten herself up the stairs no matter how weary she was.

But she seemed to fit so nicely in his arms. She murmured his name and something about being so much trouble, then helped him support her weight by sliding her arms around his neck.

His footsteps were muffled on the carpet of the hallway. She heard a door close at the far end of the hall. Hannah must be going to bed. Then she heard a second door close and realized through the layers of her drowsiness that Paul had shut the door of *her* bedroom and was lowering her ever so gently onto the high canopy bed.

His kiss, when it came, was so feather-light that she wondered if she was imagining it. Perhaps she was already asleep, and it was only in her dream that the bold professor was helping himself to a lingering, imaginary kiss. A dreamland kiss. Surrealistic.

It was a lovely dream. His lips brushed over hers, his hands softly held her face. And it felt even lovelier when his tongue began to outline her mouth—first her upper lip, then her lower, then repeated itself once, twice. So nice, it felt, that her lips parted themselves to offer the exploring tongue her sensitive inner lips to tantalize.

Involuntary murmurs of delight escaped from her throat and mingled with the touching mouths. Animal sounds, like a soft kitten asking to be stroked or a small puppy whimpering for its milk.

More. She did so want more of those warm lips and even warmer tongue. Her own lips parted still further in invitation. She waited breathlessly for his tongue to penetrate, to fill her open mouth.

But he made her wait—maddeningly. Her murmurs increased, becoming more urgent. She wanted his tongue to enter her. She was not asleep. This was not a dream. Jordan knew that now. Somehow, her sleepiness had clouded her reasoning and propelled her quickly past conscious thought, depositing her in a state of passionate need. But only if she could have this man's mouth and his tongue in the deepest of kisses could she then deal with her need. First, she must have that kiss. No other thought but that was allowed to enter her mind.

Please, her mind silently screamed out to him. And he heard her. She could tell, but he cruelly drew away and turned his attention to her neck. No, not there, not now.

"No," she said out loud, the sound startling in the quiet, and reached up to grab his hair in her fists. Ruthlessly, she pulled his face over hers.

Only then did she comprehend that he was lying on the bed with her, his head and shoulders hovering over her, but carefully holding his lower body away from her. And she understood why. He wanted her to come to him. That was why his kiss had been incomplete. He wanted her to acknowledge her need of him. She understood and was past caring.

Vaguely, she was aware that the rest of her body had awakened and was being drawn to the man like a moth to light. But she would deal with that after she had his kiss.

Her lips implored. Her tongue pleaded. A groan errupted from deep within him. She had won.

There were no longer two mouths, two sets of lips, two searching tongues. Only a blending existed, an exquisite blending of moistness and warmth and gaping need.

But the one perfect, complete kiss for which she had

so desperately longed did not answer her craving need of him. Instead, it cascaded her downstream into a roaring river and carried her along in a current too swift, too strong to resist. A flood of passion was unleashed within her breasts. A torrent of aching desire coursed through her veins.

Her body thrust itself against his, and as though that were the cue for which he had been waiting, Paul began deftly unbuttoning the front of her blouse.

Almost magically, the blouse left her body. Her bra relinquished its burden to his demands.

Hands and mouth at her breasts—it was more than she could bear, yet still she yearned for more. The turbulent cravings swept away all barriers. Uncontrollable currents hurled her helplessly toward the vague boundaries of a vast, deep sea that was waiting to swallow her into its mysterious depths.

Wave after wave of desire washed over her body, each time bringing her closer and closer to that mystical moment when the river meets the sea, when the waters merge and are one.

Flesh against flesh. She was apart from herself, apart from this room, this bed. In the entire world, there was only herself and this man and the knowledge of what awaited her—the knowledge that soon he would possess her, that he would thrust himself deep within her just as his thrusting tongue possessed her mouth again and again.

She floated with him above the world of towns and houses and returned with him to a more elemental place and time.

Nothing had prepared her for these feelings. Twenty-six years she had lived without completely entering this other dimension. It was a new world for Jordan, one she was now ready to experience completely. Never had she known such a need. She had only thought it was full-blown desire she felt those other times with those other men. *This* was desire. It was tearing her apart, showing her no mercy.

"Please," she heard her voice saying, surprised she still remembered how to speak. "I want you so," she told him desperately. But how false those words sounded. How could mere words begin to tell him what she was feeling?

And he spoke. He had words for her also. She wanted his words too. Her name! He was saying her name! And more.

"I need you so, Jordan. I can't think about anything else. Day and night. Jordan," he whispered hoarsely. "Jordan, sweet Jordan."

"Make love to me," she told him, so filled with her need she felt as though she could die of it. "Please."

"Ah, Jordan, are you sure?"

She had never been so sure of anything in her life even though there were no promises of tomorrow. Maybe this was to be a once-in-a-lifetime joining of their passion-filled bodies. But there was no room in her mind for questioning. She could no more have turned him away than she could have interrupted a dive in mid arch or stopped an avalanche from its path. The forces that would bring them together at least for one brief time in their histories had been set in motion. A need filled them both that was as natural and primeval as the flow of the rivers and the fall of the rain.

They were now apart from the civilized world of canopied beds and smooth sheets, of houses and towns. They had soared away from all but themselves. They had no names. He was man and she was woman. They joined their bodies in a union so brilliantly pure, it blinded them.

"I didn't know," Paul said softly when words returned to him.

Jordan understood. It was new. It was awesome. But it had left them both with only the power to sleep.

Paul awoke first. It was still night, but the darkness was rapidly thinning. He lay there, watching her sleep, his mind going in a dozen directions at once. He wanted to love her again and again and again. He was either bewitched or in love.

He felt like a man about to jump out of an airplane—only he wasn't sure he had a parachute. He had allowed himself to need again. To *really* need. And he was frightened by the power it had over him.

Had he gotten himself caught up in another whirlwind of emotional upheaval that would ultimately fling him away broken and humiliated and in pain?

Jordan's back was curled in the curve of his own body. Already he was so aware of her smooth skin, the aroma of her, the womanliness of her. He could feel the stirrings begin deep inside of him and warm his loins. A soft moan escaped from his lips, and she stirred.

He could sense the subtle changes in her body as she moved into wakefulness. She would feel his urgency and turn to him. Then it could all begin again.

Paul felt weak and strong at the same time. He felt tangled in a web and free-floating. He had crystal-clear visions and clouded ones.

He wanted to go slowly with her this time, so slow it would be painful. He wanted to memorize every inch of her body with his hands and his mouth. But first, he had to know what was in her mind. Was she already planning the next escapade in her busy life or did what had happened between them mean something to her?

And what about his own mind? What about Yvonne? He cared for her. There was a rightness about his relationship with the beautiful archaeologist. And it too had its passion—different, however, from what he had experienced in this bed with the small woman beside him. So very different. The intensity of what had happened with Jordan in his arms was so incredible it frightened him. It made him feel as though he had somehow stepped over a line that mere mortals were not supposed to cross.

Jordan was facing him now, her face devoid of any makeup, her hair a disheveled halo around her head. He stared at her naked face and her naked body and wanted her more than he thought possible.

She smiled a small, shy smile. His heart was in his throat, choking him.

"I have to know, Jordan," he began. "Will you give up the others? Has anything changed with you?"

"The others?" A frown crossed her brow.

"I know," he explained. "I have eyes. And I have Yvonne. I am so confused. I don't know what's going to happen now."

Jordan put her hands to her face. Paul could see her throat move as she swallowed. When she removed her hands, she was smiling again.

"Nothing's going to happen now," she said brightly. "We're adult people. You know, two ships that pass in the night. It happens all the time nowadays. We can handle it. Now, I think it would be best if you went to your own bedroom. I don't want to cause you or your mother any embarrassment in the morning."

She touched his face briefly and turned her back to him. He started to tell her he didn't want to leave. Even if it was to be a brief fling, he wanted to love her again. He'd deal with his feelings later. He'd try to accept her terms. But first, let him love her again. However, the white shoulders above the sheet looked taut and tense—as though she would jump if he touched them.

He touched her hair instead.

Jordan waited until the door closed behind him until she allowed the first sob to erupt.

Chapter Eight

Breakfast was a strained affair. Hannah was obviously puzzled by the formal politeness between Jordan and Paul. Gone was the lighthearted friendliness of the day before.

Paul excused himself before Jordan had finished her meal and already had the car loaded when she came down the steps of the broad front porch. Nothing was said about the visit to the Five Civilized Tribes Museum that had been planned for early afternoon, and very shortly the car was speeding down the two-lane highway that would return them to the Fourche Maline encampment.

The trip southward was silent and uncomfortable. Jordan's mind was full of things she would like to say to the stony-faced professor, but she could not bring herself to dignify his apparently low opinion of her with a denial. Let him think what he wants, she told herself. It's better that way. Then he doesn't have to apologize or try to explain away his actions of last night. He simply had succumbed to temptation with a willing woman.

Obviously Paul had immediate regrets after making love to her. He had been unfaithful to the woman he intended to marry and had done so with a woman he thought was promiscuous. How sordid it must all seem

to him in the light of day, Jordan realized. She almost
wished she could feel the same way. Then she would
feel only embarrassment and not have to deal with the
pain that lay so heavily against her heart.

She had allowed herself to care for him. Deeply. He
was unlike any man she had ever met before. She was
in awe of his knowledge. She respected his accomplishments. And his physical presence left her no peace.

But here was no place in his life for her. For him it
was a simple case of lust. The attraction of opposites.
The thrill of conquest. He thought she was passing out
favors to other men and he wanted his share. But as
soon as he gave into that lust, he was remorseful. After
the fact, it became for him a meaningless act.

Never again, Jordan vowed. No matter how much
she wanted him, she would never suffer the humiliation she had suffered in the dim light of early morning
when he asked her about "the others" and she learned
his love truly did belong to Yvonne.

Life had played a cruel joke on her, Jordan now realized. She had experienced the power and beauty of
lovemaking more fully than she ever had before in her
life. But Paul was full of regret. He was the man she
had allowed to tear down every barrier and every inhi-
bition left over from her strict upbringing and failed
marriage. But for him, their lovemaking had been a
betrayal of his lady and of his standards.

The trip back to the excavation was agony—endless
silent agony.

The only signs of life as they drove through Seneca
were two small girls jumping rope on the otherwise deserted grade school playground and the elderly whit-
tlers maintaining their vigil in a courthouse square near
the World War I memorial.

When at last Chester Wilson's tired farmhouse
came into view, Jordan breathed a sigh of relief. She

was more than ready for this tension-filled journey to end.

Paul's car bounced its way across the pasture, stirring up voluminous clouds of dust as it went. Obviously, it had not rained in their absence.

Jordan was surprised to see the gate at the lower end of the pasture standing open. Fortunately, none of the cattle seemed to have strayed, and Jordan closed it after Paul had driven the car through.

The river was down, and flats of ugly, slick mud were left exposed by the narrowed river and marred its picturesque beauty. The trees along the bank looked as listless as Jordan felt. Each dust-covered leaf hung limply in the still, hot air.

Jordan was staring at the circlings of a distant hawk, wondering what small animal was about to be swooped down upon, when she was startled by a violent oath bursting forth from Paul's lips. She quickly drew her gaze earthward and gasped when she saw the reason for his profanity.

The camp was in ruins!

"What in the world has happened?" Jordan asked incredulously as she surveyed the devastation.

Paul's knuckles were white as he grasped the steering wheel, and the look on his face was one of absolute rage.

"It doesn't take a genius to figure that out," he said angrily.

"What do you mean?" Jordan asked in confusion.

"The tracks," he said through clenched teeth. "Look at the ground. A track-laying vehicle has been driven through here. And the only track-laying vehicles within miles belong to that highway crew. With the river down, I guess he just drove it right across the shallows up stream. Looks like that boyfriend of yours decided to try and put an end to our dig so he could build his precious bridge on schedule."

"Larry wouldn't do that," Jordan protested, "and he isn't my boyfriend!"

Jordan stared at the maze of tracks that crisscrossed the camp. They were indeed the sort left by heavy equipment such as bulldozers. But Larry? She thought of the gentle, shy man who had taken her out and could not believe he had anything to do with this cruel act of vandalism.

As Paul walked around inspecting the damage, Jordan could sense his anger—and his disappointment. She wondered how much precious time would be lost by this senseless destruction. Perhaps they would not be able to continue. The kitchen tent had been completely torn down, as had the smaller of the three main tents where the artifacts were sorted and catalogued before being sent to the university museum. The meal tent was partially collapsed, and all of the men's sleeping tents were in various stages of collaspe. Only Yvonne and Jordan's tents on the far side of the compound remained untouched.

"Nice of your boyfriend to leave your tent standing," Paul said with biting sarcasm after completing a perfunctory inspection of the damage. "What do you think of the road builder now?" he asked, his tone bitter.

"I think he had nothing to do with this," Jordan said. "Not only would he not be a part of something like this, he wouldn't want to delay our work. What would that accomplish? He wants us finished and out of here."

"Oh, but he must have found out that I've applied to the state historical society to have the bluff and mounds declared an historical site," Paul said. "If the application is approved, the location of the bridge will have to be moved. New land will have to be acquired. It will have to be resurveyed and redesigned. Jarvis wouldn't like that one bit. It would delay the bridge for months. It looks to me like your lover boy is trying to scare us away. Well, you can tell him that I'll fight him on this thing until hell freezes over!"

Jordan wanted to scream at Paul that Larry was not her lover—and that Larry was not the sort of person who would be involved in this sort of wanton destruction. But she knew he would not believe her.

Shortly, the other crew members began to straggle into camp, returning from their weekends. Their faces each registered the same shock that Jordan had felt when she first saw the devastated camp.

"What the hell happened?" Dennis asked as he emerged from his car. "Was there a tornado?"

There was much speculation among the crew as to who was responsible for the vandalism, and the consensus was that a bulldozer was the instrument of destruction. Menacing looks were cast in the direction of the bluff and beyond where the unfinished highway lay.

When Yvonne and her three students arrived, the Peruvian woman seemed genuinely distressed over the distruction at the camp. But a disturbing thought kept nagging at Jordan's mind. Could Yvonne's clandestine visit with Frank Nicolle in Tahlequah have anything to do with this senseless vandalism?

But perhaps she had been mistaken about the voice in the back of Frank's van. Oklahoma City, where the Peruvians had been visiting, was a three- or four-hour drive from Tahlequah. How could Yvonne have slipped away from Edgar, Juan, and Miguel long enough to have accomplished such a trip?

But later, while talking to Edgar, Jordan discovered the Peruvians had spent Saturday night in Tulsa after visiting the city's famous art museums. Suddenly, it seemed far more likely that the mysterious, accented voice coming from the back of Frank's battered van was indeed Yvonne's. The drive from Tulsa to Tahlequah would not have taken very long.

However, she put all such conjecture from her mind as she joined the rest of the crew with the discouraging task of trying to put the camp back in some sort of order. Maybe she just wanted to believe the worst about the woman professor, Jordan told herself. Maybe her suspicions arose more from jealousy than fact.

Jordan was almost grateful for the hard work involved in restoring the camp. It gave her something to think about other than her disastrous weekend with Paul. She planned to be so exhausted tonight when she finally went to bed that sleep would come and not the tormented thoughts that she kept trying to push from her mind.

Jordan, like the others, felt the project should continue even if it meant sleeping on the ground and cooking over open fires for the remainder of the summer.

The head of the state archaeological society appeared, offering his condolences and apology to the crew members.

"I guess we didn't look after things like we should've," he said. "We'd patrol over here every so often. Saturday night, we chased away some sightseers who'd been canoeing the river and stopped to have a look. But I figured that after dark nobody would bother anything. They'd have to come through that farmer's yard—or so I thought."

"Well, apparently, they came across the river," Paul told the man. "We found where they crossed back up the way a bit. But I would have thought you might have heard something."

"It was windy—real windy," the man told Paul. "Thought we might get some rain for a time. Understand they did over in Wilburton. And we all took an excursion to that tavern on the edge of Seneca about ten o'clock,'' he admitted sheepishly. "It was too windy to have a campfire so we had a few beers instead. I came over first thing this morning to make sure the wind hadn't blown anything down, and—well, this is what greeted me," he said with a sweep of his hand. "You have any idea who might have done it?"

"Yes," Paul said, looking pointedly in Jordan's direction. "I have an idea. A very good idea."

Later in the day, Jordan drove the van into town to replace some of the supplies that had been destroyed by the unidentified raiders. Cookie stayed behind to salvage what he could from his bulldozed kitchen.

Jordan's first stop, however, was at the county sheriff's office. Paul had instructed her to report the raid on the camp to the sheriff.

She awakened a youthful deputy when she opened the door to the basement office. He hastily removed his feet from the desk and attempted to straighten his mussed shirt. Jordan stated her business and was assured the sheriff would be out later and have a look.

"Think I'll come along too," the young man told Jordan as he smoothed his hair. I've been wanting to see what you folks are up to out there anyway? Do you really dig up old Indian bones?"

"We excavate evidence of past human habitation," Jordan told him, "and that includes skeletal remains of human beings."

"Now why in the world would a pretty little thing like you want to go and do something like that?" he asked flirtatiously.

"We'll see you and the sheriff sometime later this afternoon," Jordan said, ignoring his question and heading for the door.

As she drove away from the courthouse, Jordan noticed a battered brown van parked at an ancient motel on the edge of the town's business district. It looked very much like Frank Nicolle's elderly vehicle. But what would he be doing in Seneca, unless...

Once again, suspicions about Paul's younger brother began to plague her. She pulled into the motel parking lot for a closer look at the van. A black, wide-rimmed hat with a beaded headband was resting on the dashboard. Frank's hat—the one he had been wearing in Tahlequah.

Could he have come to visit his brother? To apologize perhaps?

Or could Frank have had something to do with the sabotage at the camp?

As Jordan drove to a small convenience store—the only grocery open on Sunday afternoon—she tried to put her suspicions from her mind. Surely Paul's own brother would not do that to him. Surely.

But Jordan recalled the brothers' violent argument of the night before. Frank obviously considered Paul's work at the Fourche Maline site a desecration. Medicine Bluff and the burial grounds had once been sacred to the Indians—and still were to traditionalists like Frank.

When she reported to Paul what the deputy had said, she did not mention seeing his brother's van. She had no proof Frank had anything to do with the vandalism at the camp, and she did not want to be responsible for widening the gulf that already existed between the two brothers.

Perhaps the camp had been invaded by a gang of malicious pranksters. Yes. That could have happened. Why had no one thought of that? It was possible that those responsible for the destruction were intent on making michief and nothing more.

Jordan started to suggest this theory to Paul but

changed her mind. He would think she was simply trying to divert suspicion from the highway construction crew.

Well, she would leave the detective work to the sheriff, Jordan decided as she busied herself helping Cookie prepare a simple meal over a campfire. She hoped he would find that neither Frank Nicolle nor the highway builders had anything to do with the raid.

The sheriff did not come until the next morning. The deputy was wearing a freshly laundered uniform and his shoes were carefully shined. His big wink in Jordan's direction did not go unnoticed by Paul.

The portly old sheriff informed Paul and the rest of the assembled crew that he had already contacted Larry Jarvis at his Tulsa office to ask him if he knew anything about the bulldozing incident. According to the sheriff, Jarvis claimed he had no idea who had "borrowed" his equipment. His crew had all been temporarily dismissed until he got the go-ahead on the bridge construction. He had been in Tulsa since last Thursday. And yes, he could prove it.

"Well, I find it hard to believe Jarvis and his crew are blameless," Paul said angrily. "They are the only ones who would want the camp destroyed. Jarvis would like nothing better than to see me give up and leave. His firm's losing money every day that bridge is delayed."

That was true, Jordan thought. Larry had said his father's firm was counting heavily on this bridge contract to get them out of financial trouble. Their heavy equipment was sitting idle. And now he had been forced to dismiss their crew. But then there was Frank Nicolle. Paul was wrong. The highway crew were not the only ones who might want the camp destroyed.

Frank had been quite vocal in his disapproval of his brother's work here at this ancient site. And Frank had been in Seneca yesterday for no apparent reason.

And although Yvonne seemed just as outraged as the others at the destruction of their camp, Jordan wondered if the woman professor's clandestine visit with Frank Nicolle in Tahlequah had anything to do with this unnecessary setback to the Fourche Maline project.

Did she dare tell the sheriff and Paul that she had seen Frank's van in Seneca yesterday afternoon? Would she be casting suspicion on an innocent man? After all, she had no proof. And she hated to be responsible for causing trouble between brothers.

"Perhaps it was done by some Saturday-night pranksters," Jordan said.

"We thought of that," the deputy said, edging his way closer to Jordan's side. "We got some ol' boys in town who might pull something like that. A couple of weeks ago some of them got all tanked up on beer and swiped the patrol car. And would you believe, when we finally found it, they'd put the danged thing on the roof of the high school. We had a devil of a time figuring how to get it back down again, didn't we, Sheriff?"

The sheriff threw him a disgruntled look, obviously displeased with his talkative assistant. Dennis and Sam grew somewhat red in the face from stifling the laughter that seemed to be threatening to break through their studiously sober expressions.

It was funny, Jordan admitted to herself. The town's only patrol car sitting on the roof of the high school! She wondered who had to work harder—the practical jokers who put the car up there or the men who had the job of getting it down again. But a look at Paul's stern face cut short her mirth. He was obviously not amused.

The sheriff left after promising to question some of the local youths about the incident. Before following the sheriff to the blue-and-white patrol car, the deputy took time to whisper an off-color remark to Jordan and suggest they go out sometime.

The next morning the archaeological crew awoke to find that the tires on many of their cars had been slashed.

Several precious days of work were lost while the crew rebuilt the camp as best they could with the limited resources available to the project and obtained tires to replace the ones ruined during the Monday-night raid. And they had been forced to start posting nighttime guards in an effort to prevent further destruction.

The discomfort caused by makeshift beds, improvised cooking arrangements, lost sleep from guard duty, and the money they had to pay for new tires only served to increase the antagonism they felt toward whoever was responsible for the trouble at the camp.

Like Paul, most of the crew seemed convinced that Larry Jarvis had something to do with the vandalism. And Jordan's defense of the civil engineer did nothing to help the already strained feelings that existed between her and Paul since that disastrous night in Tahlequah.

Edgar, Dennis, Sam, and the others seemed to consider that Jordan was suffering from misplaced loyalties but did not hold her insistence that Larry was innocent against her.

Dennis was as flirtatious as ever. And Edgar frequently sought Jordan out to ease his homesickness with talk of his beloved Margarita. Paul's disapproving eyes seemed always to be watching her, but Jordan refused to dignify the accusation they portrayed with denial. She realized her defense of Larry had destroyed whatever credibility she had left with the obstinate professor. Paul had apparently decided what sort of woman she was, and Jordan doubted if there was any way to change his opinion of her. Perhaps she would try if she thought it would make any difference. But his relationship with Yvonne seemed as strong as ever.

While the crew was swimming one afternoon, Dennis caught Jordan in his strong arms and buried his face against her wet neck. In spite of her squealing protests, his mouth had soon covered hers, and he quite took her breath away with a kiss that was more passionate than playful.

At last she managed to wiggle free of his slippery arms, and with a well-placed splash directed toward his laughing face, Jordan scurried up the bank, not daring to look in Paul's direction. She was sure he chose to believe she had invited Dennis's advances.

At times she wondered why she did not give in to Dennis and seek comfort in his youthful ardor. At least Dennis liked her. "I know it's not love that I feel toward you," he would tell her frankly, "but what's the matter with a little friendly lust?"

But in spite of Paul's cool disdain, Jordan ached with desire for the handsome professor. She knew, however, that after a few more weeks, she would never see him again. Would time heal the ache, she wondered, or would she always feel pain when she thought of the half-Cherokee archaeologist and that summer on the Fourche Maline?

The tension between Paul and Jordan did not go unnoticed by Yvonne. And the woman professor seemed to take every opportunity to imply that Jordan's behavior was less than decorous. Jordan did not bother to refute Yvonne's constant innuendoes, telling herself that her fellow students paid no attention to them and that it no longer mattered what Paul thought of her.

As the week following the raids on the camp drew to a close, Jordan wondered what to do about the date she had promised Larry for Saturday night.

When the county sheriff had reported on Larry's supposed whereabouts during the vandalism, Jordan had not been surprised. Larry had stopped by the camp during the previous week to tell her he would be in Tulsa for seven or eight days attending to business at his firm's home office. He had invited her to go out with him when he returned.

Jordan had agreed to the date, but now, with the tension created by the bulldozing and tire-slashing incidents, she wondered if going out with Larry would be such a good idea. It could only serve to increase Paul's animosity toward her. And while the rest of the crew seemed to respect her right to defend their number-one suspect, how would they feel about her if she went out with him? It might worsen the tension that already was plaguing the camp.

But Jordan had no way to contact Larry. She knew it would be best if he did not show his face at the riverside camp even if she did decide to keep their date. She could well imagine the reception he would get from Paul and the others.

At lunch on Saturday Jordan declined an invitation from Dennis to go to a movie with him that night but asked if he would please give her a ride into town. Jordan hoped she could intercept Larry before he left to come pick her up and perhaps avoid the unpleasant situation that might arise should he come driving into camp unaware of the hostility that awaited him.

Dennis eyed her warily as he pondered her request. "Got a date with bulldozer boy?" he asked sarcastically as he helped himself to the unfinished portion of Jordan's peanut butter sandwich.

"Oh, Dennis, you're as bad as Professor Nicolle," she said in exasperation. "You heard the sheriff say Larry was in Tulsa when all the damage occurred."

"Maybe he was. Maybe he wasn't," Dennis said

with a shrug. "But that doesn't mean he couldn't have arranged the whole thing. Who else would give a damn whether or not this excavation ended now or continued for the next fifty years?"

"There are Indian groups who don't believe in excavating burial grounds and other sacred sites," Jordan told him.

"Are you suggesting that some *Indians* drove those bulldozers across the river and damaged a project of their own Paul Nicolle, Indian person *extraordinaire?*" Dennis asked in disbelief. "I don't think you realize how respected Nicolle is, Jordan. His whole family has been very influential in Oklahoma since prestatehood days and carries a lot of clout with the tribes—and everyone else in the state for that matter. Nicolle's related to Sequoyah and several famous chiefs, and to Jean Pierre Nicolle, the French trapper and explorer who was one of the first white settlers in this area. And Nicolle's got relatives who are present-day chiefs and senators and oil millionaires and bankers. No, I don't think the Indians would do that to him."

Obviously Dennis did not know that Paul's own brother was one of the Indians about whom she had been speaking, and Jordan did not feel it was appropriate for her to mention it. She was certain Paul would not appreciate her discussing his family's problems with his students.

"Look, Dennis," she said instead, "I know you don't approve of my going out with Larry Jarvis. I'm not sure it's such a good idea myself, especially if Professor Nicolle found out about it. But I have no way to contact Larry and tell him not to show up out here this evening. I'm not accustomed to standing up my dates either. So I think it's best that I keep the date—and try to catch him in town before he leaves to come out here.

I'm sure he has no idea that he's Paul's prime suspect and would not find the welcome mat out."

"He's my prime suspect too," Dennis grumbled. "I can't believe you'd rather go out with someone like that when you could spend the evening with someone as handsome and charming and sexy as me."

Dennis gave an exaggerated pout with his lower lip and did a bad job of looking crestfallen.

Jordan smiled in spite of herself. Dennis was adorable at times. "Granted that you are all of those things," she told him as she grabbed her candy bar away from his encroaching fingers. "But you happen to be wrong about Larry. I honestly don't think he had anything to do with our troubles out here. He's a nice, gentle guy—not the troublemaking sort. So, will you please give me a ride into town? I'd ask to borrow the van, but I'd have to explain why I wanted it."

"Only if you give me that candy bar and promise to drive over to Wister with me tomorrow afternoon."

"What's at Wister," she said as she handed him the candy.

"A lake—and a motel," he said wickedly as he unwrapped the melting bar.

Jordan made a futile grab to get it back, but he was too quick for her and popped the entire bar in his mouth, then ducked under the rolled-up side of the rebuilt meal tent.

Later that afternoon, as she and Dennis walked toward the row of parked vehicles, Paul stopped them and asked Dennis to mail some letters for him if he was going into Seneca. He asked them nothing about their plans for the evening, but Jordan knew from the way he pointedly stared at her freshly washed hair and brightly striped sundress that he realized she was dressed for a date and would assume she was going out with Dennis.

There would be no point in correcting his assumption, she thought. Better that Paul think she was dating Dennis than the man he had decided was his arch enemy.

Larry was still at the motel when Jordan arrived. She tapped on his door and let him know she was there, then waited for him in a lawn chair beside the small, ill-kept swimming pool.

After a leisurely drive to the nearby town of Wilburton, Larry took her to dinner in a small, locally owned restaurant that featured hearty, home-style meals. The fried okra was almost as good as Cookie's, and the apple pie would have rivaled her Aunt Sarah's.

During the drive to Wilburton and over their meal, Jordan told Larry all that had happened at the dig site during the past week.

"I'm afraid they all think you had something to do with what's happened out there," Jordan told him.

"Didn't the sheriff tell them I was in Tulsa?" Larry asked.

"Yes, but I'm afraid they still think you masterminded the whole thing to discourage further work at the site."

"And what do you think?" Larry asked, a hurt look in his hazel eyes.

Jordan reached across the small table and placed her hand on his. "I think they're wrong. You hardly seem the type of person who would run bulldozers over other people's property and slash the tires of their cars."

"Yes, but you don't really know me well enough to make that sort of judgment, do you?" he asked, staring down at her comforting hand. "After all, my family's company desperately needs that bridge contract. The delay has already caused serious problems. And now you tell me there may be even further delays if Nicolle gets the area declared an official historical site. The whole project would have to be resurveyed and reengineered. It might even be necessary for new land to be acquired. I would certainly have to find some other answer to the problems of Jarvis Engineering, Incorporated."

"But you didn't know Paul was trying to get the site designated a historical site," Jordan said. "As far as you were concerned, the archaeological project would end in just a few more weeks."

"Ah, but you don't know for sure that I didn't know about Nicolle's efforts. Such things are public record."

"You sound like you want me to believe you're guilty. Are you confessing?" Jordan asked.

"No, I'm not confessing, and I'm not guilty. I'm just trying to figure out why you're so willing to give me a vote of confidence when your colleagues out by the river are not."

Jordan withdrew her hand and took a sip of her coffee. She looked at his open, honest face. A lock of sandy hair had fallen across his forehead, and she resisted an urge to smooth it back into place.

"I don't think you always have to know someone well or for a long time to know what they're like," she said slowly. "Sometimes a feeling of rapport or trust develops almost immediately between two people—before they really know much about each other."

Larry nodded in agreement. "And you do trust me?"

"Of course. I wouldn't be here with you if I didn't."

"Good," he said with relief. "And now I hope you might want to get to know me better. I do enjoy being with you, Jordan."

"And I with you. But I'm going back to Lincoln in just a few more weeks. I'm afraid there won't be much time see you before then," she said cautiously, sensing the seriousness of his request.

"Maybe I could come see you sometime next fall," he said hopefully.

"Perhaps," Jordan said tentatively. "Tell me, Larry, am I the first woman you've gone out with since your divorce?"

He nodded mutely.

"And you're very lonesome?"

"Yes, but that's not the only reason I want to see more of you," he said earnestly. "You're a lovely woman, Jordan. And I'm ready to put the pain and unhappiness behind me. I'll admit I'm still carrying the torch for my former wife, but she's not the woman for me. I found that out the hard way, and now I need to get on with my life."

Jordan could not help but like the sincere young man. The pain he had endured was written all too plainly across his face. He wanted her to be the woman to make him forget the pain of divorce—the pain of losing the woman he loved.

She realized they were two people who were both deeply affected by someone who could not be a part of their lives—Larry, by his former wife; herself, by Paul.

Strange how her own divorce had not been nearly so traumatic for her as the arrival of Professor Paul Nicolle in her life. Her marriage had just seemed to die a natural death. One day, she realized it existed no longer. She had been far more accepting of that than she was of her feelings for Paul. She felt so foolish allowing a man who seemed at times to actually dislike her to be so disruptive of her emotions. Paul didn't want a relationship with her. He just wanted to cure the bothersome cravings he had for her body.

But then, wasn't that precisely the nature of her own problem? Wasn't that why thoughts of Paul intruded into almost every aspect of her life? Sometimes her desire for him was so intense it left her feeling disoriented and physically weak. She could close her eyes and remember the touch of his hand, the feel of his lips, the way it was to have his hard, aroused body pressing against hers. And she would discover her own lips were parted as though waiting for his tongue. Her body, too, would feel open and waiting.

And it was not just in the dark of the night that such thoughts overtook her. They came with greater and greater frequency at any time throughout her days. She would have to pause for an instant and regain control of herself, to close her eyes and wait for the dizziness to pass before going about the business of eating or working or playing.

She wondered if Paul ever had similar feelings. Or was the desire he felt for her just an occasional thing? A passing fancy? After all, he had Yvonne to satisfy his masculine hungers.

Her feelings toward Paul, she decided, were like a sickness that had nothing to do with the pattern of her life. It was just something she had to get over the best she could.

But Jordan realized that getting over Paul Nicolle was not going to be easy—and not just because of their mutual lust for one another. There had been moments when the stern, half-Cherokee archaeologist had allowed her glimpses of the sensitive, caring side of his enigmatic personality. He who could be so harsh and demanding could also stare at a soaring hawk with a look akin to rapture on his achingly beautiful face, or show an almost boyish delight at the sight of a rabbit bounding across an open field, or good-naturedly share kitchen duty with his mother.

There had been times—especially during their weekend in Tahlequah—when she had thought they could at least be friends, times when they discussed shared interests and took pleasure in one another's company.

But the chasm that had opened between them after the disastrous ending to the night they spent together would seem to indicate friendship was not possible. And the chasm had widened when she chose to defend the man now sitting across the restaurant table from her and insist he was not responsible for the destruction at the dig. Yet, she had decided not to share the special knowledge she had of the events leading up to the raid on the camp and possibly clear Larry because in doing so she would implicate Paul's own brother and the woman he planned to marry. What a tangled web life had woven around her!

Was Larry Jarvis the key to unraveling the web and putting her life in order again? Perhaps a sane, comfortable relationship with Larry would provide a way for her to deal with the myriad of emotions surrounding her feelings for Paul. Perhaps Larry could help her forget Paul.

But what if she thought of Paul every time Larry made love to her? Could she live with the dishonesty of closing her eyes and pretending the loving came from another?

And did she want to live with a man who might be thinking of the woman who broke his heart whenever he took her in his arms?

Jordan wondered if two emotional cripples such as they could bring any semblance of happiness to each other's lives. And what was the alternative? A lifetime of loneliness? A lifetime without children?

Chapter Nine

Larry stopped his car just short of the row of parked vehicles and turned off his lights. The camp was in darkness, and judging from the row of cars, everyone else but Jordan was already in.

She did not protest when Larry put his arms around her and with much tenderness kissed her good night. Guiltily, she found herself thinking of other kisses and wished with all her heart she could respond to Larry the way she responded to Paul. What was the matter with her anyway? Paul obviously did not let the attraction he felt for her interfere with his relationship with Yvonne.

What she needed was distance. When she returned to Lincoln, when she put hundreds of miles between herself and Professor Paul Nicolle, she would be able to enjoy the company of other men. Of course, she would, Jordan assured herself. Time would take care of things.

Jordan promised to meet Larry the following Saturday night but was noncommittal on his repeated suggestion that he come to visit her in Lincoln next fall.

As Jordan made her way across the rutted, moonlit parking area, she was startled by a sudden light shining in her eyes.

"Oh, Jordan. It is you," Edgar's accented voice said from behind a flashlight beam.

"Hi, Edgar," Jordan said as the light went black. "It's your turn to stand guard, I take it."

"Yes, and I was worried about you," he said with concern in his voice. "Dennis had told us you were with the highway engineer, and I was concerned for you to be gone from us so late into the night. Why do you go out with someone like this man?"

"Oh, Edgar, I'm as safe with Larry Jarvis as I am with you. He's a nice man, really—and he didn't bulldoze the camp. I can promise you that."

So everyone knew she had been out with Larry, she thought as she took Edgar's arm and allowed him to escort her across the compound to her tent. *Thanks a lot, Dennis*, she thought ruefully. She could well imagine the frosty reception she would get from Paul in the morning.

Yvonne continued her constant barage of belittling remarks about the Fourche Maline project and archaeology in the United States in general. Her evening lectures usually had little to do with the artifacts unearthed from the five riverside mounds but were about various South American excavations, especially those in Peru. She was extremely knowledgeable, but Jordan often longed to turn the discussions back to *their* project. She wanted to gain more understanding of the Fourche Maline People, not the Incas.

But it seemed that every artifact brought to Yvonne's attention received not only an evaluation but a disparaging comparison with similar artifacts that had been unearthed in Peru. The pottery, the tools, the weapons, the carvings, the dwellings of the Fourche Maline People were all unworthy in Yvonne's estimation.

One night, after a grueling, unbearably hot day in the trenches, the crew assembled with their two professors in the main tent to discuss the day's results.

At the end of the discussion Yvonne commented, "I hope someday you have the opportunity to use the techniques and knowledge you have gained here on this project on an *important* excavation."

"Meaning this one is unimportant," Jordan heard her voice challenging, realizing how very tired she was of Yvonne's archaeological snobbery.

"Well, it's not—not when you compare it with some of the exciting work that is going on elsewhere in the world," Yvonne said with raised eyebrows, obviously irritated at Jordan's remark.

"I don't understand," Jordan said even though an inner voice warned her to be still, "what right you have to sit in judgment of which parts of humanity's prehistory are significant and which are not. I don't understand how you can imply that the people who lived and loved and died here on the banks of this river are less important than the Incas in South America?"

"Oh, Jordan," Yvonne said in a condescending tone, "don't be so naive. Just compare the contribution of these primitive people to the incredible remains of the Inca empire."

"What we've unearthed here is perhaps to your way of thinking less meaningful than Inca ruins," Jordan continued, "but the people who lived here went through the same stages of civilization that the Incas went through prior to the time they built their great cities. Perhaps there are insights to be discovered at sites such as this one that will help archaeologists learn why some people developed great civilizations and others didn't. Why didn't the Fourche Maline People start building cities of masonry instead of continuing to live in earthen lodges? What about their way of life made them less enduring than other cultures? And what of their successes? We've found their unique pottery, their distinctive bone tools, evidence of closely knit tribal life. And that small skeleton I'm uncovering now—a child's remains. He was buried with great care. He was loved. Was his mother's grief less because she didn't live in an Incan city?''

Her words were greeted by a stunned silence. Her fellow students regarded her in open-mouthed wonder. Yvonne's look was one of complete rage. Before the Peruvian archaeologist had a chance to respond, Jordan turned to leave, only to find herself looking into Paul's unreadable eyes. But surely the look on his face was one of displeasure. How impudent she must have sounded, challenging so learned a professor as Yvonne DeSilvestro.

Jordan rushed to her tent, her heart pounding. It did not matter what he thought of her, she kept telling herself. It didn't matter! In a few short weeks she would be leaving. Paul would be gone from her life. He would go to Peru and become famous discovering lost Inca treasure with his beautiful archaeologist wife at his side. Jordan could read about them in *Time* magazine. She could watch them on television talk shows.

But later that night, lying alone in the darkness of her tent, Jordan faced what she had been denying ever since Paul kissed her by the river, perhaps even from that very first day when he came marching across the open field in answer to Cookie's honked summons.

It was not just physical attraction she felt for Paul Nicolle. She was in love with him.

She buried her face in her pillow to muffle the sobs that seemed to wrench themselves from deep in her heart. As knowledge dawned, as she acknowledged to herself the love she felt for this man, the pain her subconscious self had kept so carefully hidden in the nether regions of her mind made its presence known. She felt as though she would die of the pain.

Why, she asked herself over and over. Why him?

Why have I fallen in love with a man I can't have, a man who will never return my love? Why has life been so cruel? Why did she ever come to Oklahoma?

Gradually, however, exhaustion quieted her sobbing, and an acceptance of sorts began to settle over her. It had happened. There was no changing it. What she needed to do was concentrate on getting through the next weeks until the dig ended and she could go home. She must find strength to make it through those days and nights. But, oh, how difficult that was going to be. His physical presence aroused her so. She hungered so for his companionship and his knowledge. And she desperately longed for his respect.

But Jordan knew with a cold certainty that she was to be denied his friendship and respect, and her pride would not allow her to give herself to him in another meaningless sexual encounter no matter how desperately she longed for him, no matter how she loved him.

There was no sleep for Jordan that night. Life had covered her with a blanket of sadness. She felt altered. Long, lonely years seemed to stretch in front of her like a barren, empty road. Before she had expectations. Now she had none.

She could still marry, she tried to tell herself. There would still be men to love her. But could she ever love them?

She went out with Larry again. This time she asked to use the van. It really did not seem to matter if Paul knew where she was going.

It was good to get away from the camp for a time, and Larry's presence was soothing. He was gentle and kind and made no demands on her. What a sad couple they made, Jordan could not help but think. Both of them were in love with someone else and were wishing they could love the one they were with. Jordan told Larry so without mentioning Paul.

"But life must go on, Jordan, even after divorce," he said, obviously thinking that Jordan, like himself, was still suffering from the breakup of a marriage. "I don't want to be alone for the rest of my life just because it didn't work out the first time around. Maybe I'll never completely get over losing Diane, but I want to find someone else to love."

If only it were that simple, Jordan thought. She did not think it would be that simple for her—or for Larry.

Although Jordan had spent some time working in all the various trenches that crisscrossed the five mounds at right angles, the majority of her time was spent excavating the small mound near the river where she and Edgar had discovered the project's first human remains.

A total of twenty-three skeletons had been unearthed at several different levels, representing a time span of over three thousand years. Paul was certain that many more skeletons would be found and that dating techniques would eventually prove the earliest levels of the site went back six or seven thousand years, which would be the earliest evidence of human habitation yet found in the state.

But if the highway construction continued on schedule, many of the puzzles of the Fourche Maline would never be unraveled. Jordan, like the rest of the crew, found herself driven with an almost frenzied desire to get as much accomplished as possible in the short time remaining to them. Soon the summer project would be over. Paul would probably go to Peru with Yvonne. And unless this place was declared a state historical site, it would soon be covered by a highway.

Jordan was amazed at how much stamina she had

acquired over the summer. She would never be as strong as a man, but she worked just as long and just as diligently as any of the male members of the crew and the female professor.

After her challenge of Yvonne's elitist attitude about South American archaeology, Jordan had avoided both professors as much as possible given the communal atmosphere of their encampment. How irritated they both must be with her—to have spoken so disrespectfully to so accomplished an archaeologist and scholar as Yvonne DeSilvestro. But at least Yvonne's evening lectures were now free from the glories of the Incas.

Jordan was surprised when, after a week of nothing more than a perfunctory greeting from Paul, he announced that he would be working with Jordan and Edgar throughout the following week. Jordan thought Paul would have chosen to have as little to do with her as possible, but she realized the burial site—which had come to be unofficially regarded as her and Edgar's project—intrigued Paul more than any of the other facets of the excavation. Often the finest artifacts were found at burial sites. It was not unusual for the dead to have been buried with possessions that had been meaningful to them during their lifetimes, thus revealing much about their culture, religion, and status within their community.

But an entire week so near to Paul! The thought filled Jordan with panic. Now that she had acknowledged herself her true feelings for Paul, she felt as though an announcement of them was tattooed across her forehead and flashed on and of like a neon light every time she looked at him.

But he must never know how she felt. At times she found herself actually relieved that he had never found out that her desire for him was motivated by other than the blatant lust of a woman who liked having lots of men want her and encouraged their advances. Better that he feel disrespect or disgust for her than pity! Or amusement! Another coed with a crush on her professor. It probably happened to him all the time.

And he will never know, she vowed. If there was one thing she had learned this summer, it was that she was a strong person, that she had both inner resources and physical strength. And she did have her pride. She might leave this place at summer's end with shattered emotions, but she vowed that her pride would still be intact.

Edgar seemed to sense Jordan's disquiet as they followed Paul across the tent compound on their way to the smallest mound. Jordan had confided many things about herself to her loyal Peruvian friend. He knew about her father who suffered from wanderlust. He knew of her early marriage and subsequent divorce. He knew of her financial struggle to obtain an education and rebuild her life. But she had never been able to bring herself to tell the understanding young man about her ill-fated involvement with their head professor. There had been times when she had realized Edgar was staring at her with a puzzled, concerned expression on his face. At such times she had wanted to bury her face against his chest and sob out the whole miserable mess. But she didn't. Even though she knew Edgar would never be judgmental, Jordan was ashamed to find herself so overwhelmingly attracted to a man who was openly committed to another woman. She should have better control of her emotions. She should have been able to prevent this disastrous turn in her life, she admonished herself.

As the morning progressed, however, Jordan wondered if Edgar was perhaps aware of her plight. It seemed as though he was trying to function as a buffer—both physically and conversationally—between her and Paul. He usually managed to occupy a place in between them as work progressed on excavating the skeletons and artifacts. And he was more chatty than usual, keeping up a steady stream of observations about their work and posing countless questions for Paul to answer. Jordan was spared from having to converse with Paul or work next to him. At one point she touched Edgar's arm and offered him a look of mute appreciation. He patted her hand affectionately, his eyes sympathetic. But even as this moment of unspoken understanding passed between the two friends, Jordan knew it was being misinterpreted by Paul. Nonetheless, she was grateful for Edgar's presence.

But even with Edgar's surreptitious support, Jordan found it tortuous to work in such close physical proximity to Paul. She was fearful that, like Edgar, he would be able to sense the tumultuous emotions that welled up inside of her whenever he was near, and he would know she was thinking of the night in Tahlequah they had made love in the canopied bed in the guest room of his childhood home.

In spite of earlier resolve, Jordan wondered if she would resist Paul if he tried to make love with her again. Or would she go where her passions took her, even though she knew Paul's heart belonged to another and he considered her a mere dalliance?

Jordan concentrated as best she could on the work at hand, painstakingly using paintbrushes, spoons, dental tools, and even old toothbrushes to free the bones and artifacts from the packed earth without altering their present state of preservation.

Often during the course of the week, the shadow of the ever watchful Yvonne fell across the trench. Paul would usually pause in his labors and show her their most recent find. On one occasion, after a particularly productive afternoon, he told her how much he hoped the excavation here on the banks of the Fourche Maline would be allowed to continue the following summer, and even for many more summers if necessary.

"That would be nice," Yvonne said. "The university students do need exposure to fieldwork. But I certainly hope *you* are not considering spending any more time here. Leave this sort of excavation to the amateurs like Jordan," she said with a disdainful wave of her hand in Jordan's direction. "Men of your caliber should be working at more meaningful projects than this one— and making archaeological history."

Gradually, Jordan had grown more accustomed to the working arrangements and found herself less disturbed by Paul's presence. To pass away the hours, Edgar had encouraged the three of them to share and compare their vastly different backgrounds. He would talk of his experiences as the youngest son of a rigidly religious, wealthy Peruvian family.

"I was supposed to be a priest," he told them. "That is a common vocation for youngest sons of upper-class families. But I decided I was just not cut out for the clerical life," he said, tossing a knowing smile in Jordan's direction.

She smiled back, knowing he was thinking of Margarita and his plans to marry and have a family.

Edgar's reminiscences encouraged Paul to talk of his own childhood. Jordan found herself treasuring these conversations and the insights they provided about these two vastly different men.

She learned that Paul grew to manhood with one foot in the white man's world and one in the Indian's. His childhood was a mixture of wilderness treks with his grandfather and years spent at a prestigious boarding school. His father, who had been dead for several years, had been a high-ranking official in the national park system—a job that required him to be away from home a great deal of the time.

And Paul seemed genuinely interested in hearing about Jordan's parents and her vagabond childhood.

"What about your mother?" he asked. "What did she think about never having a permanent home?"

"I guess she loves my father," Jordan answered simply. "And he loves her in his way. She married a man with wanderlust. In spite of her complaints about her life, I think my mother must realize that if she insisted he change, he would no longer be the man she loves. And when we were all together as a family, we had a wonderful time. We almost never drove down highways—only back roads where we'd explore old cemeteries and deserted farmhouses. We'd fish in creeks and shop in country stores. Of course, I'll admit my mother has missed having a home of her own and a full-time husband. But I also think she and I should have gone with Daddy at least some of the time when he went abroad. There's no rule that says children have to be raised in one country."

"But children should have the security of a permanent home and two parents in residence," Paul protested as he absently fingered the turquoise nugget that rested against his bare chest. "I've always thought of it as a child's right."

And then as though he were thinking aloud, Paul said softly, "My life will always be so unsettled. Even if I remained at the university, I would be away from home for such long periods of time."

As the week drew to a close, Jordan found herself filled with a sense of sadness. Thanks to Edgar, the week had not been so difficult after all. The week had been one of shared camaraderie between a professor and two of his students. For those few days, in the presence of Edgar and joined by their work, Jordan had experienced a sense of friendship with this man who had left such an indelible mark on her heart. She felt that, for a time, they had succeeded in putting aside their past differences.

But the week ended, as all things must, and after a particularly grueling and hot afternoon, Jordan found herself alone with Paul to finish up and put away the tools. Edgar had been summoned to another trench to help extract a large rock.

Jordan did not realize how exhausted she was until the dinner bell rang and she attempted to climb out of the five-foot-deep trench. Her foot slipped from the root she was using as a toe hold, and she fell back against Paul.

And suddenly his arms were around her. Their moist, warm bodies clung to one another.

Jordan was too drained—emotionally and physically—to cope with what was happening. Her resolve to avoid any further physical contact with Paul vanished as though it had never been. She laid her cheek against the bare skin of his chest, oblivious to the sand and dirt that clung to him, oblivious to everything except the physical closeness of the man she loved.

She longed to raise her face to be kissed. He would respond—she could tell that he would. She could feel his heart pounding in his muscular chest. His breathing was quickening. It was with full-blown desire that he pressed his body against hers.

With eyes closed, Jordan tried to imprint the feel of him on her mind. She never wanted to forget how it was to live this moment—how it felt to have his strong arms engulfing her, how his damp skin felt next to hers, how his breath felt on her neck as he buried his face in her hair. But most of all she wanted to remember how her name sounded as it escaped from his mouth. He said her name with such incredible longing.

"Jordan," he whispered into her hair, his voice low, almost as though he were in pain. "Jordan," he repeated, this time fiercely, as though his jaw were clenched.

Just one kiss. Should she deny herself one last kiss? The thought of his mouth on hers made her tremble with anticipation.

Her fingers caressed his back, relishing the freedom of being able to stroke them up and down his bare flesh and being able to feel the firm, taut strength of him. He was like an animal ready to spring, his muscles tightly coiled and ready to explode into action.

His hair. She wanted to touch his hair. Her fingers left his back and wove their way into his long heavy hair. It felt wonderful. It was strong, like the rest of him.

Her face was buried against his neck. All she would have to do was lift her face to him. He would kiss her. It would be like those other times. But still she clung to him, his face in her hair, as she prolonged this moment of closeness.

Then his hand was under her chin, forcing her to look in those demanding, dark eyes. Once again he said her name. Jordan locked her hands around his neck and drew his face closer. Her lips parted in expectation. His mouth. His lips. His tongue. Oh, please, she thought. Now.

But his body stiffened. He was pulling away from her. Why? Wasn't he going to kiss her?

Then she realized that loose dirt falling near their shoulders was distracting him. A pebble fell with a thud to the earthen floor of the trench. His face turned upward.

Jordan followed his gaze with her own. Yvonne was

watching them from above, her hands on her hips, her mouth set in an angry line.

"Well, Jordan, do you let any man who wants to, touch you? How many men do you plan to have this summer?"

The air was still and heavy. And Jordan's thoughts were in turmoil. She tossed and turned on her narrow cot, Yvonne's insults replaying themselves over and over in her mind.

And Yvonne had a right to use every ugly word. Jordan had no right to encourage Paul's attention. She wasn't a child. She knew she was playing with fire. She knew how men reacted when they were tempted as she had tempted Paul. And he had never indicated to her that he wished to end his relationship with Yvonne and begin one with her. No such words had ever passed between them.

Paul was going to marry another woman. No matter how Jordan might try to justify her behavior in the throes of desire, there had been no justification in Yvonne's accusing eyes. How quickly desire had been replaced by shame as Jordan looked into those angry Latin eyes.

As Yvonne stood there, spitting out her words of condemnation, full of righteous rage, Jordan realized as she never had before that she had more than met her match in the alluring Peruvian professor.

Yvonne emitted an aura of wild, exotic beauty. Her full, tan breasts rose and fell as she raged, provocatively bulging above the brief bathing suit top she wore, along with a pair of shorts that effectively revealed long, shapely legs. Her eyes were open wide—dark, smoldering embers ready to burst into flame. The nostrils of her patrician nose were flared. Full, sensual lips spread in a sneer over flawless white teeth that con-

trasted beautifully with her smoothly tanned skin. A
wildcat of a woman! Yet, a woman who—under the
skin of a temptress—was more learned, more sophisticated, and more self-assured than Jordan could ever
hope to be.

Yvonne's hands with their long, elegant fingers rested on slim hips. And on one finger blazed a diamond-
and-turquoise ring.

Jordan had gone through the motions of dinner, but
in reality, she only pushed her food about her plate.
She heard little of the evening lecture. Her mind could
not focus on scholarly pursuits. All she could think
about was what a mess her life was in and relive repeat-
edly that horrible scene with Yvonne.

When finally she had escaped to her tent and cot, she
found she could not sleep. The heat of the afternoon
still lingered under the roof of her canvas dwelling. Her
skin was clammy, her hair damp. It felt as though there
was not enough air to breathe.

She knew sleep would be a long time in coming. And
when it finally did, fitful dreams of Paul would disturb
her rest. Her dreams did not recognize another woman's claim or even the wishes of the man himself. They
recognized only her body's aching need. Distorted im-
ages of herself and Paul projected themselves on the
screen of her dreaming mind. But no matter how ex-
plicitly her dreams dealt with her physical desire for the
man, they brought no relief to her torment.

And for Paul too, there was no rest that night. The
air was heavy and hot. He found the small confines of
his tent oppressing. When he closed his eyes, *she* was
there, her lips parted and waiting for his kiss.

How he had wanted to kiss Jordan there in the
trench. The nearness of her had been driving him crazy
all week. It was more than he could bear to have at last
been able to feel her skin, to bury his face in her hair,

to press his body against hers. He would have kissed
her and more if Yvonne had not come to walk with him
to dinner.

What a mess! Yvonne was furious with him. The
whole scene was embarrassing for both her and Jordan.
Congratulations, old man, he thought wryly. *You've
really screwed things up royally.*

He tossed for an indeterminate period of time on his
cot before finally giving up and heading for the cooling
waters of the river.

The water felt good on his overheated skin. He paddled around a bit in the dark flowing waters, then
pulled himself up on the flat rock that guarded the
bank—the rock where Jordan had been sunbathing the
day he took her to Tahlequah. He had stood there and
watched her like some smitten adolescent for the long-
est time.

The air on his wet skin felt almost cold. Nice. If only
there was some simple way like that to cool his ardor,
Paul thought ruefully. He was tired of it—tired of
thinking about the little blond minx. He wondered if
Dennis and Edgar had trouble sleeping at night because
of her. And the highway engineer. Was Larry Jarvis
tossing and turning in his bed thinking about Jordan
Marshall?

It was ridiculous for him to be this way. He was too
old to be allowing his heart to rule his head. If there was
one thing he learned from his experience with Claudia,
it was never to let that happen again. But he was out of
control. Thoughts of Jordan haunted him day and
night. He longed to make love to her again even if he
was just another notch on her belt. Never had lovemaking been so complete an experience as it had been with
her. Never. Which didn't make any sense at all. Why
had it seemed so achingly beautiful at the time?

He could almost believe Jordan were a witch and had

cast some sort of spell over him. He desperately wanted to break that spell. But even more desperately he wanted to hold her in his arms again even if it was just for one more night.

Larry Jarvis drove down from Tulsa for one last date with Jordan before she returned to Nebraska. He no longer kept a motel room in Seneca, he explained to Jordan. The bridge project had been halted until a decision could be reached on the status of the Fourche Maline archaeological project. In spite of the fact that Larry's company had already begun the bridge approach on the Medicine Bluff side of the river, it was quite possible—if the area was declared a state historical site—that the whole bridge project would have to be resurveyed and moved a hundred or so yards downstream.

"There's nothing more I can do in Seneca," Larry said, "until a decision is reached about whether or not the site is to be protected. In the meantime, I'm trying to keep the creditors off our doorstep up in Tulsa and trying to line up some smaller project to keep us from going under until we find out if we will or won't build that damned bridge."

Jordan sensed his frustration over the situation his business was in. And he was so lonely. During his years away at college most of his friends had either moved from Tulsa or were married and raising families. Larry told her he did not feel he belonged in their world. He was a divorced man with no one with whom to share his friends and his life.

But Larry seemed to believe that remarrying would be some sort of magic cure-all in his life. Marriage was supposed to help him forget about his first wife, Diane, and their young son. And he could start another family. There would be some reason to work hard and succeed.

Although Larry claimed he was happiest when he was with her, he also confessed to Jordan that Diane was constantly in his thoughts.

"Have you ever thought of trying a reconciliation with Diane?" Jordan asked.

"I used to," Larry said. "But not since I met you. When I'm with you, lovely Jordan, I know I can love again."

Once again he asked about visiting her in Nebraska. But Jordan was uncertain if it would be wise to continue to encourage the lonely highway engineer. She did enjoy his company and would love to have him come to see her this fall. But she feared that allowing him to come all that way would imply a commitment to their relationship that she did not feel. Instead, she gave him her address and suggested they write occasionally.

"Let's wait a few months and see if we really want to get involved," Jordan told him frankly. "I think you should be courting Diane, not me."

His good night kiss was more passionate than before. Jordan tried to respond.

Damn you, Paul Nicolle, she thought as she walked away from Larry's car. *Have you ruined me for life? Will I never be able to enjoy another man's kiss? Why did I have to go and fall in love with you?*

Suddenly, Jordan was overwhelmed with sadness. She sank down on a tree stump, too drained to take another step. For she knew that as difficult as this summer had been, it was going to be worse away from Paul. Yes, there was to be a worse agony than being near him and loving him and not being able to have him. At least here she could see him and hear his voice and learn from him. And here, she guiltily acknowledged, there was always the chance of another encounter—another touch, another kiss.

But after she had left the Fourche Maline, his presence would be gone from her life. He would become a bittersweet memory to invade her days and haunt her nights. A lifelong affliction—Paul Nicolle. Of that, she was certain.

Chapter Ten

Once again Yvonne left on a speaking engagement—this time to Dallas—and had taken her three Peruvian students with her. Jordan had overheard Yvonne and Paul quarreling about the trip earlier in the week. Yvonne had insisted Paul should accompany her, and he had refused.

"We've been invited to appear on a local television show," she reminded him.

"I've too much to do here, Yvonne. You go on, but I really must stay."

"Someday, Paul, my love, you will get your priorities straightened out. And when you do, you will have more invitations to appear on television shows than you can handle. Please, darling, just for one night. We would have such a lovely time."

But apparently Yvonne had failed in her attempts to persuade Paul, and she had driven off in the white van without him.

The rest of the crew had elected to work through the weekend in hopes of getting as much done as possible. There was only one more full week remaining for the project, and it was still uncertain as to whether the site would be preserved for future excavation or would be permanently buried under a highway. Several "temporaries," students who came in to work for short periods of time, were in camp for the weekend, and Jordan found herself supervising two young men from Muskogee.

Paul stopped by the small mound for a time and watched as Jordan patiently instructed the two novices on the fundamentals of archaeological excavation technique. They were helping her unearth the remains of another child—this one a real curiosity since it was buried next to the skeleton of a large canine.

After a time Paul crouched down beside Jordan and said with a broad smile, "Well, Jordan, you've come a long way this summer. And I thought you didn't have what it took to become an archaeologist! You've not only done just that, but I find you're a better teacher than I am! You may be small, Jordan Marshall, but you're mighty."

Jordan thought she would swell to bursting from his praise! With those few sincerely spoken words, he had made a summer of blisters and aching muscles and untold sweat all worthwhile.

"And now," he continued, "I think it's time we talk about your future in the field of archaeology. You have the makings of a fine scholar."

Jordan started to explain to him that it would be impossible for her to change her field of study to archaeology. It would involve so many additional years of study and would involve more of a financial burden than she could manage. But he was summoned to one of the other mounds.

"We'll continue this conversation on the way to Wilburton," he told her as he hoisted himself from the trench.

"Did I miss something?" Jordan asked. "I wasn't aware of a trip to Wilburton."

"Oh, didn't I tell you?" he called over his shoulder as he trotted down the side of the mound. "A farmer over there found some artifacts when he dug a storm cellar. I need someone to go along and take notes. We'll leave in an hour or so."

Paul strolled briskly with an easy, almost regal grace over to the largest of the five mounds where several of the crew awaited his opinion or instruction. *Even if I weren't in love with him*, Jordan thought as she stared after him, *I could not help but admire him*. His appearance, his lineage, his profession—all combined to form a unique and unforgettable individual.

She was to have some more stolen moments with him, it seemed. Of course, she could decline to go. But she wouldn't. She would go with him. How her heart gladdened at the prospect!

During the drive Paul told her once again she should be working toward a degree in archaeology and plan on a career in the field.

"I'd like that very much," Jordan said. "But after next year, I will have to get a job. I'm afraid more schooling is out of the question. But I can assure you I will have a lifelong interest in the field. Maybe I can just be one of the archaeological 'groupies' that come out to help the professionals on weekends."

"That would be a waste of a fine mind," Paul said. "Your instincts are good, Jordan. I like the way you combine the scientific approach with humanistic concerns. You measure and analyze and record. But you also think of those individuals who populated the various settlements built on that river through the ages as people—not just specimens or subjects of scientific scrutiny. You ask why they lived there? You want to know what they were like. You wonder where you would have planted your garden if you had lived there."

"I truly appreciate your words," Jordan told him. "I do have such a fascination for archaeology, but to become a professional archaeologist, I would have to earn a doctorate in the field. That would involve years of additional formal study and all the research required to write a dissertation. The circumstances of my life just don't allow for that sort of commitment right now. I don't have any money for one thing. And I don't want to live with my relatives anymore. I want to get my teaching career underway, get a place of my own, and maybe get married and have some children."

"I didn't think you were the marrying kind," Paul said almost harshly.

"What makes you say that?" Jordan asked.

"Well, you seem to like lots of men friends, and most women by the time they are your age have done something about it if they want a husband and children."

"Most, but not all," Jordan said, knowing that if Paul knew she was once married, he would assume it had ended in divorce due to some failure on her part and it would only serve to reinforce his opinion that she was not "the marrying kind."

"And about the 'lots of men friends,'" Jordan continued. "Do you expect women to only find friends among their own sex? Yes, I have friends who happen to be men, and I resent your implication that those relationships are other than just friendship."

Paul's strong hands clenched the steering wheel more tightly, and an audible sigh escaped from his lips.

"Look, Jordan, let's have a nice afternoon and not get into another confrontation. How you live your life is no business of mine. But as your teacher, I was interested in your future educational plans. And whether you marry or not, I would like to see you enter a career that suits your talents. Now, let's talk about something else. Okay?"

"Fine with me," Jordan said sullenly, wishing she had not come along.

The rest of their short journey passed in silence. Jordan wondered why he had bothered to bring her along in the first place. Perhaps it was because he considered her the most expendable member of the crew.

But after they arrived at their destination, Jordan put such thoughts aside as she helped Paul take measurements in the unfinished storm cellar. The farmer showed them as best as he could remember where he had found the five arrowheads and assorted pottery fragments. And he showed them the top of a human skull still embedded in the wall about four feet below ground level.

"I called the sheriff and showed it to him," the elderly farmer explained, "and he called out the doc who acts as county coroner. They decided the skull was real old and suggested I get in touch with you. The sheriff says you're the expert on old bones."

Using a flashlight, Paul went over the earthen wall inch by inch, pausing to dictate notes and measurements for Jordan to record. Then he carefully extracted the skull, which was well preserved and intact.

With the farmer's permission, Paul inspected the surrounding area, walking the adjoining pastures and examining the banks of a small creek.

Paul explained the different geological layers exposed in the creek bank and how such information could be used to date artifacts found in that layer. And he showed her an area of a pasture where the grasses were taller than elsewhere.

"That could indicate the earth was once disturbed in those locations," he explained. "The soil that eventually fills in ditches, root cellars, garbage pits, foundations, and other diggings is often more fertile than the surrounding soil. We suspect this when we see vegetation that appears healthier and taller than surrounding vegetation."

"What will you do about the site?" Jordan asked. "Will it be excavated?"

"That's hard to say at this point. I'll probably arrange for some aerial photographs. They often show things you can't see from the ground, such as if there is any pattern to those areas of denser vegetation. And we have a new technique that's proved most useful. Ground-penetrating radar often gives us a notion of what lies beneath the surface without having to excavate. Then, if our findings warrant it, we might make some preliminary ground probes. But it would have to be pretty promising before we would actually go to the expense of an excavation. Not only are the dollars for archaeological excavations very hard to come by, there are already hundreds of identified archaeological sites in the state. Only the ones that have the potential of making a sizable contribution to the archaeological history of the state will be explored."

"Sites like the Fourche Maline?"

"Yes. That one is a treasure. Not to preserve it for future exploration would be criminal. We've scarcely scratched the surface—literally and figuratively. I know if I just had more time, I could prove it is the oldest site of human habitation in Oklahoma. Everything points to that. But enough archaeology for one afternoon. I have some other places to take you this afternoon. Here it is almost time for you to go back to Nebraska, and you've spent most of your time in a ditch."

"Except for a lovely weekend in Tahlequah," Jordan said without thinking as they trudged across the pasture to Paul's car. But as soon as the words were out of her mouth, she wished she had not spoken them. The weekend had been lovely—until the painful ending to the night they had spent together. Paul's silence indicated to Jordan that he too was recalling that time. He had been angry that she refused to make love to him when they awakened that morning. After all, she had certainly been willing the night before. But that was before she understood why he had made love to her.

Did he still think she was promiscuous, Jordan wondered. Would he believe her if she told him otherwise? But Jordan understood it was more comfortable for him to believe she was a loose woman. It helped him explain away the attraction he felt for her if he believed she was some sort of seductress. After all, his future was reserved for Yvonne. Jordan was just passing through one summer of his life.

Jordan dared to steal a look at the man strolling at her side. Would he soon forget her, or would thoughts of her linger in his mind?

A wave of hurtful emotion swelled up in her breast as she thought of her own future and the bittersweet memories she would always carry of her summer with this magnificent Cherokee.

On the road once again, Paul did not turn the car back toward the Fourche Maline. He seemed determined to play the role of tour guide and show Jordan some of the local points of interest. It eased the tension between them as he discussed the history of the region. Paul even seemed to be enjoying himself and was quite mysterious about the nature of their next stop.

"What are we going to see here?" Jordan asked as Paul parked his car near an odd-looking building constructed into a rocky hillside outside the small town of Heavener.

"A memento left here by some visiting Vikings," he said.

"Vikings? In Oklahoma?"

"Apparently so," Paul said, grinning at her startled reaction. "This building was placed here to protect a Viking runestone."

Jordan was intrigued as they entered the building and viewed the large boulder it was built over. The boulder was deeply carved with Scandinavian runes. A nearby sign informed them that the characters—or runes—were the same as those used by Vikings, and the runes on the inscription translated to the date 1012 A.D.

"This is best known of many runestones in the area," Paul explained. "Some scholars believe the Vikings actually traveled this far inland. And no one's ever been able to disprove the authenticity of the stones."

"Has any evidence other than runestones been found that the Vikings actually visited this area?" Jordan asked.

"No, but I believe someday there will be. In fact, at one time, *I* was going to be the one to find other Viking artifacts. I first came to see the runestone when I was a kid. I think the first thoughts I ever had about becoming an archaeologist went through my head while I was standing in this very spot staring at that stone."

"I wonder if the Vikings met any of our people," Jordan pondered.

"Our people?"

"Yes. The Fourche Maline People. Maybe the Vikings and some of those souls who lived by our river met. Just think what the Fourche People must have thought when they saw big blond men with hair all over them and wearing helmets with horns growing out the sides!"

"You certainly have a knack for bringing archaeology to life," Paul said, laughing. "I rather imagine 'our people' would have been pretty shocked at such a sight—and scared."

"But maybe they became friends," Jordan continued, enjoying her fantasy. "Maybe the Vikings stayed for a time on the banks of the Fourche Maline and swam in our swimming hole and ate quail cooked over the campfires and watched the ceremonial dances. Maybe there's a little Viking blood in some of you Oklahoma Indians.''

"Oh, you think they got *that* friendly?" he said with a knowing grin.

They continued their silly banter during a drive around Wister Lake. Before long, they had names for their mythical band of Vikings and for the community of Fourche Maline People the European visitors lived among. The Vikings, they decided, never returned to their homes, but remained on the banks of the Fourche Maline, composing Wagnerian opera and racing miniature ships up and down the river.

They stopped for coffee in the tiny town of Talahina, which was named for the legendary Cherokee woman whose grave they had visited at the Fort Gibson National Cemetery, and their conversation turned from Vikings to the Sam Houston–Talahina romance.

"In his later life," Paul told her, "Houston used to talk about his time among the Cherokee as being the most idyllic of his entire life. It was said that he never forgot the beautiful Cherokee woman who refused to leave her people and follow him to Texas."

"I wonder if she regretted her decision," Jordan mused. "If she loved him, maybe she should have gone with him and at least tried to continue their life together."

"She probably just wanted a home for her child," Paul said. "Houston roamed around as much as an archaeologist. He was a proven wanderer."

Their last stop was at the old Choctaw Council House near Tuskahoma. Built in 1883, the building was the last of several capitol buildings used by the Choctaw Nation after their removal to Indian Territory in the 1830s. Nearby was the log home of Jackson McCurtain, who had been chief during the period served by the council house.

Paul continued his history lesson as they toured Choctaw Old Town near Shady Point and visited the old Choctaw Agency, which was made of hand-hewn logs.

Once again, Jordan enjoyed sharing her love of history with Paul. It seemed as though they would never run out of things to talk about, and she could not help but feel disappointment when Paul turned the car toward Seneca.

When they arrived back at camp, the dinner bell had already rung, and the crew was assembling for dinner. Jordan was surprised to see that most of the group was dressed in jeans, western shirts, and boots. Even the Peruvian students, who had bought cowboy boots and shirts during their visit to Oklahoma City, were attired in western clothing and had bandanas around their necks.

"What in the world is going on here?" Paul asked Cookie.

"I've invited everyone to a square dance in town," Cookie answered with a grin as he handed Paul the mail he had picked up in Seneca that morning. "You and Jordan hurry up and eat, then go and get ready. You wear that dress of yours with the full skirt," he instructed Jordan. "Those boys in town'll get an eyeful, won't they, Professor Paul? They'll think they died and went to heaven when they see this little angel of a gal."

Paul did not comment on Cookie's extravagant compliments, however. Yvonne was walking toward them looking slim and elegant in a citron yellow slacks outfit that contrasted beautifully with her smooth, tan skin.

"How'd it go?" Paul asked. "I didn't expect you and the fellows back until tomorrow?"

"Obviously," Yvonne said sarcastically. "The taping went well, and they finished with my part yesterday. The boys and I did a little sightseeing this morning, then drove on back. I see that you went on a little trip of your own while I was gone."

"Yes. Jordan and I went to look at that site over by Greer," Paul said evenly.

"I see," Yvonne said. "I thought you said you would need some help with the measurements and recordings."

"Jordan helped me," Paul answered.

"I suppose the farmer had a bunch of old arrowheads he had dug up," Yvonne said, her voice caustic. "I am so sick of arrowheads!"

"I know," Paul said. "That's why I took Jordan."

Not wishing to witness any more of this unpleasant exchange between the two professors, Jordan slipped away and went to pick up her meal, wondering if Paul and Yvonne were gearing up for a real lovers' quarrel. Yvonne was obviously furious at Paul for taking Jordan on the junket to Greer instead of waiting for her to return.

Very shortly, however, the professors entered the meal tent arm in arm. Yvonne was animatedly telling Paul about the television show on which she had appeared. Obviously, she had decided to be understanding about Paul's choice of traveling companion.

Much of the conversation at dinner concerned the upcoming excursion into Seneca. Yvonne was condescending about the prospect of square dancing with the "provincials." But everyone else—especially the Peruvian students—was looking forward to the dance. There was even a little off-color kidding among the male members of the crew about what to expect from the "farmers' daughters."

Dennis scooted closer to Jordan and put his arm

around her shoulders. "You guys can have the farmers' daughters," he told the high-spirited group. "I'll stick with Jordan. I'll bet there isn't another woman in the entire county that can hold a candle to her."

The crew's high spirits were enhanced even further when Paul announced he had received a very encouraging letter from the state historical society.

"Nothing definite yet," he told them, "but there's a good possibility my petition will be approved, and the site will be protected by law. That means this project can continue for years to come and be explored properly. And Medicine Bluff would be saved from destruction. We only have a short time left here this summer, but I don't need to tell you what it would mean to our cause if we could find the proof that this is indeed the oldest site of human habitation in the state. And some of the artifacts we've unearthed lately make me think we are very close to that proof. Very close indeed.

"So let's all go to Seneca tonight and have a good time," he continued. "But no hangovers, please. I want us all back in the trenches in the morning. And maybe—just maybe—this site will be spared, and some of us will have the opportunity to continue this project next summer."

Only Yvonne was unenthusiastic about Paul's disclosure. Jordan knew the Peruvian archaeologist would be against anything that might prevent Paul from returning to Peru with her. And it was very apparent that Paul was intensely interested in the Fourche Maline site. It had been his discovery, and he considered it one of the most important excavations' ever undertaken in the state. But to Yvonne, the site was inconsequential when compared with archaeological sites in her native Peru. She cared nothing about Oklahoma's archaeology, but she certainly cared about its leading archaeologist.

Jordan could not help but think what preserving the Fourche Maline site would mean to Larry and his family's company. It might very well put him out of business. But like the rest of the crew, except perhaps Yvonne, Jordan believed in the importance of the work at this excavation. It should continue. To have the mounds leveled and covered with a roadbed seemed almost criminal. And to dynamite Medicine Bluff, a sacred place to countless generations of American Indians, seemed an act against nature.

Jordan finished her meal and hurried off to change her clothes. Like the others, she was looking forward to the dance in Seneca. A square dance! What fun, she thought as she slipped into the one dress she had brought with her. It was gaily striped with a full skirt Her shoulders were tan and bare above the ruffled bodice, as were her slim legs above her high-heeled white sandals. She wore her hair down and it fell in a shimmering curtain over her neck and shoulders.

Even though she knew the others were probably waiting for her, she took the time to make up her eyes and apply lip gloss and a touch of rouge. For some inexplicable reason, she wanted to look her best tonight. She added her gold chain to her throat and pearl earrings to her ears and raced off to join the others.

The dance was in Seneca's American Legion Hall, and it seemed as though most of the town must either be on the floor dancing, gathered around the punch bowls, or sitting in the rows of chairs that lined the hall.

Cookie arranged for several of the square dancing couples to show the beginners from the archaeological dig the steps and help them through several of the dances.

Before long, Jordan was sashaying around the floor, changing partners with each dance. By the time she found herself in Paul's arms, she was flushed and slightly breathless. But such wonderful fun! The fiddlers were grand. The music was the toe-tapping sort that made one feel like dancing.

Paul was as graceful at square dancing as he was at his native American dances, Jordan thought as she twirled around the circle with him.

"Having a good time?" he asked, his dark eyes admiring as he looked down at her.

"Oh, yes! This has been a wonderful day. All of it!"

The next dance was a reel, and once again, Paul claimed her as his partner. With his arms around her waist, they skipped up and down between the lines of clapping dancers. There was more twirling and curtsying and promenading. Jordan was glad she had a full skirt to swish. And the high-heeled sandals that so embarrassed her that first day at the encampment made her feel feminine and pretty tonight—a nice feeling after weeks spent in tennis shoes and cutoffs.

Even Yvonne had been persuaded to dance, first by the exuberant Dennis, then by Paul and by each of her three countrymen. But when Jordan danced with Paul, she felt as though the exotic woman's gaze never left her.

At one point Jordan noticed Yvonne entering a phone booth located in the building entryway. But she was too busy having a good time to worry about what Yvonne was up to. She swished to the fiddlers' tunes until, at last, she had no breath left in her. The cool air coming through the hall's open door enticed her to step outside and catch her breath.

There were several clusters of people smoking and visiting in the yard of the building, but Jordan saw none of her group and made her way to a low wall that bordered the street.

With a sigh she sank onto the wall, taking a deep breath of the refreshing night air. She closed her eyes and lifted her hair from her neck to allow the breeze to cool her moist skin.

When she felt a soft kiss on her exposed neck, she said, "What's the matter, Dennis? The farmer's daughter run you off?"

But the kiss ended abruptly, and there was no answer to her teasing query. Jordan turned to see Paul's unmistakable form silhouetted against the lighted building.

"Oh, I thought you were Dennis," Jordan said.

"Obviously. Sorry to disappoint you."

"Don't be silly," Jordan said. "I'm not used to having professors nuzzle my neck. Dennis nuzzles any female neck he can find. Here, sit down by me and catch your breath."

Instead of accepting her invitation, Paul stepped over the wall and started walking down the gravel road in the direction of a small church. Jordan, without thinking, jumped up and followed him.

"I'm so glad Cookie invited us to the dance," Jordan said when she caught up with him. "Is Yvonne having a good time?"

When he did not answer, Jordan slowed her step. "Why are you so rude to me?" she demanded, not really expecting an answer. "Is it because you think I shouldn't accept the attentions of other men and save myself only for you? Only for you to do what? Have sex with a few times before you marry Yvonne? You're an engaged man, Paul. But I'm not engaged to anyone. I'll admit that you've confused me terribly, and you surely must realize how much I'm attracted to you. But if fault is to be found, it seems to me that it is equally yours. And for you to go stomping off and refuse to talk to me because I thought it was that big flirt Dennis kissing my neck instead of discerning through some sort of sixth sense that it was really my professor is unreasonable and unfair!"

She turned and started back toward the hall, knowing she had said too much, fearful that she would say more. She wanted to tell him how desperately she loved him. She wanted to beg him to love her and not Yvonne.

But she would not beg. She would not burden him with her problem.

She had only taken a couple of steps, however, when Paul was suddenly beside her grabbing her wrist and pulling her in among the shadows formed by a clump of overgrown shrubbery.

His kiss was long and hard. Jordan did not try to resist. She had wanted one last kiss. She gave herself over to it.

Her arms went around his neck as she eagerly accepted his tongue. She gave him her mouth, aching with her need to give him her entire body.

The feel of his responding body pressed hard against hers was intoxicating. Even if he did not love her, he desired her as greatly as she desired him.

Paul buried one hand in her hair and clasped the other around her waist, grasping her so tightly there could be no retreat, no escape. It was as though she no longer owned her body. His iron grip told her that she now, at this instant, belonged to him.

His hand relinquished its hold on her hair and traveled downward over her throat to her bare shoulders. His fingertips on her bare skin sent waves of sensation throughout her body. His touch was electrifying. Every part of her body longed to be touched, to be fondled, to be possessed by this man.

He pushed aside the straps of her dress and freed her breasts from the confines of the gathered bodice. An animal sound emerged deep in his throat as he cupped a full breast in his palm and rolled its hardening nipple between his fingers.

She arched her back, pushing her breast outward for his grasping hand. So exquisite was the sensation from his probing fingers, Jordan groaned out loud. She didn't want him to stop—not ever. She just wanted to be with him. She wanted time to stand still so she could float always on this cloud of intense sensation. She didn't care what he did to her so long as he didn't stop.

Then he was pushing her to the ground. He meant to make love to her here, Jordan realized, here on the ground under these bushes with people standing just a few feet away.

She didn't want this. This was not how she wanted it to be. She wanted privacy. It seemed so sordid like this.

She wanted him to love her, not take her body in an animallike coupling in the dirt with people nearby—people walking around and talking to each other while she had sex with Paul under some bushes.

But, oh, how her body cried out that it didn't matter. Here. Anyplace, her mind beseeched. All her body wanted was for him to do something about the fire that threatened to consume her.

But another voice within her argued that it did matter. The voice acknowledged that this would probably be the last opportunity she would ever have to satisfy her hunger for this man. But like this? To do so would diminish the love she felt for him.

"Not here," she gasped. "Please. Not here."

He held her so tightly against his chest she could scarcely breathe. His own breath was coming in hard, uneven gasps.

"Please, not here," Jordan whispered once again. "I don't want you to."

"Why?" he demanded in a hoarse, angry whisper. "Don't you do the same thing in the bushes by the river? Where do you and Dennis go?"

Jordan pulled the bodice of her dress up over her

bare breasts and drew away from him. "I'm sure Yvonne is wondering where you are," she told him.

When Jordan returned to the hall, she felt Paul's gaze on her as she danced with every man who asked her. She danced and danced like one possessed. She knew her color was high and her eyes shone. She knew her laughter was too loud and her smile too free as she twirled from man to man. Let him think what he wants, she told herself as men clustered about her competing for her attention. This is what he thought she was like anyway.

But later that night, in the darkness of her tent, when there were no other men to make her feel wanted, she was again alone with her pain. *Damn you, Paul Nicolle,* she said into her pillow. *Damn you! If I didn't love you, I would hate you.*

Chapter Eleven

Later, deep into the night, Jordan abruptly awakened from a fitful sleep.

That noise! It sounded like an explosion, she thought as she scrambled from her cot and peered out into the darkness. The sound of debris raining down on her canvas roof and the unmistakable acrid odor of gunpowder told her there had indeed been some sort of explosion—and it had been very close to the camp.

Almost instantly the sound of running feet and familiar voices calling to one another filled the air. Within seconds Dennis's voice was at her tent.

"Jordan, are you all right?"

"Yes. But what on earth is going on?" she asked as she grabbed a robe and slipped it over her shoulders.

"Unless I miss my guess," he told her, "someone set off some dynamite over by the mounds."

No real damage had been done, the assembled crew soon realized as their flashlights surveyed the crater left by the explosion. One wall of a recently opened trench was caved in, but none of the main trenches had suffered much damage. However, the knowledge that their project was now the victim of a dynamiting was quite disturbing to the crew.

Jordan, feeling very exposed and vulnerable, stared off into the inpenetrable blackness of the surrounding trees. Dynamite. Who could have done such a thing? No one would think it was a kid's prank this time.

But, of course, Jordan already knew who Paul would blame.

Cookie served them coffee in the meal tent as they gathered to discuss what action to take about this latest act of vandalism. Yvonne seemed as indignant as the others and somewhat shaken by the incident. And like the others, she seemed to blame the highway crew for the explosion.

"I do not know about this country," said the Peruvian woman nervously, "but in my country, it is difficult to purchase explosives. Only people with legitimate reasons are allowed to use them—people in construction and mining and things such as that."

Jordan watched the Latin woman as she spoke and was amazed at how beautiful she looked even at this late hour. She was wearing a caftan made of brilliantly colored fabric with a wild, primitive design that draped itself elegantly over her tall, slender form. Her heavy black hair hung in a smooth, shining sheet over her shoulders. Her smooth skin was flawless and golden, and her lips full over beautiful white teeth. Her nervousness seemed only to heighten her color and the brilliance of her large eyes.

Jordan realized her own appearance suffered greatly by comparison. Her pale hair was a disheveled mess, and her plain terry-cloth robe looked dowdy next to Yvonne's bright caftan.

The others seemed to agree with Yvonne's assumption that the explosion was more harassment from the road builders. Paul was silent, but Jordan could sense his inward rage. Several times she felt his accusatory gaze upon her as though to say, "See. What do you think of *him* now?"

But the dynamiting only served to bolster Jordan's

conviction that Larry had nothing to do with any of the destructive incidents at the camp. He was too level-headed ever to do anything that could possibly endanger other people. It was one thing to flatten empty tents, but quite another to set off a charge of dynamite with people nearby.

And in her mind's eye Jordan kept seeing Yvonne entering that phone booth back at the American Legion Hall. Who had she been calling at that late hour?

The next morning Jordan offered to drive into town and once again make a report to the county sheriff. She had no real confidence that the portly sheriff and his flirtatious deputy could discover who was causing the trouble at the dig or do anything to stop it. But she had a hunch. And she needed to go into town to check it out.

Jordan was far more interested in checking the vehicles parked alongside Seneca's wide, lazy streets than visiting the sheriff's basement office. A woman secretary took her report this time. Jordan quickly told her what had happened and received the woman's assurance that the sheriff would check into it.

Seneca was a small town. It did not take Jordan long to find the familiar brown van. It was parked in front of a tavern.

It took a minute for Jordan's eyes to adjust to the dim interior, but then she saw him sitting alone at a back table. He was wearing a western-cut shirt, but his shoulder-length black hair was held in place by a braided leather thong. His hands cradled a still-full mug of beer, and he seemed lost in thought.

"Hello, Frank," Jordan said, sliding into the seat beside him.

He was startled. It took a minute for recognition to dawn in wary eyes.

"Paul's friend," he acknowledged glumly, obviously not pleased to see her. "I don't remember your name."

"Jordan," she said, extending her hand. "Jordan Marshall. I'm one of the student's working out at the dig."

Frank did not shake her offered hand. Instead, he mumbled, "Nice to see you again," and stared down at his mug of beer. "I would appreciate it, Miss Marshall, if you wouldn't mention my being in Seneca to my brother. I don't have time to come out to the dig, and—well, I guess you could tell when you were in Tahlequah that my brother and I don't see eye to eye on that whole project."

"Frank, I'm here because I was looking for you," Jordan said gently. "I thought you might still be in town."

Frank frowned, a look of fear flickering across his face. "I don't understand ...," he said, his voice faltering.

"Quite by accident, I heard Professor DeSilvestro talking to you in the back of your van at the powwow in Tahlequah," Jordan explained. "I thought it was a little strange for her to come all the way to Tahlequah and not stop to see Paul or your mother, but I really didn't place too much importance on it until I saw your van in Seneca the day after the bulldozing episode out at the dig. Everyone assumed the highway people were responsible, but I don't think they were. I think you and Yvonne had something to do with it. Then last night there was a dynamiting out there, and once again, here you are in Seneca."

"Look here, Miss Marshall," he said angrily, "you're way off base. Me and my buddies were just passing through that other time. We'd stopped here to get something to eat. And I'm just passing through today too. I'm heading down to Pouteau to see my girl. And even if there was any truth to your suspicions, you couldn't prove a damn thing, and I think you know that. So just bug off, and leave me alone!"

"I probably couldn't prove anything," Jordan agreed. "And thus far I've said nothing about any of this to your brother or anyone else. I didn't want to be involved in a family problem. But after last night I feel obligated to do something. I guess that's why I'm here. I want you to help me decide what's to be done. Someone could have been injured or even killed from that dynamite charge. And everyone out at the dig, including your brother, is blaming the civil engineer in charge of the bridge project. Paul said this morning that he's going to ask the district attorney to look into the matter. Paul wants the engineer prosecuted, and the man had nothing to do with all this!"

"Well, if the guy's innocent, he doesn't have anything to worry about," Frank said defensively.

"Possibly," Jordan said. "But it was his company's bulldozer that was used. And a delay on the bridge project might ruin his business, so to Paul's way of thinking, the highway engineer is the one with the motive. It just might seem that way to the district attorney too. So you can see that if an investigation implicates this man, I'll have to tell them that you were in town right after both the bulldozing and the dynamiting. I'll have to tell about your meeting with Yvonne in Tahlequah the night before the bulldozing. And I'll have to tell them that I saw her using the telephone late last night. I don't know about the district attorney, but I rather imagine the information will cause Paul to have second thoughts. You were pretty adamant about what you think of the Fourche Maline project. He knows how strongly you oppose him."

Frank pushed away his beer and put his fingertips to his temples. The look on his face was one of reluctant surrender.

"I just wanted to push over a few tents," he said. "But my friends got carried away. There was too much beer drunk, I guess. And there was a lot of talk about past injustices to Indians and the Trail of Tears and a lot of things that happened long before anyone alive today was even born. We got pretty worked up, but I couldn't believe it when two of my friends came driving across the river in that dozer. And the whole time I kept thinking we'd get caught, that the people camping in that other pasture would hear that dozer and the war whoops, but I guess it was too windy."

"And the dynamiting?" Jordan asked.

"I know you won't believe me," he said earnestly, "but this is the first I've heard of it. Yvonne did call me last night. And she was pretty upset. She thought something more drastic was going to have to be done. She said Paul was about to get the highway changed, and then the dig would continue for years. She wanted me to come down last night, but I wouldn't. I told her I'd meet her today, and maybe we could figure out something."

"Are you suggesting Yvonne did the dynamiting by herself?" Jordan asked incredulously. "Where would she get dynamite?"

"I didn't come down here last night," Frank said miserably. "But maybe I should have. Maybe I could have prevented this from happening. You see, several of my friends weren't around when I called them this morning to see if they wanted to come along. They'd been gone all night. Really, Miss Marshall, I agree with you about the dynamite. That's dangerous and dumb— and I guess, inexcusable. But you've got to understand how riled up my people get about things like this. It's bad enough when people have no respect for Indian ways, but when one of our own goes over to the other side—"

"There is no other side," Jordan interrupted. "Paul is just as proud of his heritage as you are—of both the

Indian and the white blood in his veins. I'm sure that's one of the reasons why Paul became an archaeologist, but I suspect you're too stubborn to recognize that fact. He has a consuming desire to learn about the history of native Americans. He really cares, Frank. I know. I've seen him out there at that dig. I've seen how much this project means to him. You ought to see the reverence with which he treats the skeletons we unearth—and the artifacts. It's all just as sacred to him as it is to you and your friends. He instills in all of us who work out at the dig the humanity of the people who once lived there. Those skeletons aren's just specimens! Paul's not like that."

Frank shook his head angrily. "But then what does he do with those skeletons? He dumps them in boxes and ships them to museums! Is that reverence? How'd you feel if someone came along in a couple hundred years and desecrated your grave or the graves of your kids and put your bones in a box for people to measure and examine and theorize over?"

"Good grief, Frank!" Jordan said, "I wouldn't 'feel' a thing. I'd be long dead, and any loved ones who'd be upset by such actions would also be long dead. And would it really be so awful to have an archaeologist—a scientist—dig up your earthly remains if there was something to be learned from them, if future inhabitants of this world learned how we lived and what we believed in and where we fit into the great scheme of life on this planet? Would that really be so bad? Maybe those future people could learn from our mistakes. Maybe they'd come to appreciate our art and our culture more by examining what we left behind. Isn't understanding the people themselves more important than leaving their bones undisturbed and never finding out anything about them at all?"

Jordan impatiently waved away the waitress who was

approaching their table with a menu and waited until the woman was out of earshot before continuing.

"In a sense," Jordan continued, "we're making those people who lived out there hundreds and even thousands of years ago live again and talk to their fellow man. Without archaeologists, we would know nothing about entire eras of human existence. It would be like those people had never lived. Don't you realize that without Paul and others like him, your people would know so very little about their history? No one would understand the culture, the struggles, the migrations, the art, the crafts, the philosophy of those who walked this land before us. Archaeology stresses the continuum of human life and gives us a feeling that what we do lives after us. Just think of all those hundreds of generations of people who will live there on the Fourche Maline in the shadow of that flint bluff. Don't you want to know about the gods they worshipped? Don't you want to know what they made from the flint they took from the bluff and the clay they scooped from the riverbank? How did they live? Why did they disappear? Why did their culture evolve into another? Don't you want to know about that? You should. And you should be proud of what your brother is doing—not ashamed of it. One of Paul's students at the dig, Wolf Birdsong, is a full-blood Comanche, and he's proud to be studying with Paul and is eager to make his own contribution. A great many Indians in this state, I am told, are quite proud of what your brother is doing."

But the young man shook his head angrily, his dark eyes glaring. "I still think he's motivated more by ambition than by any real caring," Frank insisted. "If he really cared about native Americans, as you claim, he wouldn't be willing to go off to South America with Yvonne and give up his work here. He told our mother

that he was seriously considering marrying Yvonne and
joining her in excavating Inca ruins.''

As Jordan looked at the anguish on Frank's face,
Jordan wondered if much of Frank's hostility was the
result of his brother's seeming willingness to leave the
state of his birth and abandon his tribal affiliation in
order to cut a larger swath through the world of international archaeology.

Perhaps Frank did not understand how much love
can alter people, Jordan thought with a heavy heart.
Paul must love Yvonne very much if he was willing to
sacrifice his own heritage.

Jordan felt a kinship with the disturbed man sitting
across the table from her. Their love for Paul Nicolle
had brought them both pain.

"Are you sure he'll be leaving this country?" Jordan
asked. "Maybe Yvonne will decide to stay here instead."

"Not hardly," Frank said bitterly. "Yvonne would
do anything to get Paul to Peru. Her family has a lot of
influence and even more money. That's part of what
she's using to lure him there. There wouldn't be all the
constant funding problem he's been plagued with here.
His future would be as golden as the artifacts he'd be
unearthing."

Jordan was about to ask Frank what Yvonne had to
do with the incidents at the dig when she was startled to
see the woman herself, as if on cue, enter the dimly lit
tavern. Jordan watched with apprehension as the elegant, statuesque woman stood at the entrance peering
around the room.

As Yvonne's eyes adjusted to the gloomy interior,
they widened in surprise at the sight of Jordan sitting
beside Frank. She hesitated, then seemed to make up
her mind and, with an unhurried feline grace, she
strolled over to their table.

"Well, Jordan," she said in her lilting accent, "do you go after every man you meet? You have accumulated quite a collection this summer."

Jordan ignored her remark and said, "I suppose you two have 'business' to discuss, so if you'll excuse me, I'll be on my way."

Yvonne seemed to pale beneath her glorious bronze tan. She sank into the chair beside Frank and grabbed his arm.

"What have you been telling her?" she demanded, a note of hysteria creeping into her voice.

"Frank hasn't said anything about you," Jordan said evenly. "We were just talking about the incidents at the camp. I was explaining that I had seen—or rather overheard—the two of you together in Tahlequah."

"What were you doing in Tahlequah?" Yvonne demanded, her beautiful face distorted by an ugly grimace.

"Paul did not want to leave me alone at the camp and took me over there for the weekend," Jordan explained, surprised that Paul had not mentioned it to Yvonne. Or perhaps, on second thought, it was not so surprising, Jordan decided when she recalled Yvonne's displeasure over the afternoon reconnoitering trip she and Paul had taken to Greer.

Yvonne reached across the table and wrapped her long fingers around Jordan's arm, deliberately digging her nails into Jordan's flesh. "You stay away from Paul, you little tramp," she said through clenched teeth. "He belongs to me!"

Jordan jerked her arm away and rubbed the angry red marks left by Yvonne's nails.

"You needn't worry, Yvonne," Jordan said. "He only took me along because he felt responsible for me. He didn't want to leave an unattended female student at the camp."

But even as she minimized the journey with her words in order to pacify the jealous woman, her thoughts turned to what had happened in the bedroom of Hannah Nicolle's house.

Yvonne was staring at Jordan's face intently, as though she were reading the thoughts that lurked behind those turquoise-blue eyes. Jordan looked away. Was it all written there for Yvonne to see? Did Yvonne know that she too loved Paul?

"I suppose you are going to go running to Paul and tell him that his brother and I conspired against the project." Yvonne was unable to conceal the panic in her voice as she spoke. "Paul would not believe you— not about his own brother and the woman he loves."

"What did you hope to accomplish by all this?" Jordan asked. "Paul cares so much about the Fourche Maline project. Why are you trying to destroy it?"

"I didn't want anyone to destroy the excavation itself," Yvonne insisted. "I wouldn't want that to happen to another archaeologist. And Paul's worked too hard to have his dig destroyed. I just hoped someone would frighten the students, and perhaps university officials would decide the site was not a safe place for them. The dynamite certainly was not my idea!"

Yvonne turned her flashing gaze to Frank. "You young fool! I could not believe you and your rabble-rousing friends would pull a stunt like that. Someone could have gotten hurt. It's one thing to tear down some tents and slash a few tires, but dynamite! And now that dumb sheriff will be obligated to really try to get to the bottom of things. I understand he's bringing in the state crime bureau to investigate."

"I don't think Frank had anything to do with the dynamiting either," Jordan said in the young man's defense. "His friends thought that up themselves. But apparently you encouraged the other acts of vandalism at the camp. I don't understand how someone of your professional caliber could be involved in such a thing."

"But do you not see?" Yvonne asked, her eyes wide and unnatural looking. "Paul was talking about extending the project into next summer, maybe even for several years. I do not have time to wait around for him to get Fourche Maline out of his system! We have our destiny to fulfill while we are still young."

"Your destiny?" Frank asked, a wary look on his youthful face as he stared at the woman.

"Yes. Destiny. I believe it is meant to be. Individually, Paul and I would do well, but as a couple, we would be the most glamorous pairing in academe. By combining our looks, our credentials, our exotic bloodlines, our connections, our ambitions—the sky is the limit! We were meant to be together. Surely you can see that. We can combine scholarly pursuits with fame and fortune. I have already spoken with a major television network and given them a video tape of a talk show Paul and I did for an Oklahoma City station right after I arrived in the state. The network people were dazzled by it. Paul and I were magnificent. They want us for a television series after we are married—a Jacques Cousteau type of format that would have us broadcasting from the famous dig sites in Peru and around the world. We would become international celebrities. We would make the whole world care about archaeology the way Cousteau has made it care about what lies beneath the surface of the ocean."

Yvonne stared past Jordan's shoulder, her eyes seeing a private vision. The hysteria had left her voice and was replaced by a hushed reverence. She was worshipping at her personal altar, a high priestess to her own ambition. Her words seemed not so much for Jordan or for Frank, but for herself.

"In that video tape," Yvonne continued, "we were

discussing our plans for the Fourche Maline project. We were both beautiful and articulate and witty. My accent was charming. Our backgrounds lent us an exotic aura—with my being a Peruvian aristocrat with Incan royalty among my ancestors and Paul being the descendant of famous Cherokee chiefs and French explorers. We are naturals. The television people sensed it at once. They want us to begin the series with a program about the Lake Titicaca excavation in Peru. I promised the producers that Paul and I would report there by September first."

Jordan watched with amazement as the obsessed woman revealed her private dream. Jordan had no doubt that what Yvonne said was true. She and Paul could be media darlings. They would go on talk shows and discuss their latest project or book. They would make television documentaries. And Yvonne was right—individually she and Paul would still be special, but together they would be extraordinary. Dazzling. It was hard to imagine a more handsome, glamorous, and exotic couple to grace television screens or the pages of magazines and newspapers.

How different this woman is from me, Jordan could not help but think. Jordan yearned for a more private sort of life. She too could take great pleasure in sharing her work with a husband, but she also wanted children and a more normal kind of life than the one Yvonne planned for Paul and herself.

Jordan realized that a hard, cynical look had crept into Frank's eyes as he watched his brother's future wife. Yvonne seemed to sense his scrutiny and ceased her tirade as she glanced first at Frank, then at Jordan.

"Whose idea was it in the first place to vandalize the camp?" Jordan asked the black-haired woman. "Did you convince Frank and his friends to do your dirty work for you?"

The panic returned to Yvonne's eyes. She looked frantically at Frank, as though she expected him to answer Jordan's accusation.

"Even if I did as you say," Yvonne challenged in an unsteady voice, "you cannot prove anything. I will tell Paul you lie. I will tell him how you sleep with all the men at the camp."

"I'm sure you've already done that," Jordan said wearily. "And I really don't want to prove anything. I just want it all to stop. You are interfering where you have no right. It is not for you to say if the Fourche Maline project should continue. And someone is going to get hurt if this kind of insane destruction continues. It's all so foolish anyway. Did you really think a man like Paul was going to turn tail and quit just because of what you've done out there? Didn't you realize it would just make him all the more determined to see it through?"

"Ah, but there is no more funding available," Yvonne said triumphantly. "He has not been able to replace much of the equipment that was destroyed. Several of the tents were ruined. He was operating on a shoestring anyway. Of course, there is the possibility that he might get another pitifully inadequate grant and manage to continue excavating next summer. I have to put a stop to it now. It must end soon. He must give up on this silly little dig and start looking ahead to the future. And if you tell him about Frank and me, I will make Paul think you are covering up—that you were in on the whole thing with Larry Jarvis. Paul hates Jarvis, and he thinks you are a cheap little tramp. He will believe me. And just think of the embarrassment you would cause Paul if you accused his brother and the woman he plans to marry of sabotaging his project. The press would get wind of it. What would his colleagues think? And his dear mother? You would not want to embarrass Paul, would you, Jordan? I have seen the way you look at him, and I know you would not want to do that. No, I think you had best keep your mouth shut, Jordan dear, or I promise you will regret it."

Jordan experienced a loathsome fascination as she observed the face of this exquisitely beautiful woman grow twisted and ugly as she spat out her threats. Jordan had no doubt that Yvonne would be capable of doing almost anything to accomplish the fulfillment of her cherished dream. The Peruvian archaeologist wanted Paul not only to satisfy the passions of her voluptuous body, she also—and perhaps this was the greater reason—wanted him to bring her fame and fortune. Yvonne would stop at nothing to obtain her goals.

As Jordan looked at a face stripped of all feminine softness, its lips curled back in an animallike snarl, its eyes hard as steel, Jordan felt a spasm of fear knotting at her stomach. Suddenly, she desperately needed to leave this place and get as far away from this person as she could.

Yet she found herself asking Yvonne, "You'd actually jeopardize the outcome of the excavation and negate all that hard work just to get Paul to go with you?"

"I would do *anything* to prevent him from staying here in this godforsaken place," she said with a sweep of her hand to indicate the seedy bar and the town beyond. "Imagine, the talents of a man like Paul Nicolle wasted in such a pitiful place. He has to wake up and quit trying to unearth the prehistory of *unimportant* people."

Jordan heard Frank draw in his breath at her words. She could well imagine the anger he must feel for this woman—and the anger he must feel toward himself at being drawn into her sick plan.

"I think men like Paul Nicolle think all people are important," Jordan said.

"Well, he is wrong," Yvonne said, abruptly standing and tipping her chair over with a noisy clatter. "And I will show him the error of his ways. In Peru he will be treated like a prince. Here he is just a pauper begging for pitiful little grants to dig pitiful little sites. I will show him what is important, and no one is going to stand in my way. Do you understand me, Jordan Marshall? No one." She stood looking down at them, her hands on her hips, her eyes glaring.

Jordan looked up into the challenging black eyes, then turned to Frank. "Why have you helped her do these things?" she asked.

"She said it would be like a test," he said uncertainly. "If Paul went with her, she said it would prove that I was right and he really didn't care anything about discovering the past history of native Americans. And I didn't think he had the right to dig up those burial grounds. That area by Medicine Bluff has always been a sacred place. Our grandfather used to take us there and tell us about the old ways."

But Frank sounded less certain than before. His eyes would not meet Jordan's.

"Paul is finding out more about the 'old ways' than your grandfather could ever know," Jordan said simply.

"If he really cared, though," Frank said, "he'd be using his influence to keep that road from being built over the site. Do you know they plan to dynamite the bluff? People have been getting their flint for tools and weapons from that bluff since time began."

"He is doing just that," Jordan explained. "Paul has already been to Oklahoma City and started the necessary procedure to have the site declared a state historical site. It may not be approved, of course, but he thinks he can prove it's the oldest archaeological site ever unearthed in the state. If he's successful, the legislature couldn't ignore it. They would have to give it historical-site status. It would then be protected by state law. The route of the highway would have to be altered, and the bridge moved downstream."

Frank shook his head slowly back and forth. "I had no idea," he said. "No idea. Why didn't Paul tell me?"

"Maybe he never had a chance to," Jordan offered. "I'm sure he would have eventually."

Yvonne was still staring down at them, a look of disgust on her handsome face. "You two sit there worrying about some flint bluff and inconsequential site when I am talking about some of the most glorious archaeological excavations on the face of the earth. Paul Nicolle can be a nobody here in Oklahoma, or he can come with me and be internationally renowned. I think he'll come with me," she said with a haughty toss of her head.

Was Yvonne correct, Jordan wondered as she watched the woman march across the room and out the door? Would Yvonne be able to lure Paul from his homeland, from the work to which he had thus far dedicated his life?

Jordan knew the same question was haunting the mind of Paul's brother. Frank had lashed out at Paul. But he seemed to have been motivated at least in part by fear. Frank was afraid of losing his brother.

Chapter Twelve

Jordan had missed lunch, but when she delivered the groceries Cookie had ordered to his canvas kitchen, he had a sandwich waiting for her. While she was eating it, Yvonne came driving across the pasture in Paul's car.

Not wanting a further confrontation with Professor DeSilvestro, Jordan took the rest of her sandwich with her and hurried off toward the mounds.

Throughout the afternoon Yvonne seemed to be watching her every move as Jordan went about her work. Any time Jordan was near Paul, Yvonne managed to be standing or working close by. Jordan soon realized that Yvonne, in spite of her bullying threats, was worried that Jordan might tell Paul about her and Frank's clandestine mischief making.

But Jordan had already decided to say nothing—unless Paul really did try to convince the district attorney that Larry Jarvis was responsible for the destructive incidents at the camp. Her defense of Larry had already destroyed any credibility she might still have had with Paul. And Jordan knew that she would have a difficult time convincing him that Yvonne and Frank were responsible. And even if he did believe her and not think she was merely trying to turn his suspicion away from Larry, Jordan would be put in the distressing position of turning brother against brother—something she did not want to do, especially after her visit with Frank Nicolle. Frank may have acted unwisely, but Jordan was now convinced the younger Nicolle brother was not a malicious person and his actions seemed to have been prompted as much out of a feeling of alienation from his brother as from his concern that Indian traditions were not being honored.

Jordan did feel confident, however, that she had put a stop to the sabotage. Yvonne would not dare try anything else—not with Jordan knowing that she was at least in part responsible for some of the mischief that had already occurred.

She could well understand how fearful the Peruvian woman must be that Jordan would tell Paul of Yvonne's involvement and turn Paul against her.

But Jordan would not try to turn Paul against his brother or his fiancée. In one more week she would leave this place and never see Paul Nicolle again. She would leave quietly without disrupting his life.

It was almost time to break for dinner when Jordan noticed the storm clouds building up to the north. And in a very short time those clouds had rolled their way across the heavens leaving an ominous, angry sky in their wake. Paul had just given the order to cover the trenches when Cookie came trotting across the field to tell them that storm warnings had been broadcast over the radio.

"Sounds like we're in for a bad one," he yelled over the growing wind. "Maybe we'd best pack up and head for town."

Jordan had been working at the small mound nearest the river. Paul hastened over to help her just as the sky opened up and sent rain sheeting down over them. Almost at once Yvonne was climbing the side of the mound to help.

"You women'll have to manage here," Paul called out over the rain and wind. "I don't think anyone's covering the trenches on number-three mound."

The ever-increasing wind whipped her hair about her face as Jordan struggled to pull the planks over the open trenches, then help Yvonne stake heavy sheets of plastic in place. The two women were isolated from the rest of the crew by blowing curtains of stinging rain that now reduced visibility so drastically that Jordan could only see a few feet in each direction.

The river was already imitating the turbulent sky. Jordan could not believe how quickly the peaceful river was turning into a seething monster. She remembered that the river's name suggested a potential for evil, and for the first time she could understand that the name might be deserved.

The river seemed to throw itself at its confining banks and churned with an intensity that made the earth quake beneath Jordan's kneeling figure.

She felt very small and vulnerable as the forces of nature clashed about her. It was hard to believe the raging Fourche Maline had been a peaceful stream only a short time before. And the rain and wind clutched at her, fighting against her every move, making her task impossible.

"We can't!" she yelled to Yvonne. "The wind's too strong!"

Yvonne yelled something back at her, but the words were lost in the wind. Jordan made one last try at anchoring the flapping sheet of plastic with her knee so she could pound the stake through it. But her efforts were useless. Maybe if Yvonne could hold it down for her.

But as Jordan tried once again to call to Yvonne through the biting pellets of rain, she realized the trembling of the earth beneath her was increasing. The ground shuddered, throwing Jordan to the muddy ground.

Paralyzing fear shot through her veins. The earth was moving!

The segment of mound beneath her was separating from the adjacent earth! It was slipping toward the waiting torrents of the Fourche Maline!

Jordan felt her body slipping down the slanting, mud-slicked surface. She was sliding out of control toward the treacherous, churning water. Frantically, she clutched at a stake she had just driven into the ground. When it gave way, she grasped at roots, clumps of grass, rocks—but everything was moving with her.

"Help me!" she screamed at Yvonne, but her words were swallowed by the howling wind.

Yvonne stared at her from the other side of the widening crevasse, her eyes wide with disbelief.

"The boards!" Jordan screamed as she slipped still farther down the rapidly crumbling bank. "Hold out one of the boards!"

At first Yvonne did not seem to understand, then she stooped and picked up one of the heavy planks. To the frantic Jordan, she seemed to be moving in slow motion.

Yvonne extended the plank across the gaping hole of mud and swirling water. It inched its way toward Jordan.

"Closer," Jordan yelled. The bank gave way still further, dropping her closer to the murderous waters. "I can't reach it! Closer!"

Jordan managed to fight her way back up the bank. Just a few more inches. Almost. Her fingers brushed the end of the board.

But she was slipping away again. With all her strength she lunged after the escaping board. The bank was shuddering, moving. She clawed after the board.

Then there was no board. Nothing but mud and rocks. Her body joined the landslide of earth plummeting into the violently seething waters of the transformed river.

Almost instantly the water sucked her downward. She fought at the deadly currents, desperately trying to find the surface, to escape from this horrible nightmare.

At last she felt her face breaking through the surface and gasped a lung full of air before being swept under again. She was a part of the river. It owned her. It took her as easily as the twigs and leaves that swirled along with her. Her small body was no match for the raging river.

As though playing with her, the currents carried her by a log jutting from the bank. Jordan grabbed it, but it shuddered for an instant, then joined the raging torrent, sweeping past Jordan.

Once again she was plummeted downward. No breath. There was no breath left in her. Frantically, with lungs bursting, she managed to surface again.

Then downward. Her arm scraped against the bottom of the river. The surface was so far away. So very far. And she had no strength. Her arms and legs felt as though they were being torn from her body. Her lungs seemed to be exploding within her chest. But she fought on—instinctively, a small creature trying valiantly to survive, its efforts puny against so great a force.

Her head broke through the surface, and she gulped at the life-giving air. If only she could keep her body from being pulled down again. If only she could swim along with the currents. She tried. But her limbs were useless against the force of the evil river.

There was no breath and little life left in her. She knew that she was losing the battle. But she wanted desperately to keep fighting. She didn't want to die here in this damnable river!

She grabbed at a passing branch and missed. How feeble her efforts seemed. Through all her struggling, the horror of what was happening filled her heart with terror. The next time she went under, she knew she would not have the strength to fight her way to the surface again. She must stay with the currents. She must not go under again.

Go with the water, she told herself. *Don't fight it. Just go where it takes you and maybe...*

But the Fourche Maline was determined to claim her. It was ready to end its macabre game. The undertow grabbed at her, sucked at her body, pulled her from the life-giving air. Downward. The waters closed over her.

She struggled. The river would not have her without a fight. But she knew it was useless.

At first she did not realize the new force pulling at her was not an element of the ferocious river. Then she realized the new force was pulling her toward the surface, not away from it.

Strong arms were helping her. Paul. He had defied the death-seeking river to save her. But even Paul could not be strong enough. Now they would both die.

Quite suddenly, however, there was a solidness beneath her. Paul scrambled from the river and pulled her up a bank away from the river's grasp.

It was over. Paul held her in his arms to warm her against his body. He spoke soothing words to her when she began to sob. He sat there with her in the pouring rain, and rocked her back and forth as a mother would a child.

"There, there, darling Jordan," he said with lips pressed against her temple. "It's over. You're all right. Everything is fine."

She clung to him, loving him totally.

They were on the opposite side of the river from the camp, and the river had carried them a considerable distance. There was no shelter. No other human being. And the rain showed no sign of ceasing although the storm had lost much of its considerable fury.

"I've got to get you someplace dry," Paul told her, "and get you warmed up."

He moved as though to get to his feet, but Jordan wrapped her arms more tightly around his neck and pressed her body even closer against his. He had given her life when he pulled her from the river. His warmth circulated in her veins. She needed him to live. She wanted to stay in his arms forever.

Jordan realized she had started to shake, her limbs shivering uncontrollably from the chill that had settled over her body and from the horror of what had just happened to her.

Paul pushed her away long enough to rise to his feet. He pulled her up beside him, locking a strong arm firmly around her body and half-carried her up a small hill to a flooding pasture beyond.

The river had carried them a considerable distance, and they were not too far from the narrow bridge over the Fourche Maline that connected the two segments of the existing highway.

As they approached the bridge, however, the red flashing lights of a highway patrol car blinked at them through the rain. The car was parked across the road, blocking the bridge to traffic.

"The bridge must be out," Paul told her. And soon she could see a gaping hole in the middle of the antiquated bridge where a span had been completely swept away by the engorged river.

A highway patrolman quickly directed them to the back seat of his car and produced a blanket which Paul wrapped around Jordan. Numbly, Jordan listened while the rain-slickered patrolman radioed for assistance.

"I've got a couple of folks here that fell into the river," he explained into his receiver. "Can you send someone by to pick them up? And hurry. The woman's pretty shaken up."

Shortly, a second patrol car arrived. After a brief discussion with Paul, the patrolmen decided neither of the law officers could spare the time to take them the long way around into Seneca, where Paul was certain the rest of his crew would be by now. Instead, the second highway patrolman would drive them to the nearby town of Harpersville.

"There's a doc there if she needs medical help," the patrolman told Paul as they drove away from the fallen bridge. "And a boardinghouse where you can spend the night if you need to. Of course, you can call your people in Seneca to come for you—if the telephone lines aren't down, but I think you'd better get your girlfriend some dry clothes and put her to bed for the night."

The proprietress of the boardinghouse took one look at Jordan and hurried her up the stairs. "You're a lucky young lady," the elderly woman told Jordan as she ran a tub of hot water for her. "I've known of folks who've been swept away by the river, but not too many lived to tell about it."

After a warming bath, Jordan put on the gown and robe the woman had provided for her and sat by the window watching the waning storm. A glass of wine had been left for her on the bedside table, and she sipped it thoughtfully, her mind still on the raging Fourche Maline.

She had almost drowned. The knowledge kept bombarding her. If Paul had not saved her, she would be dead now. *Dead.* Her limp body would probably still be in that raging river, bobbing about like a broken twig.

With a shudder, Jordan took another sip of wine, hoping it might bring some warmth to her still-chilled body. As the realization that she had been only seconds away from death permeated the layers of her consciousness, Jordan felt altered. Her perspective shifted, and she knew that nothing again would ever seem quite the same to her.

The gift of life was still hers. It was a precious gift, and she would celebrate it with every breath she took. She would celebrate it in all its bittersweet beauty. She would not turn her back on what life had to offer.

The summer was almost over. She would be leaving at the end of the week. And she would never see Paul Nicolle again.

There was an aching sadness when she thought of what would never be. But Jordan understood that she would not wish away this summer even if she could. She was not sorry Paul Nicolle came into her life. If she had the power to erase away her memory of the man, she would not do it. She wanted that memory. She wanted to think of him every day of her life regardless of the pain those thoughts would bring.

And she still had this night—this one night. She wanted a time of togetherness with the man she loved before she left him forever. For Paul, she knew it would be lovemaking and not love itself, but after the experiences of this day, Jordan realized that an imperfect memory was better than no memory at all.

The door to his room was not locked. The small lamp on the dresser reflected pinpoints of light in his dark eyes.

His hair was black against the white pillow. His smooth bronze chest was bare above the sheet that covered the rest of his body.

"I want you," Jordan told him. "I want you to give me a memory."

There was no trembling in her fingers as she unfastened her borrowed robe and allowed it to fall to the floor. As she slipped her arms from the gown and let it slip from her body, a groan escaped from Paul's lips.

Standing before him, Jordan was proud of her womanly body and of the look of desire it brought to his beautiful face. She ran her fingers lightly over her breasts, enjoying the heightened sensation that now resided within them. Soon it would be his fingers touching them. Soon.

His gaze traveled openly over her body. It was as though he were making love to her with his eyes.

Slowly, following the path of his gaze, she moved her hands from her breasts downward over her slim waist and outward over the curve of her hips. Soon his hands would be touching her all the places his eyes were now consuming. The exquisite agony of anticipation draped itself over her body like an invisible blanket, and she was warmed by it. Her flesh fairly glowed with it. Every pore in her body seemed to feel it, to tingle with expectation of what was to come.

There was no other world except this room. There was no other person except this man. There was no other need but her need of him.

When, at last, she could wait no longer, she went to him.

Slowly, she told herself. *Make time stand still. Make it last forever. Don't think of tomorrow. There is only tonight.*

First, she must have his mouth. She leaned over his face, her hair falling in a curtain around them, and explored his mouth with her tongue. She thought of all the times she had longed to do this once again—to flick her tongue over his lips and teeth, to probe his hungry mouth, to challenge his own tongue until it came alive and began a search of its own.

Then her lips abandoned his mouth and journeyed down his neck to his broad chest. How she adored his chest. The smooth hairlessness signified his Indian ancestry, making it all the more erotic to Jordan. Relishing the role of aggressor, Jordan's fingers and tongue joined forces, dancing their way across the muscular, brown expanse of his torso. So strong. He could crush her with those shoulders and arms if he chose.

Little groans of passion erupted from his lips. He was a prisoner of his lust for her. It was she who now had power over him. The masterful professor was under her spell.

Suddenly, she pulled away from him and looked upon the full length of his aroused body, feasting her eyes on his manliness. Then, with a featherlight touch, she traced the landmarks of his body—his lips, his neck and shoulders, his chest, navel, and thighs.

He cried out with pleasure as her fingers left no part of him untouched, except for where he wanted her touch the most.

Jordan closed her eyes, imagining the throbbing hardness of him, then slowly allowed her fingers to have their way.

He was filled with desire. The power of knowing that she had done this to his body was arousing beyond belief. It was as though the world would end if she did not feel him within her, yet she waited, not wanting to relinquish the sensations—the feel, the taste, the sound of him. She was intoxicated with her desire for him, yet she knew this encounter would be the last in a lifetime, and she wanted to experience as much of this man as their mutual passion would allow.

At last, however, Paul's patience came to an end. He had allowed her games, but now he took command. With one motion, he rolled her to the bed and pushed her shoulders against the pillow.

His mouth was hard on her breasts. He tugged at her

erect nipples bringing a sensation just short of pain, yet causing her to arch her back and cup her desire-swollen breasts in her hands to offer him more—and to cry out when his mouth pulled away.

Now it was his turn to explore, his turn to possess her body with hands and lips and tongue. At first, she touched his face, his shoulders, his hair, but then she abandoned herself to his ritual with arms flung outward and the palms of her hands open and exposed in a gesture of supplication. Her need of him was complete. She could bear it no longer, yet he made her wait. He was unhurried. He lingered. She floated on a sea of desire somewhere in the region between pleasure at its most extreme and yearning at its most severe.

Yet when, at last, he lowered himself over her body, she placed her hands flat against his chest and held him back. "Say you want me," she demanded breathlessly. "I know you don't love me, but tell me at this moment, you want me more than anyone else."

He looked down into her eyes. For one horrible instant Jordan thought that he would leave her. But then his face was buried against her neck. And she felt her body opening to him, their bodies joined in one pulsating unit as the desire she had endured for so many days and nights concentrated itself in wave after wave of ecstasy.

Jordan melted into his fire as its heat spread over her thighs and throughout her entire body.

How was it possible? A miracle was taking her to its outermost limits. Yes. A miracle.

When it was over, when she had left his bed and returned to her own, she wept into her pillow, knowing with a cruel certainty that she would never have him again, knowing that no man would ever make her feel like that again. Even she had not realized the depths of her own love for him.

When they returned to the camp the following morning, it appeared that the destruction begun by the militant young Indians was now completed. Most of the camp had been washed away by the flooding river, which had now retreated into its banks leaving mud and devastation in its wake. Some of the trenches had caved in. The others were full of river silt. It was hard to tell that the site had ever been an archaeological excavation. Only the meal tent remained standing. Several tents were collasped mounds of soggy canvas, and several—including Jordan's—had disappeared altogether.

Larry Jarvis was there with the sheriff and a handful of local citizens trying to help the beleaguered archaeological crew, but other than stack up the equipment and personal possessions that had not been washed away, there seemed to be little anyone could do.

Everyone clustered about Jordan, welcoming her back with hugs and endless questions about her ordeal.

"You can't imagine how relieved we were when we heard you and our heroic Professor Paul were okay," Cookie told her after planting a kiss on her cheek and a hearty slap on Paul's back. "By the way, you've got a visitor, Jordan," Cookie continued. "Some fellow who says he's your husband came out with the sheriff this morning looking for you."

"Clayton? Here?" Jordan asked.

"Yes," Cookie said, a puzzled look on his face. "He's having coffee in the meal tent. Says he's come to take you home."

Her Aunt Sarah was ill and in the hospital, Clayton explained. Fearing the worse and not knowing what else to do, Uncle Joe had asked Clayton to go after Jordan.

There was nothing to pack. There was nothing left of her tent or its contents. She quickly said her good-byes. Larry was first.

He and his wife had decided to try a reconciliation, Larry told her.

Jordan hugged him and said, "I knew you were still in love with her. No matter how hard you tried to convince yourself otherwise, it showed."

"I'll never forget you, Jordan," Larry said, returning her embrace. "You gave me the courage to try again with her. Now you find someone to love. Okay?"

"Don't worry about me," Jordan said with forced cheerfulness. "I'll be fine. You be happy, and raise lots of kids and build lots of highways."

And there were hugs from Dennis and Edgar. Edgar promised to write. Dennis told her she missed her chance with the world's greatest lover.

She shook hands all around with the group of people with whom she had spent the most memorable summer of her life. Even Yvonne stepped forward to offer a farewell.

But there was no farewell from Paul.

Jordan allowed herself one last long look at the proud half-Cherokee professor as he stared out over the destruction wrought by the Fourche Maline. Jordan knew it would be important to her in the years to come to remember the way he looked when last she saw him.

For a time it looked as though her aunt would die from the stroke that had felled her, but slowly, she began to grow stronger and the danger passed. In just two weeks Jordan and her uncle were able to take Sarah home to her own bedroom.

Sarah continued to improve, but it soon became apparent to Joe that the old two-story house on Maple Street was no longer an appropriate home for an aging couple who could not look after themselves adequately much less a large house. It was Joe who gently con-

vinced his wife that it was time for her to leave the only
home she had ever known and move into a retirement
home.

Jordan reluctantly helped her uncle sell the old
house and make the move. Using money from a student loan, she enrolled late for the fall semester and
moved herself into a boardinghouse near the campus.

She had no room in her schedule for any more elec-
tive classes in archaeology and anthropology. It was im-
perative that she finish her degree as soon as possible,
and she took only required courses. With the help of
the ten hours of credit she had earned working at the
Fourche Maline excavation and by taking correspon-
dence courses and an intersession class, she would be
able to graduate at the end of next summer's session,
and she hoped she would have a teaching job by next
fall.

She was enrolled in only education classes this semester with the exception of one history class: The
Settlement of the Great Plains.

It was the first class meeting after the midterm exam
when Jordan entered the lecture hall for her history
class and saw Paul standing at the podium. For an instant she seriously wondered if she was losing her
mind. Surely she must be hallucinating, Jordan told
herself, so firmly convinced was she that her path and
Paul's would never again cross.

Oh, she had fantasized about seeing him again, about
being with him again. She thought of his arms about
her each night before sleep came, and his face haunted
her dreams. She had long ago realized that if she was
not consciously thinking about Paul, thoughts of him
were hovering just beneath her level of consciousness,
ready to surface and surround her. But she had learned
to live with the specter of Paul Nicolle in her life much

like one learned to tolerate a handicap or chronic illness. Acceptance must come or life was not worth the living.

So she had accepted the fact that Paul's memory would be with her always. She would die thinking of him. And if she found another love along the way, it would not diminish what she felt for the professor in Oklahoma. In a way she felt sorry for her future love—if indeed such a man existed at all. Already her ability to enter fully into a relationship with him was altered, and they had not even met. But then, perhaps there was no man waiting in her future. Perhaps she was sentenced to journey through life alone with only her memories of a love that never was.

And, in a way, Jordan had even reconciled herself to that possibility. A life of loneliness might be her lot. If that was to be the case, she resolved, she would live a useful life, finding her joy in books and teaching and travel.

As she stood there in the back of the lecture hall, and knowledge dawned that it was indeed Paul Nicolle in front of the room—not a fantasized Paul Nicolle but the real flesh and blood man—Jordan cursed the cruel joke fate had decided to play on her. His being here could change nothing except erase the acceptance that the months since summer had brought and hurdle her back to that agonizing time of leaving him forever.

Her first impulse had been to flee, but quickly that resolve faded. She found herself incapable of leaving no matter how disastrously Paul's presence would affect her. It was a large hall. He would never notice her among all these other students. She slipped into the back row and sank into a seat.

Her heart was racing furiously, and an uncomfortable light-headedness swept over her. She buried her face in her hands and concentrated on calming her tremulous emotions.

"Are you all right?" a man's voice asked from the next chair.

"Oh, yes. Fine. Just a little tired," Jordan told her concerned classmate and forced herself to sit up straight and face the front of the room. The wall behind her head helped. And she wouldn't open her eyes just yet.

Distinguished archaeologist Dr. Paul Nicolle was in the state for a series of lectures, Jordan heard the professor tell his class. Dr. Nicolle had agreed to speak to the class today on the prehistory of the Great Plains area and discuss the impact of white settlement on the culture of the Indians of the Great Plains.

Paul's lecture was apparently brilliant judging from the spontaneous round of applause at its end, but Jordan had not been able to concentrate on his words. She had heard his voice and relished its fullness and timbre, but his words had no meaning for her. Only his presence in this room had meaning, and her memories of those strong, expressive hands that had gestured in accompaniment to uncomprehended words, and her memories of his lips, his tongue, his flesh.

If anything, she had forgotten how beautiful he was, how commanding his presence. His hair was shorter, and there was no beaded headband across his forehead. He was wearing a tweed sport coat and white turtleneck sweater with the ever-present turquoise nugget dangling against his chest on its chain of silver. She sensed the impact he had on this room full of listeners. For that hour, they had been his. He had woven them into his spell.

Paul acknowledged the applause from the class with a smile that showed white teeth contrasted against bronze skin and softened his stern handsomeness for an instant. As he left the hall, the entire assemblage seemed to collectively relax and sink back in their seats as though exhausted from their hour of rapt attention.

The history professor once again addressed his class, reminding them of papers due, making an assignment, announcing a meeting of the history club, and asking Jordan Marshall to stop by his office after class.

The sound of her own name forced Jordan mentally to retrace the professor's words and come up with the reason why her name had been spoken in front of the class. What had he said? Stop by after class?

But it was Paul who waited for her behind the cluttered desk. He did not rise. She stood just inside the door of the small office, trying to fathom what she was doing there.

"Why didn't you tell me that you and Dennis were just kidding around?" he demanded. "Did you intentionally try to make me think the two of you had something going on?"

Taken aback, Jordan did not reply. What right did he have to come here and taunt her like this? But then, he could not possibly know what torture this encounter was for her.

"And what about Larry Jarvis?" Paul continued, his hands clenched on the desk in front of him. "He tells me you encouraged him to try again with his wife—and that they are now remarried. Why did you allow me to believe your interest in him was of a romantic nature?"

With a forced calmness in her voice, Jordan said, "You seemed intent on believing the worst about me. I did not feel then, nor do I feel now, that I had to explain my friendships—but if I had, you would have chosen not to believe me."

A deep sigh escaped from Paul's lips. He rose and stood in front of the room's only window, staring out at the winter-bare trees and students scurrying by in jackets and coats, their breath making white vapor as they hurried to their next class.

With his face in profile, his gaze still fixed on the scene outside the window, he said, "Your're right. I wanted to think the worst about you. That made it easier for me to believe what I was feeling was only lust for a beautiful and immoral woman and that she was like another woman I had known before. Then I didn't have to make a place for her in my life."

He turned and stared at her face. "Those eyes. Never have I seen eyes that color. It was like an omen, but I refused to heed it." As he spoke, his fingers touched the turquoise nugget that rested against the wool of his white sweater.

"Edgar and I had a talk before he left for Peru," Paul continued almost as though he were talking for his own enlightenment. "Or perhaps I should say that Edgar gave me a talking to before he left. I discovered lots of things from Edgar. I discovered that Dennis was a pest, and that you had married young, and the man who came to fetch you after the flood had not been your husband for over two years. And I discovered that I can't live without you."

Jordan could not believe what she was hearing. Surely she misunderstood his meaning. "But what about Yvonne," she stammered. "I thought you were going with her to Peru."

"She tempted me—and my ego. Before Frank told me of the mischief he and Yvonne were responsible for, I had already realized she was not the sort of woman I wanted to marry. You see, a wonderfully wise and desirable young woman had slipped into my life. She helped me understand where my destiny lies. And I find that I want to seek out that destiny with her at my side. I want to journey through time with her—to travel into the past with our shared work, to share our present, to be together always. I want to look into those wondrous turquoise eyes for the rest of my life."

Was it only a dream, Jordan asked herself. Or was it a dream come true?

Whatever—she wanted only to feel those strong arms around her, to bury her face against his chest and dream on.

ARLEQUIN *Love Affair*

Now on sale

THE LAST KEY   *Beverly Sommers*

After eight years, Toby had almost stopped expecting him. Hidden away in Key West, running a charter fishing boat, Toby had changed her hair, her clothes—even her walk. But when she saw Mac McQuade, she knew she had never been safe.

Toby. No birth certificate, no fingerprints on file, no identification at all. But Mac thought he knew who she was. She wouldn't slip through *his* fingers. Funny, she didn't look the type—her proud, determined spirit fascinated him. Yet lives were at stake and his duty was clear. He had to bring her in!

WINTER'S BOUNTY   *Muriel Jensen*

The Christmas reunion in Astoria, Oregon, was a boisterous gathering of love in many forms, but Marijane Westridge was a stranger to all of them. Her mother's recent wedding, her older sister's tempestuous marriage, her younger sister's irresponsible affection for her child—all left Marijane bewildered.

At least until she looked at James Sullivan's love for his adopted son and beheld a kindred spirit. James radiated the kind of love that increased joys and lessened sorrows. Marijane had only to take his hand to share a lifetime of that wonderful emotion . . .

CHEROKEE SUMMER   *Anne Henry*

Jordan Marshall's days, divided between her job and her graduate-school courses, had fallen into a dull routine and the archaeological dig near Seneca, Oklahoma, held the irresistible promise of ten weeks' excitement.

The reality of the excavation was a shock—blistering sun, back-breaking work, the most primitive facilities imaginable . . . and Professor Paul Nicolle.

Paul Nicolle, who had expected a male student, angrily implied that Jordan was a starry-eyed incompetent. Jordan refused to be intimidated. She would do her share, she promised him. But silently she prayed she would survive the ordeal . . .

HARLEQUIN *Love Affai.*

Next month's titles

WHEN LOVE ISN'T ENOUGH *Kathleen Gilles Sei*

They were one of Washington, D.C.'s rising couples. Janet v rapidly gaining recognition as the creative writer at a sm advertising agency. Wiley, like his father, was making his name a respected lawyer.

But while Wiley strove for position and power, Janet yearned a real home, steeped in love and filled with the laughter children. Then Wiley took on a case for one of his firm's m important clients, a case that was to shake the foundation of th love and awaken them to the real meaning of their marriage!

DARE TO DREAM *Modean Moon*

D.J. Simms had never feared a man so much. Undaunted by D. chilly facade and intimidating reputation as one of Tulsa's b lawyers, Nick Sanders had uncovered the woman who ne spoke of her past, who moved numbly through the present—a offered her understanding. Nick traced the scar along D. hairline, watched her flee from a child's innocent laughter—a offered her comfort. Nick spoke of the future and offered I love.

But love was her enemy, an unbearable reminder of the wom she had been and of the world she had lost!

THE OTHER HALF OF LOVE *Jacqueline Ashley*

With his California good looks and his fascination with physi fitness, Patrick Phipps was a decided affront to Murph's sensib ties. Patrick was the kind of man who was so concerned with icing that he didn't deserve the cake.

Unlike her young patients, who loved Murph for herself, Patr was just the sort to notice little things like tattered stockings a missing buttons and to object to Murph's comfortably me home. Murph wasn't the least bit interested in Patrick—until informed her that he wasn't interested in her type of woman.